The Cat, the Wife and the Weapon

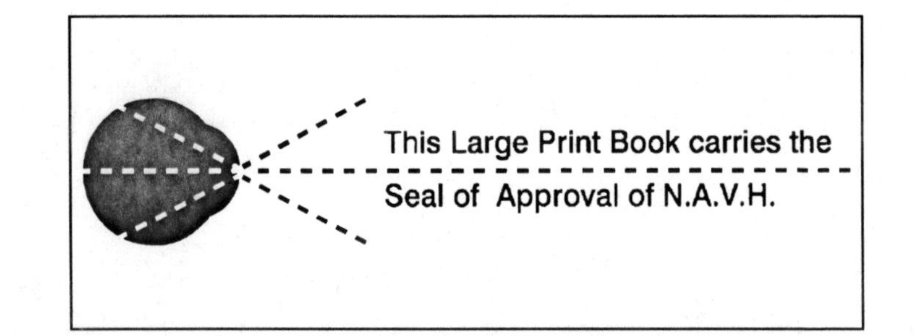
This Large Print Book carries the
Seal of Approval of N.A.V.H.

A CATS IN TROUBLE MYSTERY

The Cat, the Wife and the Weapon

Leann Sweeney

KENNEBEC LARGE PRINT
A part of Gale, Cengage Learning

Detroit • New York • San Francisco • New Haven, Conn • Waterville, Maine • London

GALE
CENGAGE Learning

Kennebec Large Print® Superior Collection.
The text of this Large Print edition is unabridged.
Other aspects of the book may vary from the original edition.
Set in 16 pt. Plantin.

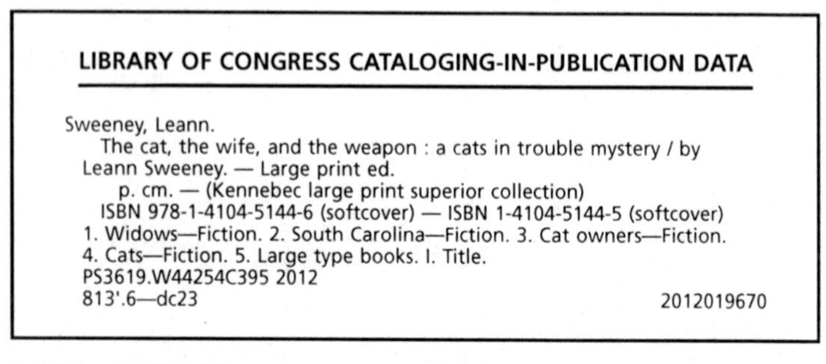
LIBRARY OF CONGRESS CATALOGING-IN-PUBLICATION DATA

Sweeney, Leann.
The cat, the wife, and the weapon : a cats in trouble mystery / by Leann Sweeney. — Large print ed.
p. cm. — (Kennebec large print superior collection)
ISBN 978-1-4104-5144-6 (softcover) — ISBN 1-4104-5144-5 (softcover)
1. Widows—Fiction. 2. South Carolina—Fiction. 3. Cat owners—Fiction. 4. Cats—Fiction. 5. Large type books. I. Title.
PS3619.W44254C395 2012
813'.6—dc23 2012019670

Published in 2012 by arrangement with NAL Signet, a member of Penguin Group (USA) Inc.

Printed in the United States of America
2 3 4 5 6 17 16 15 14 13

This book is for Morgan Elizabeth.

ACKNOWLEDGMENTS

A book is a journey never traveled alone. Without the help of my husband, Mike, my writer's group — Kay, Dean, Amy, Bob, Laura, Heather and Millie — as well as Susie, Charlie, Isabella, Enzo and Curry, I would have been very lonely. A special thank-you to the "cozies," wonderful readers on the cozyarmchair Yahoo group, as well as all the other readers I've met through Facebook. My three kitties and my wonderful dog have been beside me as I typed every word. Lorraine and Jennifer, you have wrapped your arms around me and helped me through so much. Thank you. My agent, Carol, I thank you, too; and Claire, I could never thank you enough for your support. Lastly, a special shout-out to my two friends waiting on the Rainbow Bridge. My beautiful Himalayan, Indigo, and my tuxedo cat, Archie Goodwin, are right there. Rest in peace, dear, dear friends. You're forever in my heart.

"It always gives me a shiver when I see a cat seeing what I can't see."

— Eleanor Farjeon

ONE

Cats don't worry, I thought as I pulled two of the three pet carriers from my minivan and lugged them to my back door. I disabled the security alarm and carried a couple fur kids inside. *Cats are brave, sometimes afraid, always curious, but they do not worry. How wonderful that must be.*

Worry had plagued me my entire trip home to Mercy, South Carolina. For the last week, I'd been on a business trip, traveling across a few Southern states selling my handmade cat quilts at craft fairs and cat shows. November can be a sweet month in South Carolina, weatherwise, and offers lots of opportunities to sell my wares. I'd had a successful tour, but my cell phone had not rung once during my journey home. I'd left at least ten messages for my friend Tom Stewart. Maybe more. Why wasn't he calling me back? Had I left too many messages and he'd gotten tired of my calls? Or had there been some kind of emergency?

With concern a background thrum in my head, I carried in the last cat and the suitcase into my house. As for my three kitties, their plaintive meows to be released from captivity told me Syrah, Merlot and Chablis felt only relief that their journey was over. No, they weren't worried at all.

I opened their crates and set them free, then watched them slink into the kitchen. I loved how cautious they were. Not worried, just careful. After all, who knew what creatures might have invaded the house during our absence? They might need to be pounced upon and eliminated. All three cats gracefully crept around the kitchen, noses and tails twitching.

But it was the invisible invader that continued to bother me — the one inside my head. I went outdoors again. This was the first real wintry day I'd experienced in a week, cold wind blowing, gray skies above. I unloaded the quilts left unsold, again rolling through possibilities as to why Tom was not returning my calls.

I went back in the house and set my suitcase by the washer. Before the trip I'd left a large box in the utility room and now, as I carefully packed away the remaining quilts, I recalled what had happened the night before I'd left town. Tom and I had enjoyed a nice dinner and then watched a DVD while cuddled on my couch. He said he would miss me. I knew I would miss him too.

I talked to him on the phone the first five nights while I was away. Then my calls started going straight to voice mail. *Was it something I said?* Problem was, I was so tired during our last conversation, I couldn't even remember what we'd talked about. Did he think I was blowing him off?

Merlot pressed against my calf, his warbling meow pleading for me to quit standing around and provide him with food and water. He's a big boy, a red Maine coon cat with a giant appetite. I opened the pantry and took out three cans of tuna cat food, thinking how I should have followed through — phoned my stepdaughter, Kara, and asked her to see what was up with Tom. Kara worked part time for Tom's security business when she wasn't running the *Mercy Messenger,* our small-town newspaper — or when she wasn't supervising the construction of her new house on the outskirts of town.

I snapped open each can, and the noise brought the other two cats racing from wherever they'd been. Chablis, my seal point Himalayan, and Syrah, my amber Abyssinian, were as hungry as Merlot. They never ate much when I took them with me on business, but their semi-fasts ended as soon as we arrived home.

Why not call Kara now? I thought, setting three dishes of food and a stainless-steel pan of water on the floor in the utility room. I always used stainless or glass because plastic dishes are toxic to cats and can give them mouth sores or make them sick.

Kara is my stepdaughter, my late husband's only child, and though she was an observant young woman and probably knew exactly how I felt about Tom, I never wanted to seem too romantically interested in him. She liked him, worked well with him, but the whole thing between Tom and me seemed awkward when it came to Kara. I felt as if calling her to ask about Tom would be like saying, "Hey, have you seen my boyfriend? The one who is slowly taking your father's place?" No one could ever take her father's place in my heart, of course, but it might seem that way to her.

"Oh heck," I said aloud. "Quit with the mind games and do something." I had to find out what was going on. Now.

I took my phone from my jeans' pocket and stared down, gripping it as tightly as

Chablis hangs on to her banana catnip toy. *Call Kara. Do it.*

She answered on the second ring. "Hi, Jillian. You home yet?"

"Just got in. Listen, I have a question. Is there something wrong with Tom's phone?"

"Why?" she said.

I explained about the unreturned calls.

She said, "Maybe he didn't take his phone with him, or forgot his charger."

"Take it with him where?" Even though I couldn't remember much from our last talk, I was certain he'd never mentioned a trip.

"He called me a couple days ago, asked me to handle any jobs or clients. Said he had to go away for a few days."

"Oh." A quiet "oh," a small word that failed to hide the surprise and disappointment I felt that he hadn't shared his travel plans with me.

Kara must have picked up on the emotion because she quickly said, "I got the feeling it was a last-minute thing, and he didn't offer me any explanation. He sounded rushed or distracted or . . . something."

"Oh," I repeated. The worry was back. If there was one thing I'd learned since my husband's death two years ago, it was to rely on my instincts. I knew Tom. I trusted him. Something was definitely wrong.

"You're sure he's not back in town?" I said.

"I'm sure. He'd call to find out about any new customers, Jillian," she said. "I expect we'll hear from him soon."

"Maybe I'm overreacting," I said, "but I'm concerned. What if he never got out his front door?" Thoughts of my husband's collapse right here in this house, his instant death from a massive heart attack, flashed through my mind.

"Really? You're jumping to worst-case scenarios?" I could picture her lovely, indulgent smile, so like her father's.

"Maybe, but —"

"Okay," she said in a take-charge tone. "Clearly you're beyond stressed about this. Did you try his landline?"

"I didn't have the number with me. He hardly uses that phone. But maybe his cell is damaged or lost. Thanks for the suggestion. I'll call his house right now." An ounce of relief washed away some of my anxiety.

"Call me back after you talk to him — either now or later," Kara said. "I don't like to hear such strain in your voice."

I hung up, the chill in the house making me shiver. No afternoon sun to warm things up. The murky, cloud-dulled day meant the cold would linger on. After I turned the thermostat up to seventy, I went through the living area and down the hall to my home office. I took my address book from my desk drawer. All three cats followed and jumped up on the mahogany surface to check out what I was doing.

Merlot crooned his concern — he has a special sound for intense interest in my state of mind. When I'm upset, all three of them seem to sense it and follow me everywhere. If I were to sit down on my sofa right now, they would be all over me.

First thing I did was add Tom's landline number to the contacts on my cell phone. Then I hit call. His answering machine picked up.

Darn it.

I didn't bother to leave a message, just disconnected. His voice on the answering machine greeting, so engaging and cheerful, made my stomach clench.

Trust your instincts. This disappearance isn't like Tom.

I looked at the three curious feline faces staring up at me. "I have to do more than make phone calls, friends. I'm sure you'll take much-needed cat naps while I'm gone."

Tom lives about a five-minute drive away in a secluded neighborhood within walking distance from his mother, Karen's, place. *His mother.* While I was traveling home, I'd considered calling her. But Karen is an odd bird. If I alarmed her unnecessarily, Tom would end up receiving endless visits from her when he did come home — or she might even take up residence in his guest room for a while. No. I couldn't call her. Not yet.

The first thing I noticed when I turned on to Tom's street was that the work van he used for his security business sat in the driveway. But rather than his Prius parked next to it, I saw an unfamiliar car. A white Ford sedan. Had he traded in his beloved little car for something so generic?

But wait. Maybe he'd had car trouble and this was a rental. It sure looked like one. But if so, it still didn't explain his lack of contact.

I pulled in behind the Ford and was soon knocking on the door of his red brick home. The November wind had picked up just in the last few minutes. I pulled my barn jacket closer around me and turned up the brown corduroy collar. Arriving here on this familiar front porch made me think of Tom's cat, Dashiell. His big tabby was recently diagnosed as diabetic. If Tom was out of town and left the cat behind, someone would have to be giving Dashiell his insulin. Maybe the car belonged to a cat sitter, a role I would have taken on had I been here.

The forty-something man who answered the door wore navy sweats and his feet were bare. He looked more like a guest who had made himself comfortable than a pet sitter.

He smiled and said, "I was hoping for company, and it seems as if my prayers have been answered." He looked me up and down. "And answered in a very fine way. How can I help you?"

That voice. So like Tom's voice. But he appeared a tad younger than Tom, had blond hair rather than dark hair and was maybe four inches taller. A good six foot four if he was an inch.

"I — I — I —" Words wouldn't come.

"I'm not scary, am I? 'Cause you look like your panty hose are quivering," he said.

What? I had to deal with a wise-guy stranger now? As politely as I could, I said, "I'm sorry, but who are you?"

"Bob Cochran." He had a crooked smile, perfect teeth and broad shoulders — the kind of guy women fell for instantly. Especially with his bad-boy vibe. Younger women, that is. Not me. Being in my mid-forties may have brought a few wrinkles, but I'd gained wisdom and an eye for trouble. I liked the trade-off.

He went on, saying, "I take it you came to see Tom, but he's not home. You're welcome to come in, though."

The wind whipped my hair across my face and I brushed it away. But though I was cold and more than a little confused, I didn't know this man from Adam. I wasn't about to go inside the house with a stranger. "Where's Tom?"

"Good question. My brother hasn't shown his face since I arrived two days ago."

"Your *brother?*" I said. That explained the resemblance.

"Guess he never mentioned me. Figures. And you are?"

"Jillian Hart. Tom's friend."

He offered his charismatic smile again. "A friend with benefits?"

My cheeks heated up and I started to turn away. "I'll come back when Tom's home."

Bob Cochran grabbed my elbow. "Wait. Sorry. That's not any of my business. But maybe you can help me out. See, I expected Tom to be here and I'm a little puzzled he hasn't shown up. Especially since he left his cat."

Dashiell. Tom left Dashiell alone? I withdrew from Bob Cochran's grasp but didn't leave. I couldn't now. "How is Dashiell?" I craned my neck to see past the man's wide frame.

"He left instructions for a neighbor to care for the animal — the old lady next door. Mostly illegible notes about food and medicine. She came over, said something about how she could give the cat his shots and test him since she and this cat had the same problem, whatever that meant. But the stupid animal slipped by me when I let her in. Haven't seen the thing since."

"What?" I almost shouted around the lump of panic in my throat. "When did this happen?"

"Two days ago. I told the neighbor I'd come and get her if the cat came back." He cocked his head and smiled again. "It's only a cat. They always come back to where the food is."

I had no time to enlighten this idiot about Dashiell's medical problem.

I had to find Tom's cat *now.*

Two

I turned and scanned Tom's yard, looking toward the red pines and ashy shagbark hickories that hid the creek running along the edge of Tom's property.

Taking off toward those trees, I shouted Dashiell's name but slowed as the lawn sloped toward the water. *What if Dashiell's blood sugar plummeted? Or went sky-high from him eating birds, or even fish from the creek? What if he fell into the water? What if he was swept away?*

Tears filled my eyes. Ever since Tom's big sweet Dashiell had been diagnosed, he'd had major swings in his sugar levels. But Tom was now an expert at testing a drop of blood from the cat's ear and keeping him as well as possible. What would two days without insulin do? Or would lack of food be the bigger problem? My gosh, was he *dead?*

My heart sped even faster at the thought.

First Tom is incommunicado, and now this.

I reached the trees and called Dashiell's name again, this time in a more gentle tone. I shouldn't transfer my fear to him, especially if he was nearby and in trouble.

No meows in reply.

I scanned the blanket of decaying leaves and russet pine needles. Cats tend to stay close to where they feel safe, especially when they're sick, and I was counting on that. Dashiell's brown stripes would camouflage him out here, though.

I took deep breaths, calmed myself. *Focus, Jillian.*

Deciding I needed to block out the distraction of the gurgling creek water tumbling over rocks toward the lake, I stood as still as a statue and took several calming breaths. Then I let my gaze sweep slowly over the grass and leaves, as far to the right as I could see, then to the left where a fence separated Tom's yard from his neighbor's, then to the right again.

There.

Oh my gosh. There he was.

Fear rose again to take a choke hold on me. I felt paralyzed. Dashiell lay, unmoving, maybe twenty feet away on the steeper bank leading to the creek.

He couldn't be gone. He couldn't.

Help him, Jillian. Help him now.

I crept toward him, whispering, "Dashiell, baby. It's Jillian. Are you okay, buddy?"

No response. Even when I knelt and stroked his head, he didn't move. I lifted his limp body and held him close, willing him to be okay.

He was not okay. But despite the cold air, he felt warm. I remembered Tom's description of the first time he knew something was wrong with his cat. He'd found Dashiell unconscious.

Unconscious. Not dead.

I moved his paw aside and pressed my hand on Dashiell's chest.

And smiled.

I felt his heart beating. Felt the rise of his abdomen as he breathed.

I unbuttoned my jacket, carefully tucked him close to me and raced back to the house. Bob was still standing in the doorway, watching me with what appeared to be amusement.

What a jerk, I thought. "Please get out of my way," I said, pushing past him.

Karo syrup. Tom kept Karo syrup for when Dashiell's blood sugar dropped.

I ran through the living room into the kitchen. The syrup was sitting on the counter next to the scrawled note Tom had left for his neighbor.

I laid the nearly lifeless cat on the counter and opened the syrup bottle. Then I stopped for a second to think this through.

Tom's words came back to me: "You can never be sure with Dashiell. He can pass out from low sugar or be halfway to a coma because his blood sugar is too high."

If I used the syrup and his sugar was high, I could kill him.

I sensed Bob's presence behind me. Standing way too close. "Please leave us alone," I said through clenched teeth.

He backed up and said, "Sure. Just like seeing you playing cat rescuer. It's kind of sexy."

Ignoring him, I glanced around on the cream ceramic tile counter, looking for the black leather case holding the equipment to test Dashiell's blood sugar. There, an arm's length away.

With shaky hands I removed the small blood sugar meter, picturing how I'd seen Tom test Dashiell. There were little needles and a cleansing pad inside the case. Like I'd remembered Tom doing, I cleaned the outside tip of Dashiell's ear and stuck him with a needle. I winced when the small drop of blood appeared, but Dashiell didn't even twitch.

At first I put the test strip into the meter the wrong way, but finally got it right and the digital display appeared. I pressed the test strip against that tiny bit of blood. The meter beeped and after a few seconds the display showed the number twenty.

Twenty. So low. Tom always said one hundred twenty was a good number.

I swiped my index finger around the inside rim of the syrup bottle. Then I rubbed the sticky stuff along Dashiell's gums and repeated this about three times.

Slowly, Dashiell's eyes opened.

Yes. Good baby. Yes.

He blinked and tried to meow, but no sound came out. I decided another dose of syrup couldn't hurt, so I repeated the gum rub. Then I gathered Dashiell into my arms again, picked up the Karo bottle and hurried out of the house, passing the man with the stupid smile.

How could he be related to my Tom?

I'd called Mercy's only vet as I sped to his office. The white-haired Doc Jensen met me in the waiting area and immediately took the half-conscious Dashiell from my arms. He headed through a door to the back of his clinic. Tom's cat was in expert hands now and I felt my shoulders slump in relief.

"Where's Tom?" the receptionist, Glenda, asked.

She was a fairly new employee, always cheerful — a caring, sweet lady with highlighted hair who wore colorful, pet-themed scrubs and always had manicured nails with painted-on paw prints.

"I — I'm not sure," I said. "But I'll pay, if that's what I need to do. I left my purse in my van." I started toward the exit.

"Wait, honey," Glenda said. "You don't have to be concerned about money now. First we have to get our Dashiell shipshape. Then we'll think about the bill. I was just wondering why Tom couldn't come. Work, I suppose."

"Yes," I muttered. "Work."

Maybe that's all his absence was about. A PI or a security installation job outside of Mercy. But he left without fully explaining to Kara? Nope. He wouldn't do that. The worry, temporarily replaced by Dashiell's emergency, settled into the pit of my stomach again.

I sat down on the built-in Formica benches lining the wall and realized for the first time that Martha, the owner of Mercy's quilt shop, the Cotton Company, sat in a corner with a quilt square in her lap. She was appliquéing what looked like a Baltimore Album flower. An empty pet carrier sat on the tile floor next to her.

"Hi, Martha," I said.

She looked up and her kind smile relaxed me at once. "Hey there, Jillian. Didn't see you come in. I was so engrossed in my stitching they could have dropped a bomb in the parking lot and I wouldn't have noticed. Did you sell a lot of kitty quilts on your trip?"

"Yes — but is Crazy Quilt okay?" I glanced at the carrier. She'd recently adopted another calico cat fittingly named Crazy Quilt not only because of her wildly patterned white, gold and black fur, but because she'd been known to shred bolts of fabric in minutes — that, and tear other things to bits. Crazy Quilt never visited Martha's shop anymore.

"Crazy's had her teeth cleaned and I'm waiting to pick her up. But where are *your* friends? I always wondered how you managed to take three cats to the vet when I could use the help of a Navy SEAL just to get my baby into a carrier."

I smiled, almost forgetting my distress. Almost. "I brought Tom's cat in. He's sick."

"Ah. Tom left town in a hurry and I guess he's not back. You watching Dashiell, then?" She refocused on her handwork.

"Sort of," I said, surprised. "How did you know Tom left in a hurry?"

"Saw him in his cute little car racing down Main Street a couple days ago. Had some man with him. Thought surely he'd get stopped for speeding."

"Do you remember what time you saw him?" I asked. Urgency colored my question and made Martha look up from her work.

She cocked her head. "Something wrong, Jillian? You seem . . . upset."

"Just worried about Dashiell," I said. "You say Tom was speeding. What time of day?"

"I was walking down Main Street to get my morning fix at Belle's Beans. Always buy my coffee right before the quilt shop opens. Tom didn't even wave. Not like him to be impolite."

"No . . . not like him at all," I murmured. I shouldn't have been surprised she knew more than I did. This was Mercy, after all. Small-town America doesn't need the Internet or Twitter to get the word out.

Doc Jensen's vet tech, Anthony, appeared and waved to Martha. "We're gonna need your carrier, Miss Martha. And your help, I'm thinkin'."

Martha planted her needle in her quilt square, folded her work and put it into her bag. Carrier in one hand and purse in the other, she walked toward Anthony. As she passed me, she said, "You need to get you some rest, Jillian. Your trip looks like it's taken a toll."

I forced a smile, then clasped my shaking hands. The adrenaline that had pumped through me after finding Dashiell was wearing off. I was left trembling as well as wishing I had a giant box of Tums.

Doc Jensen smiled when he came out into the waiting area a few minutes later. He gestured me into a cold, immaculate exam room that smelled of disinfectant and alcohol. Dashiell wasn't sitting on the stainless table. Despite the vet's relaxed expression, that could mean the poor boy was still in trouble.

Nodding reassuringly, Doc Jensen said, "You got to him in time, but his blood sugar remains low. He needs to stay with us overnight. Can you get Tom on the phone and see if that's okay?"

How I *wished* I could get him on the phone. "Um, Tom's out of pocket so I'll be making the decisions. Do whatever Dashiell needs. That's what Tom would want."

"Will do. You go home and have a glass of wine, Jillian — 'cause it sure looks like you could use one. Say hi to your three amigos for me, pet them and relax. Stroking a cat gets your blood pressure down, you know. We'll take fine care of Dashiell."

He turned and left through the door leading to the back of the clinic while I went in the opposite direction and into the waiting area. I passed Glenda, who waved good-bye.

Once I'd climbed into my van, I thought, *What next?*

But the answer came immediately.

Find Tom. Find Tom. Find Tom.

Three

Before I left the vet's parking lot, I took my phone from my purse, hoping Tom had left me a message. No such luck. I sighed heavily, staring at the screen. I touched the app for my cat cam. Watching my cats' antics or just seeing them nap in the slivers of sun that striped the living room in the late afternoon always soothed me.

Maybe because there was no sun today, my fur friends weren't lounging in their usual spots. I switched to the kitchen feed and the bedroom feed, but they were nowhere in sight. Perhaps they'd decided hiding from the woman who might come home and cram them back into those carriers was a good idea. That's what I'd do. Hide.

I put my phone away and started for home, but as I turned onto Main Street I saw a Mercy PD patrol car parked in front of the best coffee shop on the planet — Belle's Beans, with its green awning. Every shop on Main Street had exactly the same awning. Tradition and continuity were important parts of this small Southern town.

I knew who drove that particular squad car thanks to the dent in the right front fender — my best friend, Deputy Candace Carson, and her partner, Deputy Morris Ebeling. I'd meant to call Candace about Bob Cochran's presence in Tom's house, but had forgotten all about him until I saw the police car. What the heck was brother Bob up to? How had he gotten inside the house? Was the man even who he said he was?

What a relief my brain seemed to be functioning logically again — asking the important questions. I pulled into a parking spot near the coffee shop and hurried over to Belle's Beans. Candace would want the same answers I did.

Today's barista, or the "Belle of the Day" as owner Belle Lowry always said, greeted me with, "Hey there, Jillian. Vanilla low-fat latte?" She wore a BELLE name tag, but then, every barista who worked here sported one while on duty. Her real name was Beth.

"Nothing right now, thanks." My gaze swept the crowded café. The quiet conversations and the familiarity of the place would have been comforting on any other day. Not now, though. The high glossy wood tables for two lining the periphery of the coffeehouse were all occupied. The center tables seating four were almost all filled as well. Belle had added free Wi-Fi last month, and several people were working on their laptops. I spotted Candace and Morris in a far corner and, as I navigated between tables, I heard acoustic music playing softly, piped in through overhead speakers. Another new addition.

Belle, a wise lady in her early seventies, always wanted her customers to feel comfortable. Sure, the coffee was the best I'd ever had. Plus, the refrigerated glass case filled with homemade pies, scones and cakes made the shop all the more popular — especially to someone like Morris. But music and technology could only improve a small business seemingly unaffected by the economic downturn. Yes, leave it to Belle to keep her shop thriving.

Candace stood before I even reached their table, her expression showing her concern. "What's wrong?"

Morris said, "She looks right as rain to me, Candy. Or are you thinkin' of becoming a psychic or somethin'? Oh yeah, I can see your shingle now. Candace Carson, Psychic Forensic Investigator."

"Shut up, Morris," Candace said, her stare locked on my face.

"Can we talk?" I said.

"Oh boy." Morris rolled his eyes. "When I hear the words *can we talk* I know there's a passel of hassles headed our way."

"Sit." Candace dragged a stool from an adjoining table.

The squeal of the legs scraping on the floor made my already frazzled nerves light up even more. Candace and I both sat and she took my hand. "You're as cold as a corpse. What has you so upset?"

I took a deep breath and released the air slowly. "Might help me get this all straight in my head if I begin by telling you about my trip. I feel as if I have a jumble of computer wires for brains right now and I need to unwind them. Put everything in a straight line."

"What you need first is coffee." Candace turned to Morris. "Get this woman some coffee, would you?"

"Why, of course, boss girl. I'm thinkin' I don't want to hear this anyways." Morris looked at me. "Your usual, Jillian?"

I nodded and started fumbling in my pocket for the twenty I always keep in my jeans. "Guess I *could* use a latte."

But he waived off the cash and made his

way to the counter. He sure must be anxious to get away from me, considering he'd offered to pay. Morris never paid.

"Go on. Tell me." Candace swiped at a wayward blond hair on her forehead. She rested her elbows on the table and supported her chin with both fists. She may be twenty years younger than me, but she is an old soul. Guess being a cop made her more mature than the average young adult.

I quickly explained about Tom's unreturned phone calls, his rush out of town, the sick cat and my concern about finding Bob Cochran in Tom's house.

When I was finished explaining, Candace said, "Did you call Tom's mother and ask about this man who claims to be her son? Or ask if she knows where Tom is, for that matter?"

"I wasn't sure if that was wise," I said. "Karen is well — *unpredictable* is the word that comes to mind."

"Nutcase, you mean," Morris said, setting a steaming vanilla latte in front of me.

"She's no such thing, Morris Ebeling," Candace said. "Free spirit, a little odd, but not crazy."

"Nutcase." Morris reclaimed his seat. "Please tell me we don't have to pay her a visit 'cause she's gone and painted her house a funny shade of orange or set some life-size sculpture in her front yard that leaves nothin' to the imagination."

"Nope. I think we'll be making a call at Tom Stewart's place." Candace adjusted the two-way radio clipped to her forest green uniform shoulder. She then attached her cell phone to her belt. "Come on, Morris. Wrap the rest of your red velvet cake in a napkin and let's move."

He didn't budge. "This is our break, Candy. We get thirty minutes."

She placed both palms on the table in front of him and leaned close. "Tom Stewart might need our help. He's more important than your cake break." She pushed my latte closer. "Finish this and go on home. Chill out if you can. I'll call you."

Morris grumbled as he wrapped his cake in a napkin. Then they left.

But the relief I thought would come from having put this situation in Candace's competent hands didn't sweep over me, or even calm my stomach the tiniest bit. Still, I resolved to take her advice. I picked up my coffee, grabbed a to-go lid on the way out and headed for home.

I felt my shoulders sag with disappointment when I found myself at my back door and remembered I'd failed to set my security alarm. Too rushed when I'd left earlier today, I guessed. Thanks to Tom, I now had a remote on my key chain for just that purpose, seeing as how I always seem to forget to arm the thing if I am in the least bit of a hurry.

I unlocked the door — at least I'd locked up — but no cats sat waiting in the utility room. They were always there to greet me, but not this time. Hiding from another possible road trip, perhaps?

I tossed the empty coffee cup into the trash can under the utility sink and stepped into the kitchen, surprised the well-caffeinated latte hadn't made me feel more agitated than I already was. Syrah slinked up from the basement through the open door — a door always left open since my cats get irritated and whine when it's shut. Maybe that's where they'd been when I checked earlier. An occasional mouse did sneak into the basement.

But when Syrah sat in the doorway and meowed rather than come to me, I felt a new tingle of adrenaline beneath my skin. My cat was telling me something — but what, I wasn't sure.

Since Syrah's hair wasn't standing on end and his ears weren't laid back, he obviously didn't feel threatened. A good sign.

Then I heard heavy footsteps on the stairs and my heart skipped a beat. But when the voice I heard finally answered my most pressing question, I felt the wave of relief I'd been needing.

"Don't worry, Jillian. It's just me," Tom called.

I was so happy to hear his voice I thought my legs would give out.

Chablis raced through the basement door ahead of Tom and into the kitchen, followed immediately by Merlot. The man I'd been so concerned about appeared a second later.

Before I could rush over and throw my arms around him, I froze at the sight of his face. What the heck happened to him? His left cheek was bruised and swollen, he had a cut over his eyebrow and his blue eyes were bloodshot.

"I showered downstairs," he said. "Didn't want to mess up your guest bathroom — because I sure would have. You can close your mouth now, by the way."

I walked over and gently touched his bruised face with the tips of my fingers. "My gosh, what happened?"

"Kind of a long story," he said. "I could sure use a beer while I tell you."

"Certainly," I answered, unable to take

my eyes off him. His dark hair was wet and he hadn't bothered to button his ripped, blood-streaked shirt. "I might even have a beer myself."

He grinned. "I don't believe I have ever seen you drink a beer. Do I look that awful, or is something else going on?"

Avoiding the question, I said, "Have you been to your house lately, by any chance?" I turned my back and headed for the fridge, deciding what I had to tell him should wait. All three cats followed me, hoping for something besides a beer. Cheese? Turkey luncheon meat?

"Haven't been home yet," he said. "My ride only took me this far."

"Your ride?" I said. Since his car was missing and Martha saw him leaving town in the Prius, this didn't fit. But his car hadn't been in my driveway, either. So I was confused as I opened the fridge door.

I felt Tom's hand on my shoulder. He leaned close and whispered, "I'll explain everything. But you didn't set your security system. You know how that bothers me, Jilly."

I grabbed a Miller Lite from the fridge door, and held out the can. Looking up to meet his gaze, I felt tears begin to flow. "I was frantic. You didn't call me and I was sure something was wrong and I —"

He pressed his index finger to my lips. "I'll tell you everything, but if you don't mind, there's something I need first." He took me in his arms, the icy can of beer the only thing separating us.

His kiss was exactly what we *both* needed.

Four

Tom's kiss reassured me that whatever happened to him had nothing to do with the two of us. After I found one of my late husband's old Texas A&M T-shirts for Tom to replace his torn and bloody shirt, we settled on the couch. He let out a sigh before slugging down probably half his beer. I'd already finished off a much-needed glass of sweet tea while he'd changed shirts. Once we sat down, cats immediately arrived and planted themselves in their usual spots. Syrah sat on the sofa top behind Tom and me, Chablis climbed into my lap and Merlot settled next to my hip.

"I don't know what to ask first," I said. "Start with the cuts and bruises, maybe. Or your car. I didn't see the Prius in the driveway. Where *is* your car?"

"If I start with the car, it would almost be like telling you the punch line of a joke first. But let me assure you, this was no joke," he said. "Somebody will be damn sorry once I get home and use every tool in my technology box to get answers to what the heck is going on with those crazy jerks."

"Crazy jerks?" I said. "What crazy jerks?"

"People I used to know. People I thought I'd never see again." His jaw muscles tightened and those blue eyes darkened.

People from his past. The past he'd refused to talk about since I'd known him. I said, "I don't think I've ever seen you this angry."

"Oh, I am more than angry. But anger is wasted energy. Maybe talking about this with you will straighten everything out in my head and help me get rid of the anger." He chugged the rest of his beer and set the empty can on the coffee table. He reached over Merlot and took my hand. His fierce grip was cold and wet from the beer and I shivered a little. He went on. "I've been pretty good in the past at keeping stuff locked away in a corner of my mind, but there's a couple of things I should have shared. Problems. It's time, I guess."

"Go for it." I turned a little more on the sofa, tucking a leg underneath me. Merlot squeaked his displeasure but moved to accommodate me. He knew I was stressed and wanted to be as close as possible. Sort of like Tom, I thought.

He smiled briefly. Then his eyes seemed to focus beyond me, as if he were remembering. A few seconds passed before he spoke. "I was married once to a woman named Hilary. You'd think a cop would know a liar right off the bat, but I was stupid in love."

A small voice in the back of my head was asking, *A wife? This is big. Bigger than I imagined.* "How many years ago?" I said softly.

"The marriage or the divorce?" He didn't meet my gaze.

"Either, both. It doesn't matter." I squeezed his hand. "If you start talking and keep going, the telling might get easier."

He met my gaze. "You are nothing like her and that is so good." He took a deep breath. "Okay, here goes. I met her while I was still on the force in North Carolina. I'd moved around a lot. Been on several different police forces. See, I followed my mother. Felt like I had to protect her from herself. She'd marry every man she'd meet, get tired of the husband of the month and move on after the divorce. Did that five times. The last man was actually decent, though. Helped her get sober, gave her a good life and then he up and died. The only time she didn't run off, and the guy dies." Tom shook his head.

"All this happened in North Carolina, then?" I asked.

"Yes."

"But," I said, "she's been with Ed now for a while. They seem to care a lot for each other." Ed owned Ed's Swap Shop and was one of the most generous, kindest men I'd ever met. Strange guy, yes, but he had a big heart and was no more strange than Karen.

"I guess I'm not including Ed since he's part of the here and now," Tom said. "He's the reason I ended up in Mercy. Following Mom again. She met Ed when he came to an antique auction in North Carolina, and they had an instant connection. She moved here, bought a house and when I decided I was done with police work, done with Hilary, I came here, too."

"I have to say, you are a good son, looking out for your mom for so many years," I said.

"My mom didn't always make good choices, but she and I were always close," he said. "She's settled in for the long haul with Ed and I am so glad she found another decent man. Guess I'm talking about her past because I don't want to talk about Hilary. I better share what happened in the past few days, though. Maybe then I'll have the wits to solve a few pressing problems."

"Start with when you met Hilary or I might get confused. You said this was in North Carolina?" I prompted.

"Yes. In court. I was testifying on a case," he said with disgust. "That should have been a red flag. She was a witness against her former boss. His business was more than a little illegal since money was being laundered every other hour. I told myself she'd been a pawn, had no idea what her boss was doing until he started asking her to shred anything shredable. Thinking she was innocent was my first mistake. She had these eyes, this way about her. I was toast the minute I saw her."

"How long before you two married?" I asked. Something in my voice must have bothered Syrah because he reached a paw out and rested it on my shoulder. Syrah was right. Hearing about Tom's marriage bothered me. No, the fact that he hadn't told me before today is what bothered me.

"Three months after we met, we tied the knot. Three short months. Same pattern my mother followed. But the love affair wasn't simply with her. She had a twelve-year-old kid. I cared about Finn — short for Finnian — and missed another red flag. If his mother was as fantastic as I thought she was, why was Finn the most melancholy kid on the planet?"

Not only an ex-wife, but a boy he loved. Wow. "Bet you made Finn less sad. You do that for me all the time."

For the first time since we sat on the sofa, I felt Tom relax. He even smiled. Chablis wasn't fooled by the smile because she crawled off my lap, over a disgruntled Merlot and onto Tom's. She sensed he needed comfort. He stroked her champagne-colored fur with his free hand. "Finn and I bonded. Did all the father-son stuff. Baseball, Nintendo, hiking, camping. Looking back, meeting Finn was the best thing that came out of marrying Hilary."

Though he needed to know about the other problems, like the half brother who had taken up residence at his place and his sick cat, my news could wait. Tom had lots more to say about the past. "How long were you and Hilary married?" I asked.

"A year," he said. "Her true colors came out — and hers were mostly black. What did Shakespeare say? Something about smiling and smiling and being a villain? That's Hilary."

"Those irreconcilable differences caused the divorce?" I asked, worried I was wandering too far into painful territory.

"That and the fact she cheated on me with

my partner, Nolan Roth." He closed his eyes, jaw tight. "I almost stayed for Finn's sake, because I understood why he was so miserable. She felt nothing for him. But I knew the marriage couldn't work. When we divorced, leaving him with her was the hardest thing I've ever done. I feel guilty about it to this day. But I had no choice. I hadn't adopted him — though I should have — and had no parental rights. Now he's disappeared and Hilary and Nolan think I encouraged him to run away." Tom stared down at the purring Chablis. "I didn't, but I wish I had. Wish I'd found a way to take him away long ago."

"He ran away? How old is he?" I said.

"Just turned eighteen," he said.

"And why would those two think you had anything to do with his disappearance?" I asked.

"Because even though I had no legal standing as far as Finn was concerned and was warned to keep my distance — because Hilary said I was a 'negative influence' — I've kept in touch with him. I thought Hilary didn't know. Obviously she did. Her jerk of a husband took me by surprise the other day. Came busting into my house."

"Like *broke in?*" I said. "How frightening."

"Yup. He had a gun," Tom said. "Searched my house, looking for Finn. Said he logged on to Finn's computer and saw all the e-mails between us — e-mails going back a long time. Stupid to use e-mail, but Finn told me those two completely ignored him, couldn't have cared less about what he was doing in his spare time."

"You hadn't heard from Finn, though?" I said.

"No. What Nolan told me was the scary part — how Finn went missing in the middle of the night. I asked a lot of questions and got no answers except for a pistol whipping. Long story short, we drove in my car all the way to North Carolina to where he and Hilary and Finn lived." Tom parted his dark hair near his temple and I saw a large gash.

I winced. "Looks like you could have used stitches."

"Too late for doctoring now, but you can guess I was pretty messed up. He tied a rope from my knee to the steering wheel and cuffed my right hand to the other side of the wheel. We drove for hours like that."

"What about *his* car?" I was thinking about the white Ford I saw at Tom's place, but I had assumed it belonged to Bob. "And why did Nolan need to take you all the way to North Carolina?"

"Okay, going where Nolan and Hilary lived was my idea. A stupid one, looking back. See, I was afraid Nolan was aware how close Finn and my mother were and that he'd end up at her house. Maybe he'd terrorize *her* trying to get information. I had to protect my mother from him."

"There's nothing stupid about protecting Karen," I said. "How did you convince him to leave Mercy with you?"

"I told him how I was in the security business and could hack into Finn's computer and discover information from instant messages or any social networking sites Finn frequented, maybe find him through his Internet friends. I called my neighbor to take care of Dashiell and phoned Kara and asked her to handle the business."

"Why did *you* drive, though?" I said.

"I told him in this small town people would know I'd disappeared if my car and my van were in the driveway and I was out of touch," he said. "So we ditched Nolan's car near the creek and came back to my house. I was dumb enough to think we'd take my van with all my tools. I told Nolan I needed them. But remember, he was a cop once. He knew I probably had at least one gun in the van, not to mention communication equipment. He wasn't about to offer me any opportunity to get the jump on him. Plus, Nolan figured we wouldn't have to stop if we took the Prius. For the first time ever, I was pissed off about having a full tank of gas."

"Did you find anything on Finn's computer once you got to their place?" I asked.

"I pretended to go through the motions, checked out files and chat rooms and Web sites and told him there was nothing. About then the lightbulb finally came on for Nolan. He figured out I was stalling. So the beatings started — and they weren't because he thought I could tell him anything. He hated me for sending him to jail." Tom gave a mirthless laugh. "He enjoyed the heck out of kicking my ass, too."

"*You* sent him to jail?" I said, feeling my eyes widen in surprise.

He nodded. "Oh yeah. Nolan Roth was a dirty cop and I turned him in. He was sure it was because he was sleeping with Hilary. It wasn't. I'd already made plans to leave her. Nope, I ratted him out because there's no place on any police force for common criminals."

"How hard was it to do something like that?" I asked.

"I never lost any sleep," he said.

"Okay, so what about your ex? Did she . . . *participate* in your . . . *abduction?*"

"She was too smart to show her face once we arrived at their house. But she probably had a hand in this. Lucky for me, the second night I was there, Nolan drank too much and passed out. I'd been working on those zip tie restraints every chance I got and they finally gave. I took off. Would have been easier if I'd left in my own car, but Nolan had my keys, my phone and my wallet. I couldn't risk waking him to get to them."

"Why didn't you go straight to the police?" I said.

"Are you forgetting I was a cop, too? I know from experience that going to the North Carolina police would put the focus on an ex-con's assaulting me rather than on finding Finn. I'd be spending time doing paperwork and talking to one person after another. Nope. I need to find Finn. That's my priority."

I was silent, trying to make sense of all he'd told me.

"I know. I know," Tom said. "I should have told you all this before, but I — I couldn't. I kept it locked away, afraid to open that particular compartment in my brain. I left a kid with a woman I hated, left Finn in what I should have predicted would turn out to be a bad situation. How I wish I'd done things differently."

"You kept in touch with Finn. You cared. Now I'm wondering how I can help. Because this is awful," I said. "Do you know if this Nolan Roth or Hilary went to the North Carolina police about Finn's disappearance before Roth came after you?"

"I doubt they'd do anything even remotely responsible. Plus, Finn's of legal age. Thousands of people disappear every year, most often by choice. Cops always consider kids Finn's age to be runaways rather than missing persons unless there's absolute proof of foul play. I don't like the attitude, but more often than not, it proves to be true."

Tom stroked Chablis gently. He seemed more like the Tom I knew now that he'd gotten some of this difficult story out — a man in control and ready to problem solve.

These revelations were troubling, though, and I said, "This missing kid is not a priority to the police, and the people searching for him are . . . well, plain mean. Any chance Roth really cares about Finn and wants to find him?"

"Not a chance in hell. I don't know what my ex and Nolan are up to, but I intend to find out."

I gently touched his swollen cheek. "So

Nolan came straight for you — and came hard," I said.

"Not because he cares about Finn, though. A lot of his actions were focused on revenge. But I'm wondering if Finn might have taken cash they'd stashed in the house. Missing money would have motivated them, for sure. Could have been serious money, too, since Nolan might still be working for his drug-dealing friends. See, he went to jail for stealing drugs from our busts and then selling them."

"Sounds like a terrible man." My gaze traveled over his battered face. "He did all this to you?"

"Yup. I'll say this: The coward had to restrain me or he'd look worse than me right now." He held out his hands to show me the angry red marks from the zip ties.

"You've got to tell Mike Baca about this right away," I said.

Tom shook his head and was vehement when he said, "No. I'm handling this."

I could see he was getting upset again. I touched a bruise with the tip of my finger and said, "I know you want to deal with this on your own. I'll help you. But first, there are a few things I have to tell you."

He pressed a hand against his right rib cage and grimaced. "Whoa. I'm feeling

Nolan's boot in my side all over again. Is something as wrong as your face is telegraphing?"

I took a deep breath and offered a small smile. "It's not *all* bad news. See, I was so worried when I couldn't reach you that I went to your house."

"Uh-oh. Is Dashiell all right?" he said.

"Good news there. See, Dashiell did have a little blood sugar trouble, but he's with Doc Jensen now and he'll be fine." I rested a hand on his forearm. "There's something else, though."

"My mother? Did Nolan come back here and —"

"No. It doesn't concern Karen — well, not directly. When I went to your house, I met your brother. Seems he's made himself at home."

"*Which* brother?"

FIVE

Which brother? Yet another surprise. “Bob,” I said.

Tom’s jaw muscles flexed. “Figures. I’m not sure I want to hear anything about Bob right now. Let me call Doc about Dashiell and then maybe you can give me a lift home. I’ll deal with my brother face-to-face.”

“Of course,” I said. “There isn’t much to tell except he seems to have made himself comfortable over at your place.”

“Sounds like the same old Bob. Can I use your phone?” Tom called Doc Jensen at home — it was after six now — and learned Dashiell was doing well and could be released tomorrow.

I set out treats for the cats before Tom and I left, feeling guilty about dragging them around in the van all last week. We still had one more trip coming up in a few days and I was already considering leaving them at home. Maybe Kara would care for them.

Though I asked Tom about any other brothers as we headed toward his house, he said he just couldn't talk about his family right now. I respected this. Though I had no ex-husbands in my past, I'd never mentioned my parents' divorce or me moving in with my grandparents when I was a child. But I vowed to do so once the current problems were solved — and I was sure Tom would find Finn. He wouldn't quit until he did. We'd only gotten halfway to his house when Candace and Morris's patrol car flew by us heading in the opposite direction, lights flashing and siren squealing.

"I wonder what's happening," I said.

"If I'm lucky, they're taking Bob to jail for breaking into my house," Tom said. "Though I doubt they'd fire up all their lights for something so mundane. Nope, whatever it is, it's more important than Bob Cochran — which will probably be a shock to him."

"You're confirming what I'd already decided about him," I said. Okay, but I was still curious about the family members he'd never mentioned.

"My brother Bob is — *What the hey?*" Tom said. He pointed up ahead. "Look. On the side of the road."

My headlights revealed a figure walking on the shoulder. He wore a dark hoodie and seemed to be burdened by a heavy backpack. Trotting beside this person was a dog.

"I sure hope that's who I think it is," Tom said. "Pull onto the shoulder ahead of him, okay?"

"You recognize this person?" I asked.

"Nolan mentioned Finn's dog was missing, too. He even looked for dog poop in my backyard when he was sure Finn and the dog were at my house. Finn once texted me a picture and the dog was white with spots — just like this one."

We closed in and indeed it was a small, spotted dog. I slowed and carefully steered off the road in front of them.

Once I'd come to a halt, Tom said, "Let me check on these two. Can you stay in the van?"

"No problem." I watched in the mirror as he approached the small-framed young man. Within seconds, he wrapped the boy in an embrace. The little dog rose on its hind legs and jumped like a jack-in-the-box beside them. The sight melted my heart.

Soon Finn and his dog climbed into my backseat. He pulled down the hood of his sweatshirt and I saw he had big brown eyes and sandy hair, which was longish and messed up from being trapped under a hood. I greeted them with a smile and a Carolina, "Hey there." I wanted to reach out to the dog so he could smell me, but he was panting and focused so intently on Finn, I figured a greeting could wait.

Tom reclaimed the front passenger seat. He sounded almost giddy with elation when he said, "This is my good friend I always talk about, Finn. Jillian Hart. Jillian, this is Finn and *his* best friend, Yoshi."

Tom had gone from angry to anxious to exuberant in the span of a couple hours. He may have hidden his emotions from me in the past, but they were out in force now. He cared about this kid. A lot. His excitement was contagious and I found myself grinning.

I turned on the back overhead light so Finn could get his dog and his belongings settled. "Rough journey?" I asked. His young face looked road weary, that was for sure.

"Not too tough," he answered in a low, soft voice. His gaze wandered from the floor to the dog and then to Tom.

After all he'd probably been through lately, he had to be tired. But I saw what looked like a bump topped by a small cut on the right side of his forehead. The injury might be another reason he seemed foggy.

"Are you okay?" I asked.

Tom laughed, but it was a nervous laugh. "Sure he's okay. He's with me now. Isn't that right, Finn?"

"Sure," he said. But his *sure* came out slurred and slow.

"Tom," I said quietly. "Look at his head." Yoshi yipped several times as if he agreed with my suggestion.

Then I noticed something else and my heart skipped. "And his hands."

In the dim overhead light, Finn's knuckles appeared to be rusted by what looked like dried blood. Or maybe it was just mud. Finn could have fallen in the dirt and hit his head.

Yoshi barked a few more times and bounced up and down on the seat. Indeed, it seemed as if he'd been waiting for someone to notice the kid had a problem. He was a darling little dog, white with brown patches and darker brown spots circling both eyes. His ears were erect and I guessed he was some kind of terrier.

"Uh-oh," Tom said under his breath as he took in Finn more carefully. "What happened, son? How did you get hurt?"

"I'm not hurt," he said. "Just looking for a ride to Tom's house. I think it's up ahead."

On closer inspection, the bump seemed even bigger than I'd first thought.

"To *my* house, right?" Tom's concern came through in his tone.

"Yeah, that's right," Finn said with a laugh. "To *your* house."

"Let's give the kid his wish, Jilly." Tom then mouthed the word *Hurry* to me.

Five minutes later, I pulled in behind brother Bob's Ford. I pushed the button for the van's automatic side door to open and Tom scrambled out his side of the vehicle to help Finn. I came around and took Yoshi's leash from Finn's grip. I'd had my fill of escaping pets for one day. Now I had something else to worry about — this young man.

Tom said, "Glad you knew how to find me, kid."

Finn's brown eyes searched Tom's face. "Yeah, this is where I was headed." He pulled a crumpled piece of paper from his jeans pocket. "Got these directions from . . . somewhere. Maybe at the last truck stop." He began smoothing out the paper.

"Did a trucker give you a ride?" I asked.

"I can't quite . . . remember. Probably 'cause I got this headache that won't quit." Finn squinted even though the sun had gone down thirty minutes ago. "Kinda clouding my brain."

"We need to get you inside. Then we'll figure out the next step." Tom hoisted the backpack over one shoulder and said, "What you got in here? Rocks?"

"I was thinkin' it's kinda heavy. Not sure what all I brought with me," Finn said.

The front porch light came on and Bob opened the door. "About time you showed up, bro."

"Don't use *bro* with me," Tom called. He draped an arm around Finn's shoulders and they walked into the house.

Bob raised his hands in mock surrender. "Hey, almost half of the word *brother* is *bro.* Seems about right." He laughed.

As I followed behind Tom and Finn, hanging tight to a surprisingly strong Yoshi, I again wondered how Tom could be related to this insensitive man.

Yoshi seemed determined not to let Finn out of his sight. Hostility had filled the space between Tom and his brother and probably brought out the protective instincts of this little dog.

When he passed Bob, Tom said, "Gather whatever crap you brought with you and get out of my house. And don't you dare land at Mom's place."

Bob, still smiling, said, "Look at your face,

Tom. Seems like you had a can of whoop ass explode all over you and it's got you pissed off."

To his credit, Tom ignored Bob. He knew we had more pressing issues than an uninvited guest.

Tom dropped the backpack inside the door, put both hands on Finn's shoulders and guided him to the black leather sofa. "Take a load off, kid. You look tired."

"I got this headache, man." He sat and pressed his hands against his temples. Yoshi jumped on the couch next to him and began licking at what sure did seem like blood on Finn's hands.

I knelt in front of Finn, hoping he'd make eye contact. That would sure be a good sign. "Can I check if you're bleeding somewhere?"

He looked straight at me for the first time, but he was still squinting. "Huh?"

Yoshi's full attention remained on Finn. Tom sat on the edge of the sofa on Finn's other side, leaving the dog where he was. "We want to see your hands, okay? You could have a cut somewhere."

The side of Finn's right hand was smeared with blood, too, but I couldn't see a cut or a scrape anywhere.

I looked up at Tom. "We need to get Finn

checked out by a doctor. His headache could be —"

"She's right. The kid doesn't look so hot," Bob said. "Hope it doesn't have anything to do with this." Bob had opened Finn's backpack and was pointing at something inside.

Uh-oh, I thought. *Drugs?* Drugs would explain Finn's dazed behavior.

Tom said, "What makes you think you can mess with Finn's stuff?"

"I don't expect *you* to tell me what's going on," Bob said. "Figured I might find answers by myself. Is your former kid the reason you're all beat up? The gun tells me maybe so."

"Gun?" Worry filled Tom's eyes as he looked at Finn. "You brought a gun with you?"

Finn started to shake his head but grimaced and stopped. "I don't have a gun, Tom. All I've got is a headache."

I stood. Finn was traveling alone, probably hitchhiking. Maybe he'd thought he needed a weapon. But now he couldn't even recall bringing one with him.

I said, "Finn needs help. Maybe Marcy is off duty." Marcy was a paramedic friend of ours. "She could check him out if you're worried about taking him somewhere too . . . public."

"Bet every paramedic in town is at the car wreck that just sent the cops racing out of here," Bob said. "By the way, do I have you to thank for a visit from Mercy's finest, Jillian?"

"Shut the hell up, Bob," Tom said evenly. He seemed to be trying hard to be patient, but wasn't succeeding. "This is none of your business." He looked down at Finn. "You might need more than a paramedic."

Tom walked over to where Bob was and, with his index finger looped through the trigger guard, he lifted a small gun from the backpack.

"Before we do anything else, I'll lock this up." He hurried past us through the small living room. I knew he kept a gun safe in his office.

Meanwhile, Finn was examining his hands, turning them over and back as if fascinated.

His behavior sure bothered me.

When Tom came back, I said, "He definitely needs to see a doctor."

Tom nodded. "I'll take him to the emergency room, say he's a runaway. Maybe then I won't have to give anyone his name." He craned his neck so he could look at Finn's face. "Can you forget your name for a while, son?"

Finn didn't respond for several seconds. "There seems to be a few things I can't remember. Guess I could lose my name, too."

"Okay, good. We're gonna get your headache fixed up." He cupped Finn's elbow to help him up, but Yoshi, who had been sitting quietly, growled.

Finn patted the dog's head. "It's okay, boy. He's good."

Yoshi seemed to settle with Finn's touch and I held my hand out to the dog palm down. He sniffed at it briefly and I could see his small, muscular body relax even more. In a gentle tone, I said, "It'll be fine, Yoshi. You can come, too."

He stared at me and cocked his head. If dogs could smile, I'd just seen it happen.

I picked up the leash, deciding to handle Yoshi so Tom could help Finn. Just as I did, the sound of a cell phone playing the *William Tell Overture* blared from its spot on the end table beside the sofa.

Bob answered, remained quiet for a few seconds and then said, "Our missing man is right here. Talk to him yourself." He held the phone out to Tom. "Deputy Candace Carson wants to speak to you in the worst way. Seems you've got every hot woman in town on your roster and I must say, your deputy friend is smokin'."

Tom walked over and snatched the phone from Bob, his patience close to completely evaporated. "Tom here," he said abruptly.

He listened intently and his expression grew troubled. I saw him glance at the backpack before he said, "Yes, I know him. You want me to come to the scene and confirm?" A few more seconds passed and he said, "I'm on my way." He clicked off the phone and handed it back to Bob.

"What's happening?" I asked.

Tom glanced down at Finn, who was now leaning back against the cushions looking groggier than ever. Yoshi's head rested in his lap. Tom took my arm and turned us away from Finn. "Can I ask a huge favor?" he whispered.

"Whatever you need," I said.

"Get Finn medical help. I don't care how; just get him checked out. If you can avoid giving his name, that's good, but I know you have to do this your way."

"Sure. But what did Candace want?"

Tom stared at the floor. "She found my phone. Nolan had it."

"Okay," I said slowly. "But you said something about identifying someone?"

"Nolan wrecked my car," Tom said.

"Oh boy. Not good about your car, but it could be good in another way. They can arrest him for kidnapping and assaulting you. They can —"

"Damn hard to arrest a dead man."

Six

Tom took off immediately in his work van without a word to Bob, the obviously unwelcome brother who showed no inclination to follow Tom's earlier instructions to leave the premises.

As I helped Finn to his feet, I looked over at Bob and said, "If a woman named Hilary calls or comes by, I don't think Tom would appreciate you telling her anything."

Bob smiled. He always seemed to be smiling and it was getting on my last nerve.

He said, "I know Hilary. I won't say anything about her kid being here."

Finn peered at Bob. "Who are you?"

"You and I met once or twice a long time ago, Finn," he said. "I won't hold it against you that you don't remember me. Go with the nice lady and get yourself fixed up."

Bob knows Finn and Hilary. Makes sense, since Tom was married to Hilary. How much more of Tom's past will spill out before the end of this very long day? Seems like years since I came back to town earlier today.

Making sense of Tom's relationships with his family could wait. Right now, I had to help Finn. I took Yoshi by the leash and cupped the kid's elbow with my other hand.

Bob held up the backpack. "Don't forget this," he said. "I saw a few treats for the dog in there."

I grabbed it on our way out and slipped it over one shoulder. Even with the gun gone, the pack was still heavy. Seemed as if Finn brought along everything important to him when he made the journey here.

The night was unpleasantly cold, the first bite of winter snapping at us as I urged Finn into the backseat where he could lie down. I always have at least one quilt in my car and I covered him up. Yoshi whimpered as he settled alongside his best friend. I started the engine and turned on the heat.

Since taking Finn inside an emergency room with a dog in tow would be frowned upon, to say the least, I pulled out my phone and called Shawn Cuddahee for help. He and his wife, Allison, owned the Mercy Animal Sanctuary and had become my good friends. I was hoping Shawn could separate Yoshi and Finn with as little emotional trauma as possible.

Allison answered.

"What can I do for you, Jillian?" she asked.

I explained I needed a spot for a dog, hopefully just for overnight, because I had to take a young man to get medical treatment.

She said, "Oh no. I am so sorry. I'm not at the sanctuary. I'm getting help for a pregnant bulldog. They always have difficult labors and she'll need a C-section. I'm at the vet clinic. Are you on the road already?"

"I will be in about thirty seconds. I guess I'll have to leave the dog in my van when I take the kid in to see a doctor. It's not terribly cold out and —"

"You heading to the hospital?" she asked.

"Too far. I think there's a new emergency clinic about twenty miles north," I said.

"You're right. Just opened in a strip center near the interstate. Since you have no idea how long you'll be, I'll meet you in the parking lot and pick up the dog. Doc Jensen has the situation under control here."

I put the phone on speaker and started to back up. "You already have an emergency of your own. I can call Kara if I get in a bind."

"This happens all the time with bulldogs, so it's not an emergency. I will meet you," Allison said firmly. "See you soon, sweetie."

She disconnected.

On the drive out of town, I glanced in the rearview mirror every so often. Finn's eyes were closed and Yoshi's head rested on his arm. When I finally pulled into the small shopping center, I was surprised to find the lot nearly deserted. But a neon sign flashed *24 Hour Emergency Care* in the storefront at the far end. I saw Allison's truck pull in right next to me when I parked. What timing.

Even with the heat on, the van was chilly. Good thing I had a quilt to cover Finn. All he wore for a jacket was his black hoodie. I wondered then if it was stained with blood, too. Impossible to tell.

I unlocked the van and Allison climbed into the front seat. With her eyes trained on Yoshi and Finn, she said, "You want me to take the dog to the sanctuary?"

"If you can," I said.

She was staring at Yoshi with a kind but take-charge expression. I'd seen her work miracles with animals using that look.

"Who's this?" she asked, never taking her eyes off the dog.

"Yoshi," I said.

"Yoshi's a rat terrier, I see," Allison said. "This might be a challenge. Very possessive dogs." She still smiled, still stared and kept her tone even.

"I need to get this kid inside." I tried to keep the urgency I felt out of my voice, but wasn't sure I succeeded.

"Hey, Yoshi," Allison said. She reached her hand between the front seats. "Everything's gonna be okay. Have a sniff, friend."

Yoshi's neck stretched and he smelled her hand. His ears flattened and he started to blink. He suddenly looked incredibly sad.

"I'm here to help you and Finn, baby," she said. Then she thumped the side of her chest with her right hand. "Yoshi, come."

Tail wagging, he wiggled between the seats and into Allison's arms. "Jillian's gonna take care of your friend and you're gonna stay with me, baby."

Yoshi started licking her face. *The Dog Whisperer's got nothing on you, Allison,* I thought as I pushed the button to slide open the van's side door.

"I think it might be better if we waited here," Allison said cheerfully, her arms wrapped around Yoshi.

I left the van running and roused Finn who, thank goodness, was just asleep and not unconscious.

With my arm around his waist, I helped him through the emergency center door — an emergency room next door to a Subway.

Never thought I'd see something like this.

Inside, a mother sat holding a flushed baby, but they were the only patients in the waiting area. The place had been open only a few weeks, as far as I knew. I was so glad we'd lucked out and wouldn't have to wait too long.

When the young woman at the front desk saw me come in supporting Finn, she looked at him with concern and immediately told us to come through the double doors to my left.

A man in blue scrubs seemed to arrive out of nowhere once we passed through and he said, "I've got him." He took my place supporting a wobbly Finn. "You can check him in, ma'am. Head injury, perhaps?"

I nodded.

He said, "I'll begin his neurological assessment but we'll need his medical history, so talk to the receptionist and —"

"I don't know his medical history. He's visiting me," I said.

The man — Dr. Stanley, I read on the picture ID hanging around his neck — looked at Finn. "What's your name, kid?"

"Finn," he said.

"You got a last name?" the doctor asked.

"Hart," I said, before he could answer. I could at least make this a little easier for

Finn and Tom by keeping questions to a minimum.

Stanley turned his attention back to me. "Tell Regina at the front desk everything you know — including where we can reach a relative." He was already assisting Finn into a curtained cubicle. A woman in pink scrubs came hurrying from another cubicle to help him.

"I am a relative," I said. But to my own ears, the claim sounded hollow. Would anyone believe me?

Soon I was telling the light-skinned black woman who'd ushered me through those doors what little I knew. She had hazel eyes and a warm smile, but of course her main concern was who would be financially responsible.

That's when I knew with certainty that to get this kid the care he needed, I would have to tell a few more lies. My stomach clenched at the thought and I remembered something my grandmother used to say: "A lie may take care of the present, but it has no future." Such would be the case today. But still, I needed to aid a boy who'd trekked all the way from North Carolina to find Tom. I am an honest person, but honesty needed to be put aside, at least for now.

"His name is Finnian Hart," I began. "We

don't have insurance. Can I pay with a credit card?"

Thirty minutes later, paperwork complete, I walked out to the van. I opened the driver's-side door and saw Yoshi curled in Allison's lap. He sat up, ears pricked, when he saw me.

"How's Finn? What did they find out?" Allison said.

"I don't know yet. They said the examination would take a while. I said I was his aunt and his parents were out of the country and unreachable. Can they sue me for telling fibs?"

"You told me on the phone he's a runaway, right?"

I nodded.

"In that case, you did what you had to do, Jillian. It's like when we take in lost animals at the shelter. Someone has to care for the strays in the moment of need. We worry about the emergency situation first and the people part later."

I smiled, liking her analogy. "Exactly."

"He looked like he's what? Seventeen? Eighteen?"

"Tom said he's eighteen. He looks younger to me, but he's legal age and probably could have signed off on all those papers himself if he had his wits about him. But he doesn't."

Allison stroked Yoshi's head. "We're fine here, so go on back inside and wait. Yoshi and I have already shared a granola bar. Never go anywhere without a granola bar, I say."

I noticed Allison had the quilt wrapped around her shoulders.

"You warm enough?" I said. "I have another quilt if you need one."

"We're fine," she said. "You go on, now."

Turned out, I waited only an hour before they called me to the back. Dr. Stanley was with Finn in his cubicle. Somewhere, in another curtained-off space, a child wailed.

Stanley held a clipboard and quickly told me Finn had a minor concussion, nothing that needed hospitalization unless he vomited, had seizures or his headache became severe. The treatment was simple — let him rest and allow him to have Tylenol or Advil starting tomorrow morning. He should follow up with a neurologist and the clerk Regina would give me a list of a few in the area.

Then the doctor looked straight at me for the first time. "As for his memory loss, it's to be expected. But where did the blood come from? The cut on his forehead is small and he has no other injuries."

"I have no idea about the blood on his hands and shirt. But he does remember hitchhiking. Maybe he got in a fight with someone." I glanced at Finn, wondering if a fight explained the bump on his head.

Stanley said, "All he could tell me is he came to visit this person, Tom. Tom is . . . ?"

"His uncle," I said quickly.

"Yes, you're the aunt. I forgot." Stanley cocked an eyebrow. "Anyway, blood from something or someone seeped through his sweatshirt and onto the shirt underneath."

"I wish I had answers," I said. "The only thing I know for sure is he has this memory gap."

The doctor gripped Finn's shoulder and smiled. "Aside from the concussion, he's a healthy young man. Not remembering is, as I said, very typical after a concussion."

"But he'll remember in time?" I asked.

Stanley shook his head. "The information is probably gone forever, so you might have to help him solve this mystery. I'm guessing you're probably right about a fight, though he's so subdued right now, it's hard to picture him getting aggressive. At any rate, he's all yours." Dr. Stanley turned abruptly and left us, mumbling, "I'm coming, little girl. I'm coming," in response to the supersonic screams the child somewhere beyond had now resorted to. I hoped she would be okay.

Finn whispered, "Tom said Hart is your last name, right?"

I nodded.

"Thanks for doing this," he said. "But, you know, when the lady was helping me take off my clothes, I couldn't find my phone. Do you have it?"

"No, but maybe you dropped it in my van. Come on. I hate you having to put dirty clothes back on, but you can't leave here in a hospital gown, even though it's oh so attractive."

With that remark, I'd managed to nudge his first real smile — and it was a nice one.

"Are we heading back to Tom's?" Finn said. Though he still slurred his words a tad, he was considerably more alert. The nap in the car probably helped. How long had he been on the road without sleep?

"Since Tom's been called away," I said, "let's stop at my house. We can phone him from there." All I could think about was Bob, still camped out at Tom's house. We'd be better off at my place. "You hungry?"

His sleepy eyes brightened and now he offered a genuine grin. "Hungry? You bet."

Once we returned to the van, Allison turned Yoshi over to Finn and put one of her business cards in his hand. "If you ever want to help out at an animal shelter in sore need of volunteers, call me."

Finn smiled and put the card in his backpack. "I love animals."

"I can see that," she said. Then she hugged me good-bye and took off, but not before showing me a picture of the four puppies that Doc Jensen had sent to her phone. They were tiny little things and Finn couldn't take his eyes off them.

After a hunt for the missing phone we never found, Finn fell asleep again on the trip to my house, his terrier by his side. As we pulled into the driveway, I had the feeling that a caffeine-overloaded energy drink might give me the boost I would need when my fur friends met Yoshi. How would I convince three cats a dog visitor would be just what they needed? What was to come might be the biggest challenge of the day.

I couldn't be sure Finn had the strength to keep up with the dog, so I took the leash as we got out of the car. Once we reached the back door, I disabled the security system.

Taking a deep breath first, I led the way inside. Or should I say I led briefly before Yoshi raced into the house, his leash nearly slipping from my hand.

We were greeted by a trio of loud hisses.

SEVEN

I wrapped the leash around one hand, shortening it considerably, and flipped the utility room light on with my free hand.

Syrah and Merlot, their fur standing on end and their backs arched, guarded the entrance to the kitchen. Chablis was nowhere in sight. Wispy cat hairs drifted around us — a result of all three cats' agitation at this invasion by, of all things, a *dog.*

Finn stood so close behind me his head was next to my ear. He said, "What cool cats."

"They're not always this, um, *fluffy,*" I said. "Can you handle Yoshi? Because I get the feeling that though your dog is small, he could pull me to the floor."

"Yoshi, down," Finn said loud enough that I nearly jumped.

The dog obeyed instantly, but he didn't take his eyes off my cats. And they didn't take their eyes off Yoshi.

"Do you think he'll stay put for a few minutes? Or maybe we could attach his leash to —"

"He'll stay until I release him. We did obedience class and he took the prize for best student." I turned and saw Finn smile again, with pride this time.

"I have to say, though there may be an obedience class for cats, mine have never attended. They do what they want to, when they want to. Pretty typical behavior, I'm afraid." I unwound the leash and handed it to Finn.

"You apologizing for your cats being cats?" Finn said with a laugh.

I grinned. "Shouldn't do that. You're right."

"The big one is almost Yoshi's size," Finn said. "What's its name?"

"He's Merlot and the other one is Syrah. Syrah is my protector, just like Yoshi is yours."

"Funny names," Finn said. "French or something?"

"I'll explain later. Right now, I have three cats to tame," I said.

Syrah would be the biggest challenge. I could tell from his laid-back ears and the wide-mouthed hisses that just kept coming, he was very unhappy with what the humans had dragged in.

"Maybe it's the concussion, but I only see two cats," Finn said.

"The other one is hiding. She does that. If you're sure Yoshi will stay, we can go into the kitchen."

"He'll stay. He likes cats, by the way. We have a few in the apartment complex and he . . ." Finn's voice trailed off as if sadness had taken hold. Leaving home is never easy, even if home is a miserable place.

"Come on," I said. "I'll bet you haven't eaten in ages."

"You got that right." After Finn ordered Yoshi to stay one more time, using a hand signal with the command, he took a spot at the breakfast bar.

I filled a bowl with water and set it near the dog. He hadn't been offered a drop since we'd first met. Finn said, "Take it," and Yoshi lapped water like he'd been left in the desert. As soon as he was finished, Finn repeated his command to stay.

I made peanut butter and jelly sandwiches and gave Finn a bag of potato chips and a glass of milk. After he downed the milk in several long swigs, I set the remaining half gallon next to him. While I knelt and petted my two boy cats, I heard about Finn's hitch-hiking trip to find Tom. He did not, however, mention his mother or his stepfather. I wasn't about to tell him that the man he might have once called *Dad* was dead. His journey to this point had been difficult enough.

When he was done telling me about the truckers who had given him rides, as well as one teenage girl who he said was "cute" but talked too much, Finn said, "Can you call Tom now?"

I'd been thinking the same thing, but then I remembered I couldn't. Tom's phone had been found with Nolan. I said, "He'll call us when he's free. He had some business that couldn't wait."

"Okay. Cool," Finn said. But I read disappointment in his eyes.

Meanwhile, neither of my fur kids had moved. Syrah and Merlot would not be dissuaded from their vigil at the utility room door, not by offers of catnip or cat food or treats. They'd settled into what I called the "meatloaf position" — hunched up like I'd just patted them into a football-size oven-ready meal. They kept their intense stares on Yoshi, resting patiently like cats tend to do while watching prey — and waiting for their chance. I decided to leave the animals to sort this out. My interference might make them more nervous than they already were.

I said, "I'll bet Yoshi is hungry. But I don't have any dog food."

"No problem," Finn said. "I have some in my backpack." He'd set his pack on the floor by his stool at the breakfast bar and now he went to get it.

The minute Finn got the food out and released Yoshi with an "okay," the dog came racing by the cats. Syrah took a swipe at him and Merlot stood and arched his back. Yoshi ignored them and ran to Finn's side. The dog barked repeatedly, but his eyes were focused on the food.

"I'll get a bowl," I said.

Finn set the baggie of dog food on the counter and held out his arms. The dog jumped up into them and started licking the kid's face. What a bond those two had. From what I'd learned from Tom about Finn's mother and latest stepfather, he probably needed his dog as much as I needed my cats.

Before I could even retrieve the bowl from the cupboard, Syrah leaped onto the counter, his whiskers and nose in action. A cat's sense of smell is nowhere near that of a dog's, but it's still about fourteen or fifteen times stronger than a human's. Syrah approached the kibble as if all things edible in this house needed his inspection and approval. He was the alpha around here, after all.

Then Syrah spotted the backpack and withdrew a few steps as if surprised by this strange new object. But his whiskers kept twitching. Syrah liked anything remotely resembling a bag or a box and I was sure he was contemplating whether this was a safe item to thoroughly explore — like, climb right inside and explore.

By the time I poured the food into the bowl, Merlot had joined Syrah in his fascination with the backpack. Their focus made me remember the gun, the one Tom put in his safe back at his house. Seemed like a long time ago. Heck, this day seemed like it had lasted a hundred years. Did Finn really have no idea where the gun came from? Might as well ask.

"Do you remember anything about the gun?" I said.

Finn shook his head vehemently. "Not my gun. No way. I hate guns. But Nolan sure had enough of them. My preferred weapon is a sword in a video game."

I nodded. "When was the last time you looked inside your pack?"

He squinted, as if trying to imagine when he might have done this. "Besides just now? I fed Yoshi last night. I can't remember any time today — but there's a lot about today I don't remember."

"You didn't see the gun last night, wherever you spent the night?" I asked. "Gosh, where *did* you spend the night?"

"This guy let me and Yoshi crash in his truck. But I never saw any gun. Something like that kinda grabs your attention, you know?" I detected strain in his voice, perhaps born of impatience with my questions.

Yoshi reacted by licking Finn's face again.

"Yes, they certainly do. Sorry if I've upset you," I said. "You've been through enough and I want you to know I'm your friend. At least we know someone put the gun in your pack between last night and when we picked you up."

"Yeah. Makes sense. Whatever screwed up my brain happened today. You didn't upset me, by the way. I'm just mad at myself 'cause I can't remember." He stroked Yoshi but didn't look at me.

"Which is not your fault." I handed him the bowl of kibble Yoshi was staring at intently.

"Maybe it is. Maybe I did something stupid . . . or knocked myself stupid," he said.

"Quit beating yourself up." I glanced at

the dog. "You plan to feed your poor animal?"

"Yeah, right." He set both the dog and the food on the floor next to him.

I peered over the raised breakfast bar. Yoshi was making short work of his food. Meanwhile Syrah now had his head in the backpack while Merlot supervised this exploration.

Finn laughed. "I've never had a cat. But from what I've seen tonight, dogs need a boss, but cats *are* the bosses."

"You got that right." I looked down at the dog. "Let me get him more water."

"Can Yoshi and I crash?" Finn picked up the empty dish and handed it to me. "I'm pretty tired even though the sandwiches and stuff made me feel better." Finn's pale cheeks did have a bit of color now. "And I didn't thank you for helping me. Sorry. Thanks, Mrs. Hart."

"Call me Jillian. And no thanks needed. I have the feeling you'd do the same for me if our positions were reversed." I smiled. "Now, come on. You deserve a real bed to sleep in rather than the backseat of my van."

First, I set Finn up in the bathroom with a fresh towel. After he'd showered, he put on the clean T-shirt and sweatpants I'd provided. He was thin enough to wear mine.

Honestly, he looked more like a fifteen-year-old than an eighteen-year-old. I almost felt like tucking him in once he and Yoshi were settled in the guest room. Instead, I brought in Yoshi's bowl of water, and a glass for Finn, too. After I wished them a good night's rest, I closed the door.

Now to hunt down Chablis. I found her in her favorite hiding place, under my bed. She didn't seem anxious to come out. But with a few "I love you's," words she could never resist, she was soon in my arms.

When I came back out into the hallway holding her, I saw Merlot and Syrah positioned outside the guest room. Syrah was pawing under the door and Merlot was sitting like a statue, observing this game. The two of them hoped to engage the dog in a little paw peekaboo, I was sure. For my three cats, a closed door is a challenge, and a fun one at that. They could always lighten my mood, and today, though it had been an awful day to say the least, they cracked me up. Kudos for cat behavior, I thought.

I nuzzled Chablis as I walked into the living room, and again wondered why Tom hadn't called yet. We left for the emergency clinic at dusk and now it was close to midnight. He was obviously concerned about Finn and would want an update, and yet I hadn't heard from him. I could call his house, but a call might mean a conversation with Bob — which was the last thing I wanted right now.

Unfortunately the *very* last thing I wanted was about to happen. I'd changed into flannel drawstring pants and a long-sleeved T-shirt, not exactly dressed for company — but company arrived. The knock on the front door made my heart skip. Kara, Candace and Tom are back-door friends. So who could this be?

I checked the peephole and almost moaned out loud when I saw the person standing on my front stoop.

Lydia Monk. The craziest assistant coroner on the planet.

EIGHT

I sighed heavily and unlocked the door. "Hey, Lydia," I said with far more enthusiasm than I felt. "I was about to head off to bed, so —"

"Let me in," she said brusquely.

No *please,* no *may I,* just Lydia being Lydia. Nor did she wait for me to step aside before brushing past me and marching on her high-heeled black boots into my living room. I noticed her bleached hair was held back by a large jeweled clip — plenty of rhinestones and a variety of brightly colored fake gems to be had, enough to decorate a tiara.

She sat on my sofa, dropping her patent leather bag beside her. There seemed to be no dress code at the county coroner's office, or perhaps the coroner himself was too afraid of this woman to address the issue of her gaudy wardrobe. What kind of assistant coroner wears skinny jeans and a leather jacket to the scene of an accident? I assumed that's where she'd been — the spot Tom had also been called to. She'd probably spoken with him and something he'd said upset her enough to bring her here — because she was certainly on a tear. Lydia's obsession with all things Tom never failed to surprise me. One day, when I wasn't exhausted, I'd love to sit down and have a heart-to-heart with her about when she first fell "in love" with a man who never gave her any encouragement in the romance department. Maybe I'd learn more about what made Lydia tick and even begin to understand her.

She didn't waste any time letting me know just how upset she was. "Jillian Hart, when will you learn to stay out of the murder business? You should be the one sitting in the police station right now, not Tom."

My eyes widened in surprise. *Tom was still at Mercy PD after all this time?* And did she say *murder?* "I'm not sure I understand what you're talking about, Lydia," I said as evenly as I could. But my stomach was doing somersaults.

I eased myself into my late husband's recliner, hoping to find comfort in his old leather chair. I was still holding Chablis and clutched her close. From the corner of my eye, I saw Syrah sitting on the foyer tile at the entrance to the living room, his gaze fixed on Lydia. Those two had a little history and did not like each other one bit.

"Before Candace and Morris put Tom in the squad car, I heard him tell Candace to call you." Lydia's ruby-colored lips tightened. "Why would he tell her to do such a thing?"

Though Lydia had never had so much as a cup of coffee alone with Tom, she was fixated on him and had decided I was a threat to their imaginary relationship. "He probably told Candace to call me because we're friends?" I stated it as a question, hoping to avoid bringing up Finn. Tom probably wanted Finn to know he was delayed so he wouldn't think Tom had abandoned him.

"Nice try, Jillian. You heard about that car wreck and you know something about the victim, don't you? Tom was sending you some kind of message."

"W-why would you think that?" But my slight hesitation apparently stirred even more paranoia in the Queen of Paranoia.

"Are you sure you want to lie to a county official?" she said. "I'm betting your best buddy Candace has already called you."

"Haven't heard from her," I said a little too forcefully. I had to keep my cool. It was always better to try to get more information than I gave when it came to Lydia. I could never tell what she was up to. "I understand Tom's car was in an accident and there was a fatality. That's all I know."

Lydia leaned back on the sofa with a satisfied smile. "If you didn't talk to Candace, how did you find out?"

"Tom told me after Candace called him to help identify the victim. But I know nothing about any murder and I certainly had no idea Tom was still at the police station."

I swallowed, trying to make sense of this. *Why is he still there after so many hours?* I went on, saying, "You, of all people, realize he would never murder anyone."

She smiled smugly, gloating, I supposed, over my acknowledgment that she was a friend of Tom's — even though she really wasn't. But then she blinked slowly and I saw her glittery purple eye shadow was smeared, almost giving her eyes a bruised look. "He must know something or Candace wouldn't still be interviewing him. What has he told you, Jillian?"

So she'd come here to learn why Tom was called to the scene — information I didn't have. I desperately wanted to get Candace on the phone and learn what the heck was going on. Maybe Lydia was making this all up to find out what I knew. After all, she believed Tom was her soul mate and I somehow stood in the way of their being together. I finally found my voice — and tried to sound conciliatory. "Please, Lydia. If you know why Tom is still at the police station, you know far more than I do. Why is he still there after all this time?"

"I'm not at liberty to say." She leaned forward and pointed a scarlet-tipped finger at me. "I'm an investigator on this case. Goes with the job description. You need to start talking, lady."

Oh, jeez, now she was resorting to her tough-guy routine. What a kaleidoscope of personalities Lydia Monk possessed. "What do you want me to talk about?" Chablis, now curled in my lap, lifted her head in surprise at my tone, and Syrah bounded from his spot in the foyer and came to a stop in front of Lydia. He slowly sat and gazed up at her with slitted golden eyes.

She recoiled. "You know how I feel about your *animals.* Get that thing away from me."

"Please tell me what you know about Tom," I said, making no move to rescue Lydia from my cat's presence. It's not like he would ever hurt her.

"I suppose your stepdaughter will be printing it in the paper tomorrow, so you'll find out anyway. Tom has information about the dead man. But all I've been able to learn is the victim was his ex-partner. Now, remove this cat. I know he bites."

She'd actually drawn her knees up and, fearing her spiked heels might hurt Syrah, I called, "Here, buddy." I patted the arm of my chair.

He complied, but not before rubbing his body on the sofa to leave his scent and let Lydia know who owned this place.

Once Syrah was sitting next to me, Lydia said, "You've admitted to being present when Candace called Tom to the scene. Tell me what you know and maybe Tom will be allowed to go home. You could start with how he got those cuts and bruises and why his ex-partner was driving the Prius."

"The only thing I can tell you is what you already know. The man was Tom's former partner on some police force a long time ago." I hoped she wouldn't get back to the cuts and bruises. I didn't want to answer that particular question since I had no idea what information Tom had shared. He was the one who should be telling the story about what Nolan Roth did to him, not me.

"You are being intentionally difficult, Jillian Hart. Tom wouldn't tell me anything at the scene, and I'm beginning to think you're probably the reason why. Have you ever met this Nolan Roth person?"

"No. Never," I said.

"Really? I'm not sure I believe you, but time will tell. It always does when it comes to crime. As for Tom, I suppose he has his reasons to keep quiet." She smiled at me — a forced smile, in my opinion. "What you don't seem to understand is that sometimes he needs help to understand what's best for him. That's not you, by the way. We both know who he really cares about."

I barely restrained myself from rolling my eyes. I certainly didn't feel as if I had to say anything more. I most certainly didn't have to tell her about the kid sleeping in my guest room. "I'm sorry, Lydia, but I can't tell you what I don't know."

Lydia's features softened. "You're being stubborn, probably because you believe in your heart you have a chance with Tom. You don't, but that's beside the point. Let me reassure you that if you're worried I'm gonna run to Candace and give up information, you should know me better. I'll help Tom any way I can, but you could help, too."

This new tactic reminded me of a caramel apple — all sticky-sweet on the outside and sour on the inside. Did she believe I'd fall for this? I said, "Lydia, I know next to nothing about Nolan Roth and nothing at all about the accident."

"Not an accident. Murder, remember?" She raised her eyebrows expectantly.

"Why do they think this man was murdered? All I heard about was a car accident."

"*Think* he was murdered? I, the assistant coroner in this county, do my job well. A bullet hole in the skull with the absence of a weapon at the scene tells me this is murder. But here's the thing — and I told your BFF Candace this, too. I know Tom owns a Glock, not a revolver. The fatal injury came from a much smaller caliber weapon than a Glock. Maybe a .38." She raised her chin. "Seen my fair share of gunshot wounds, so I *know* what I'm talking about."

I could feel the blood drain from my cheeks. I thought again about the gun found in Finn's backpack. Was it a .38? I swallowed hard. "He was shot? How horrible."

"News flash, Jillian. Murder is horrible."

Despite the sarcasm, Lydia was finally giving out information. If she kept telling me things she probably shouldn't be saying, then maybe I wouldn't have to answer more questions. I didn't want to offer anything else. Nothing. I felt protective, not only toward Tom, but toward Finn, too.

Finn. Why did I feel so protective? But I knew the answer. The kid was hurt, vulnerable and Tom cared about him. Still, I couldn't stop the questions now filling my head.

I began to string the day's events together. When we picked Finn up on the side of the road, he seemed dazed and was obviously injured. Could the bump on his head have come from being in a car accident? Perhaps. So, did Nolan drive the Prius to Mercy and find Finn on the road before we did? Did Nolan pick him up and the car crashed? Maybe when Finn pulled a gun on him? I shook my head to free myself of these thoughts. No. Finn couldn't have done such a thing. After our conversation and seeing him interact with his beloved dog, I trusted this kid wasn't holding back. He didn't know where the gun had come from — of that much I was certain. Or at least, he couldn't remember. Could he have forgotten he killed someone, though? Perhaps in self-defense? I wanted to scrub such a thought from my mind, but I couldn't. The gun could have belonged to Nolan Roth, there could have been a struggle and —

"What's going on, Jillian? I can tell your wheels are turning," Lydia said.

I blinked several times, determined not to

dwell on possible scenarios before I had all the facts. "I — I'm simply tired and I'm picturing my nice, comfy bed. I drove back here this morning from the craft shows and —"

"Oh, right," she said with a sarcastic smile. "You're a *businesswoman.* How does making those cat blankets, or whatever it is you do, give you enough money to keep you in this nice house?"

I wasn't about to tell her that when John died, he left me enough to live comfortably even if I never made another cat quilt in my life. It was none of her business and, besides, mentioning John's name in her presence seemed . . . *wrong.* "Sorry, I'm not sure what my financial status has to do with why you came here tonight."

"Just always wanted to ask how you maintain this comfortable lifestyle. You're saying you were gone part of today? What part?" she said.

Where was she going with this? "Why do you need to know?"

"You say you were out of town and yet you were with Tom when Candace called him," Lydia said. "Do you always head straight for him when you come home? Because I'm certain he wasn't waiting here for you."

What would she do if she knew he actually *was* waiting here for me earlier today? I wasn't about to offer that piece of information and set her off. Did she even realize we were at Tom's house when the call came? Did she know anything about Bob? I decided it wasn't my responsibility to enlighten her about anything. If I mentioned Finn, Tom's being kidnapped, or the gun, I was certain Lydia would take the information, twist it and end up making Tom, Candace and probably the police chief pretty darn angry.

No, I would call Candace the minute I got Lydia out of here and tell *her* what I knew.

Get her to leave, Jillian, I told myself. Finn might wake up and walk out here, or Yoshi might start barking.

But she seemed settled in, even comfortable, so I said, "Do you think Tom will be free to go soon? It's getting really late."

Her demeanor changed abruptly. "If you'd tell me what I need to know," she said with fire in her eyes, "I could relay information to Candace and he could go home in a New York minute. But if you don't come through with anything helpful, they might make him sleep in the jail tonight."

Now she was trying to make me feel

guilty. I wanted to scream with frustration. Instead I repeated, "I don't know anything more." To myself I added, *Because you, Lydia, aren't the one who holds the key to him leaving the police station. It's Candace.*

"Back to my earlier question. How did Tom get so banged up? Was he in the Prius when it crashed?" she said.

I wanted to thunk myself on the forehead with my palm. Of course. Candace and Lydia could be assuming his injuries came from being in the car with Nolan when it crashed. "You're an expert at seeing folks who've suffered injuries. Did his face look like he'd been in a wreck, Lydia?"

She sat straight up and leaned toward me, realization brightening her face. "No. Absolutely not. For once we're on the same page. Now that I think about it, his face looked like he'd been in a fight, not in any car accident."

"But Candace wants to hear what happened directly from him. Makes sense to me," I said. "Could be he's helping her piece evidence together and it's taking longer than you expected."

She pointed at me again. "You *know* something. Why won't you help me help Tom?"

For once her instincts were right. I knew

about a troubled, sleeping eighteen-year-old in my guest room. What I didn't know was if he was somehow connected to Roth's death. And I wasn't about to speculate on that with Lydia Monk. Fortunately, Merlot ambled in from the hallway, probably having grown tired of waiting outside the guest room door for the dog to reappear.

Lydia threw up her hands in disgust. "Oh, for crying out loud, here's the other cat. I have got to get out of this . . . this cattery." She stood. "I hope you can sleep tonight knowing you refused to help a good and decent man who is supposed to be your friend."

She stood and took a wide path around Merlot since he had stopped and was staring up at her, his big tail twitching at the tip.

"Bye, Lydia," I called after her.

She responded by slamming my front door after she went out.

I'd left my phone in the bedroom when I'd undressed earlier. I picked up Chablis and went to my room, the other two cats beating a path ahead of me. They were ready to settle down for the night.

I sat cross-legged on my bed and dialed Candace. Her phone went straight to voice mail. Since I knew Tom didn't have a phone, I decided to call the Mercy Police Station.

B. J. Harrington, a part-time dispatcher, answered.

"Hi, B.J., it's Jillian," I said.

"Hey, Mrs. Hart. You got a problem over at the lake?" He sounded concerned.

Such a sweet kid, I thought. "No problems," I replied. "I'd like to talk to Candace, if she's still there."

"Oh, she's here. Everyone the city council hasn't laid off is here." He lowered his voice to a whisper. "There's been a murder."

"I heard, which is kind of why I wanted to talk to her," I said.

"You know something about this case?" he said.

"I don't know anything directly. I just need to talk to Candace as soon as possible."

"Sounds like you *do* know something," he said.

"You practicing what you're learning in those criminology classes on me now?" I said with a laugh — though I'd never felt less like laughing in my life.

"Guess I am. Sorry, Mrs. Hart, but I can't interrupt Deputy Carson's interview. She's been collecting evidence, trying to find witnesses and has been talking to Tom. She'd have me for lunch if I stuck my head in the interview room."

"You're right. Candace might get upset," I said. "Is Chief Baca there, too?" I asked. "Maybe he could —"

"He's in the room with Tom, too. I can have one of them phone you back. How's that?"

"Sure," I said. "Have Candace call me when she's free."

I disconnected, feeling disappointed. All three cats had settled on their cat quilts at the foot of my bed. But Syrah lifted his head and looked at me when I just sat there, phone in hand.

"How will I ever get any sleep? Tom's been hurt and must be exhausted. He should be home by now," I said.

Syrah stood, stretched and walked over to me. He rubbed his head against my knee and then sat and meowed quietly, as if telling me everything would be okay.

As I stroked Syrah's silky coat, I considered getting in my van and driving to the police station. Then reconsidered. Tom wouldn't want that. He would want me to stay with Finn.

I turned off the light and slipped under my winter quilt.

Sleep would not come. After an hour of

tossing and turning, I took the flashlight from my bedside stand and got up. The cats didn't budge. This had been a long day for them and they were sleeping soundly, but they would probably wake within minutes of me leaving them. I made sure to close my bedroom door so they wouldn't follow me.

I went to the guest room. Though Finn had appeared to feel much better when he turned in, I wanted to make sure he was okay. I slowly turned the knob and immediately Yoshi barked.

"It's me, Yoshi," I whispered through the small opening in the door.

Seconds later, his muzzle appeared in the crack. I knelt and petted him, whispering for him to stay quiet. I opened the door wider and, keeping the flashlight trained on the floor, I peered into the room.

Finn apparently hadn't heard the dog because he was snoring softly.

He seemed comfortable and at peace. The only way I could help Tom was to make sure someone he loved was safe — at least for now.

NINE

After a fitful night's sleep, the sound of my cell phone woke me at seven a.m. It was Candace. Before I could say more than hello, she told me she was on the way to my house and disconnected. She sounded abrupt, to say the least. My guess was, she was tired, too.

Since Mercy is small enough that the longest drive is about five minutes from one place to the next, she'd be here soon. I got up, splashed water on my face and changed into jeans and a rose-colored henley T-shirt.

The cats had already left my room. Dawn and dusk are the busy times for felines. I wondered if they'd been sticking their paws under the guest room door to bother Yoshi. More likely, however, they were sitting by various windows, checking out birds and squirrels and anything else on the move outdoors. That's how they usually began their day, and nothing was as important as routine in their animal world.

As I walked down the hall I heard Yoshi whining and guessed he needed to go outside. I cracked the door and he squeezed out into the hall and took off. I checked on Finn and he was still sleeping. I shut the door and hurried after the dog before he and the cats got into a fracas.

But Yoshi made a beeline for the back door and was doing his jack-in-the-box thing as when I'd first seen him on the side of the road. Merlot and Syrah sat outside the utility room door observing his actions with interest. Though cats can jump up to seven times their height with ease, they don't bother unless their life is in danger or they're playing with feathery objects. A cat's philosophy is this: Why expend energy if not absolutely necessary?

I attached Yoshi's leash, disabled the security alarm and the dog nearly dragged me down the porch steps and out to the backyard. The temperature was maybe in the high forties and I shivered while Yoshi lifted his leg on the first white oak he came to. After his urgent need was satisfied, he stood like a statue, his stubby tail wiggling, his nose busy sniffing the air.

The lake was still, the rising sun spreading shimmering autumn hues across the glassy surface. I started walking him down my sloping back lawn toward the lake, but about halfway to the shore, Yoshi stopped and started to bark repeatedly. At first, I thought he'd seen something I hadn't. Then I realized his frenzy seemed to be directed at the water. Maybe he'd never seen a lake before.

"Not sure about big water, huh?" I said.

He answered by barking again. Since sound carried well to the nearby houses, I decided to take Yoshi inside before he woke the neighbors.

I'd just reached the back steps when Candace arrived. She wore her uniform and her ash-blond hair was pulled back and twisted into a bun at the nape of her neck. Then, rounding the house, I saw a tired-looking Tom as well as Liam Brennan, the assistant county DA. I smiled, glad to see all my friends, even if they looked worse for wear than I felt. "Hey there," I said. Yoshi started barking at the new arrivals.

Candace turned to Tom. "This is the dog, huh? Very cute, but I've had some bad experiences with dogs. They don't always like cops. Does he bite?"

Tom said, "I haven't had a chance to find out. I've been visiting with you since around dusk yesterday." He looked at me, and though he was tired the last time I saw him, now his whole body seemed weighed down by fatigue.

Yoshi barked again, probably not wanting to be ignored.

"You sure he's okay with a uniform around?" Candace said to me.

"He's been fine so far, and despite the uniform, you don't give off a menacing vibe," I said. "I wouldn't worry."

Liam said, "Since we've determined this fierce beast is probably no threat, can we go inside?"

"Most certainly. Chilly morning," I said.

They followed Yoshi and me into my kitchen.

Syrah swiped at Yoshi's muzzle as we passed the cats, but the dog didn't seem bothered. In fact, his little tail wagged. As soon as Chablis saw Yoshi, she took off so fast tufts of her champagne-colored fur fluttered in her wake. Yoshi strained against the leash, wanting to give chase. The other two cats didn't budge, staring at the dog with inscrutable faces.

I offered the leash to Candace. "Make friends by hanging on to this guy while I make coffee, okay?"

Candace took the leash with some hesitation. "You're sure he won't bite?"

"He's not the aggressive type — unless you were to mess with a kid he loves dearly. And Finn's asleep." I glanced at Tom. "Candace knows about the dog, so I'm assuming she knows about Finn."

Tom nodded solemnly. "She knows."

"She *finally* knows," Liam said. "Been a long night, Jillian. Sorry to start your day so early — but we need to talk to Finn." Liam Brennan's eyes seemed weary, too. He and Kara were dating, so he'd spent quite a bit of time in my house over the previous months. I'd come to like him. He was as passionate about the law as Candace was about evidence.

Candace said, "Liam wants to be here when I speak with Finn. Not the assistant DA's usual duty, but we're kinda short on the force with all the budget cuts."

"Where's Morris?" I asked, unsure her partner's absence was the entire reason Liam was here. Substituting a lawyer for a police officer didn't make sense to me.

"He had to take the day off or be paid overtime." Candace rolled her eyes. "Wouldn't want the city council to hear about us *wasting resources*. Can you get Finn to come out here, Jillian?"

"Could we let him sleep a little longer?" I looked at Tom, who had knelt and was scratching Yoshi behind the ears. "See, he suffered a concussion. He could use the rest."

"You got him to a doctor, then?" he said. "Will he be okay? Is there anything else we should do for him?"

As I poured ground beans into a filter and made the coffee, I explained to the three of them about the doctor's diagnosis and Finn's memory loss.

"Tom said Finn didn't seem like himself — that is, after I got him talking. If I learned anything last night, it's that Tom is protective of those he loves," Candace said.

"Hey," Tom said. "You kept me hanging around while you booked evidence and went over witness statements. Can you blame me for not being all that cooperative right away?"

Candace led the dog around the counter and took a seat at the breakfast bar. "Let's say it was a long night for all of us."

Tom smiled at her. "I did grab a nap while I waited on you, and I know you didn't have the luxury of even a few minutes' rest." He opened the fridge. "I am starving. Got any eggs?"

"I have bread, yogurt, peanut butter and some bananas I put in the freezer before I left town," I said, while Liam and I pulled mugs from the cupboard. "I haven't had time to visit the Piggly Wiggly since I came home."

"I haven't eaten, either," Liam said, meeting Tom at the pantry.

Soon they were making breakfast for all of us with what few items I had to offer. While they were doing this, I joined Candace as the coffee brewed.

She said, "You managed to locate Tom after we talked at Belle's and yet I never heard from you. Were you too busy helping the kid to call?"

"Once I knew Finn would be okay, I had to get him settled in here. Then I tried to reach you," I said. "When I couldn't get you on your cell, I talked to B.J. at the station and left a message for you to call me. When you didn't phone, I figured you were busy."

"B.J. never told me," she said. "We kept him late answering calls and he got pretty frazzled — had an early class this morning and was afraid I'd keep him all night. He practically ran out the door when I finally realized he needed to go home. My bad."

"I did call the station late, though. There's a reason, too," I said. "See, I had a little visit from Lydia last night. Of course, you understand it wasn't exactly a friendly visit. She tried to pressure me into telling her things she seemed to think I knew."

Candace closed her eyes. "That woman. What is *wrong* with her? Doesn't she know she's a coroner and not a cop?"

"Good question, one I'm not sure will ever be answered," I said. "She told me about the murder, about Tom having to hang around the police station. She made it sound like you were about to arrest him for murder."

"Typical Lydia drama," she said. "Still, a man is dead — brutally murdered. He was found in Tom's car and Tom didn't like the guy one bit. I was concerned where the evidence would lead me, as you can surely understand. I get it that Nolan Roth wasn't exactly an upstanding citizen, but he deserves the same justice everyone else is entitled to. I'm counting on you, on Tom, on Liam and even on this kid to help us get this thing solved. That is if Finn is who Tom thinks he is — the greatest young man who's ever walked the earth. Are you with me? Will you help me get the truth?"

I reached out and rested my hand on her forearm. "I am totally on board. Until Lydia came here, I had no idea Nolan Roth had been murdered. I was on a mission to help Finn. He *is* a good kid, Candace. Sometimes you just know when someone's good and decent. I'm with Tom. Finn deserves all the help we can offer."

I felt her arm muscles relax beneath my touch. "You understand I have to make my own decision about the kid's character, right? Because both Tom and Finn were more than a little unhappy with a man who ended up murdered and I can't ignore that. You get where I'm coming from?"

"Of course," I said. "But I know you, Candace. You'll see what we have already seen when it comes to Finn. I'm sure of it."

"You know what? You are the best thing that ever happened to this town," she said. "You can put things in perspective in an instant." She snapped her fingers for emphasis.

Hearing the sound, Yoshi sat at attention. Wonder what he thought was about to happen?

"Coffee's ready," Liam said.

"Toast coming up," Tom said. "You have the following gourmet choices: peanut butter on toast, peanut butter and frozen bananas on toast or your always delicious dry toast." He pulled four slices from my toaster and hastily dropped them on to a plate.

I helped Liam pour us all coffee. Soon we were sitting at the small table in the nook, munching our food and gulping coffee like it was water from an oasis.

Yoshi sat at Candace's feet. She'd dropped the leash and put her foot on it to make sure he stayed close. I didn't have to tell her the cats and the dog hadn't quite managed to come to an understanding yet. Yoshi almost had this worried look — ears down, blinking a lot. Poor guy. He seemed to understand he was in the middle of a big mess.

At some point, Syrah had taken a spot on the window seat in the living room. This offered him a good vantage point to observe the dog while still keeping an eye on whatever bug was moving outside. Merlot, however, surprised me by plopping down about two feet away from Yoshi. He started what I called his "inquiring" chatter — something Maine coons are known for. Poor dog just kept cocking his head from side to side as they stared at each other.

While Tom started another batch of toast, Liam refilled our coffee mugs.

"I could get used to good-looking men waiting on me," I said.

Liam sat down and said, "I have three sisters. Comes natural to take care of the ladies. Back to business, however. Since Finn isn't with us yet and you spent more time than anyone with him yesterday, did he say anything about the gun?"

I said, "Finn says he never put any gun in his backpack."

Candace looked at me as if I wasn't ready to graduate from kindergarten. "Sure. So someone else just put it in there when he wasn't looking. I hate when that happens."

"You're going to give him the benefit of the doubt, remember?" I said. "In my opinion, he's being as honest as he can. And I'm not saying the gun isn't his. I'm saying he doesn't remember ever seeing it. You had a concussion last summer. Remember how you felt afterward?"

She briefly closed her eyes, as if recalling the blow to the head that put her in the hospital. "I do. I understand he might not remember. But how far back does his amnesia go?"

Tom hovered near the toaster, but I could tell he was listening to every word.

Candace went on, saying, "The kid was walking around with a loaded gun and a head injury. I have to completely understand what brought Finn here and how the gun ended up in his possession — hear the explanation from Finn himself."

"So Tom told you about the gun right away?" I said.

Tom said, "I didn't. My brother decided he wanted to *help out.* He told her when he called his new best friend Candace at the police station looking for me."

"Ah," I said. "Bob. How nice of him."

"Time to interview Finn," Candace said. "Unlike you and Tom, I don't have the luxury of trusting Finn's character and I can't make decisions about guilt or innocence until I've gathered and evaluated all the evidence. Does that make sense?"

I nodded. "I know. But let Tom and me help you with him. He sure trusts Tom and I think he's starting to trust me."

"We do need your help," Liam said. "But if the outcome isn't what you want, if he did harm Roth, you should be prepared."

Tom set more toast on the table. The smell of it, combined with the aroma of fresh-brewed coffee, would have been comforting on any other day, but Liam's words made my stomach tighten. I could hear a hint of desperation in my voice when I said, "You're the one who should be prepared — prepared with an open mind, Liam. He could never kill anyone."

Just then, Merlot crept closer to us, his eyes on the dog, but I was sure he'd heard the worry in my voice. My cats were so protective, and I relaxed a tad just thinking about them.

"Please wake the kid up, would you?" Candace said.

Tom said, "Can we let him sleep a little longer? He's injured and —"

"I need to interview him before his mother arrives. We, of course, called her and expect her in town this morning. Even though the kid's eighteen, has a North Carolina driver's license and I don't need her to be present, she might insist. I sure as heck don't want to argue with a brand-new widow. Is he in the guest room?" Candace stood, probably ready to wake Finn up. Too bad she forgot she was supposed to be keeping Yoshi on his leash.

He had his chance and took it.

When he ran, it wasn't toward the back door or down the hall to the guest room. No. He started racing around my living room, Merlot right behind him. I was about to intervene, but then realized those two were actually playing a game. Yoshi had the advantage. The little dog could turn on a dime. Finally he stopped dead, whirled and faced Merlot. He lowered onto his front legs, his butt in the air. From growing up with my grandparents' various dogs, I knew this was a "play position" and smiled.

Syrah, meanwhile, was staring with complete disdain as this commotion unfolded. He wasn't about to make nice with a dog. Merlot must have caught a look from his feline friend because he turned and walked away from Yoshi. But there had been no hissing or swiping, just some much-needed fun.

"What's going on?" a sleepy-eyed Finn said from the foyer.

Yoshi took off and leaped into Finn's arms.

Candace said, "I take it you're Finn. I'm Deputy Candace Carson of the Mercy Police."

He looked at me. "You called the cops on me?"

Ten

Finn sounded and looked defensive when he said, "If you're here to arrest me as a runaway, you can't. I'm old enough to leave home."

"You're right," Candace said. "You're an adult in the eyes of the law. A few things have happened I need to talk to you about, though. I came here as part of an investigation and need to ask you a few questions. As I said, I'm Deputy Candace Carson. I came here with Mr. Brennan from the county district attorney's office."

"Hold on. What kind of investigation?" A touch of panic tinged Finn's voice.

Yoshi squirmed to get closer to Finn and licked his cheek.

"Something bad has happened," Tom said as he and Liam joined us in the living room.

"Tom. You're here." Finn smiled and his pale cheeks took on some much-needed color. Then he focused on Liam and the flush drained away. "Is this guy a lawyer? Is he planning on turning me over to my mother? Because he can't. I'm legal."

Candace nodded. "We all understand you were free to leave a bad home situation. But right now, we need to sit down and talk. Will you do that?"

Finn shrank back, clutching his dog to his chest.

Liam walked over to Finn and offered his hand. "I'm Liam Brennan, and yes, I am a lawyer. We just want to talk to you."

Finn simply stared at Liam's hand.

Thank goodness Tom took over then. He walked to Finn's side and put an arm around his shoulder. "Liam's a good guy. A friend. So is Deputy Carson. These people want to help and you must know Jillian and I do, too."

"I — I do know. But this is kinda freakin' me out," Finn said.

Merlot sat in the middle of the living room, a silent observer of this tense human interaction. Syrah went to his scratching post near the entertainment center to sharpen his nails and, I decided, to convey his lack of interest in this gathering. That didn't mean he was disinterested, just that he wanted us — or should I say Yoshi — to think so.

The little dog was trembling. Too many strangers for him, it would seem.

"How's the head?" Tom brushed aside a lock of Finn's sandy hair to examine the cut and bruise on his forehead.

"Ouch," Candace said. "How did that happen?"

"I told you last night — or was it this morning? — he doesn't remember," Tom said through gritted teeth.

Uh-oh, I thought. The last thing we needed was for Tom to get tense and overprotective right now. I looked at Candace when I said, "Finn's probably hungry, and though I know you have lots of questions, maybe we can get some food in this guy first?"

"Sorry," Candace said. "You're right. Guess I was hoping Finn recalled more details now that he's had some rest."

"I don't get it. Details about me coming here?" Finn looked at Tom. "Tell me what's going on. I left home, sure. And I didn't tell my mother. It's not a crime."

He thought this was about him leaving home. I wanted the poor kid sitting down when he heard the news this wasn't about running away. I said, "You're right, Finn. It's not a crime. Before we talk about why these people are here, you need to sit down, maybe eat something." I glanced around the room. "Is that okay with the rest of you?"

Liam nodded and Candace said, "Sure."

Tom led Finn, who still clutched his dog tightly, to the sofa.

"Tom makes some mean peanut butter toast," I said. "What about something to drink? There's fresh coffee, but —"

"No Dr Pepper, I guess?" Finn said as he and the dog settled back on the couch.

"Sorry," I said, watching from the corner of my eye as Liam and Candace took the chairs opposite the sofa. "After we're done talking, I intend to fix that problem."

Finn gave a small smile. "Milk is cool."

Liam said, "Your dog's name is unusual, but it sounds familiar."

Finn told him about the little dragon in the Mario Brothers game and Liam smiled.

"I used to love playing Mario Brothers," Liam said.

While they talked about video games, I could tell by Candace's tapping foot and her grip on the chair's arms that she was getting impatient. But to her credit, she allowed the guys to bond a little.

After Finn had his toast and milk and we were all on our third round of coffee, Tom took a deep breath and said, "These folks coming here? It's about Nolan, not about you leaving home."

"Oh, yeah? What's with him?" He bit into the toast.

"He died yesterday," Tom said quietly.

Finn's eyes widened in surprise and he quickly swallowed his food. "But he's, like, younger than you, Tom. Did he get sick or something?"

"Someone killed him," Tom said.

"Wow." Finn blinked several times and repeated, "Wow."

Yoshi, who'd been curled up next to Finn, sat up and nuzzled Finn's neck and began licking his face again. This was certainly a perceptive dog. Almost as perceptive as a cat.

"We know you were injured yesterday," Candace said. "We understand you can't remember part of the day. Do you recollect seeing Nolan at all?"

"Easy question. Since Nolan's in North Carolina and —"

"He came *here,*" Tom said. "Probably looking for you."

"Nolan died in *this* town?" If Finn had been surprised before, he now seemed stunned.

Candace leaned toward Finn, her hands between her knees. She spoke reassuringly when she said, "Finn, do you remember being in Tom's car yesterday?"

Finn looked up at me. "Tom's car? No way. I was in Mrs. Hart's van. She can tell you. She and Tom picked me up. I saw a white car in Tom's driveway when we got to his house. Is that the car you're talking about?"

Tom went into protective mode again, saying, "Like I tried to tell you back at the station, he's never even seen my car before."

Candace ignored Tom, her focus remaining on Finn. "Sounds like you remember part of yesterday, which is good. But there's a big problem and it's bothering me. I was told there was a gun in your backpack."

"Oh yeah. That was, like, so weird. I have no clue where the gun came from." Finn went silent then, his expression changing. A realization was taking hold. He slowly put his unfinished toast on the coffee table, wrapped his arms around Yoshi and drew him close. "Nolan was shot, wasn't he? And you think I did it."

Candace said, "We aren't sure what happened. We're just gathering information."

Liam added, "The police have a job to do, Finn. They need to find out what happened to Nolan. Anything you can remember might just help us straighten out this mess."

"I didn't see Nolan. At least I don't think

I did." He stopped and I saw uncertainty on his face. He couldn't remember.

Finn went on, saying, "I came to this place to be with someone who gives a rat's ass about me. Tom said I could come anytime I wanted." Finn stared straight at Liam. "You want to know what I remember? I remember how Nolan treated me. And I'm not sorry he's dead."

Oh boy. Not the best choice of words when the police had reason to suspect him of a crime. I was sitting on the floor with Merlot, whose keen interest in Yoshi had not waned, and my body tensed after Finn said this. My cat's claws dug into my knees and then retracted in response to my body language. Merlot looked up at me with concern.

Tom's uneasiness was evident, as well, and he said, "You didn't kill him, though. No matter what you can or cannot remember, I know you didn't."

Candace said, "Maybe we should let Finn talk."

Finn raised his chin. "Tom's right. I may have hated Nolan, but I wouldn't kill him. I wouldn't kill anyone."

I believed him and I hoped Candace felt the sincerity that seemed so evident to me. I said, "The doctor said you will never remember parts of yesterday." I glanced around at the people in the room. "You can check with the doctor if you want, but those were his words. It doesn't mean Finn hurt anyone during that period of time. Concussions don't change who he is."

"You can take that to the bank, Candace," Tom said. "This is a good kid who had the courage to leave a bad situation."

Candace said, "I understand. Doesn't change the fact we need answers. A man has still been murdered, and I need to find his killer. If Finn can't remember anything, I need to do more investigating, find out if anyone saw Finn during the hours he seems to have lost. I sure as heck want to find out how he got the head injury."

Liam stood, and Candace followed his lead. He said, "I think we're done here. You've had a long trip, Finn. So far, we don't have any evidence indicating you harmed your stepfather, so don't —"

"*Stepfather?* I never called him anything that included the word *father.* He was just Nolan." Finn paused before saying, "Does my mother know what happened to him?"

Candace nodded. "She's on her way from North Carolina."

Finn hung his head. "Great. Just great."

"It's okay," I said. "Maybe you won't have

to see her."

Liam said, "Tom, we need the gun. Should Candace get a warrant, or will you hand it over?"

Tom's jaw tightened. "I said I'd cooperate as long as you give this kid a chance. He's not your bad guy." Tom's gaze hadn't wavered from Finn. He sounded more than a little testy, and I noted that his eyes were still bloodshot. He hadn't gotten any rest last night aside from the nap he mentioned — or in the nights before when he was trapped in North Carolina, for that matter.

"There's something else." Finn looked at me. "Did you tell them about the blood on my shirt?"

I shook my head. "To be honest, I forgot." Too many things happening too fast had my brain muddled. But the blood on Finn's shirt could be important.

Tom said, "Maybe you got a nosebleed or something when you hit your head."

"Maybe," he said. "I'm not sure where it came from, and I was thinking the police could figure it out. Help me remember, 'cause not knowing is kind of freaking me out."

Candace cocked her head when she looked at Finn. "Thanks for telling me about the shirt. It could help us understand what happened to both you and to Nolan. Do you get my meaning?"

"I'm not stupid," Finn said, a hint of defiance returning. "You're a cop and you want evidence. You don't know me; you don't trust me when I tell you I wouldn't hurt anyone. So take the shirt, okay? I know you're not going to leave me alone until you find the real killer."

"I don't think you're stupid," Candace said quietly. "Not for a minute. You willing to give me DNA, too, then? I can't do anything with the blood unless I can compare it to your DNA."

"Sure. Whatever," Finn said. "Make sure and compare it to Nolan's DNA, too. But you were gonna do that anyway, right?"

Candace nodded. "Yup. You seem to know that's how it works."

Liam turned to Tom. "A more complete statement about Nolan Roth's assault on you before your ex-wife arrives in Mercy might help. She'll probably have an alternate version of the events, if what you said about her is true. We need every bit of information you can give us."

Finn said, "What's he talking about, Tom? Did Nolan mess up your face?" He had no idea Tom had been held by Nolan. Now he was surprised again.

Tom avoided Finn's gaze, looking uncomfortable. "I'll explain later." He turned to Candace. "Let's get this gun business over with."

"Sure. I'll collect the shirt and the DNA and we're on it. I'll need my evidence kit from the patrol car." Candace hurried out through the kitchen.

"What if it is Nolan's blood on my clothes?" Finn said to Tom. "Does it mean I did something I can't remember?"

Tom said, "Finn, don't worry. We both know you didn't hurt Nolan. Like you said, let's just help them figure out who did. I'm turning over the gun, you're giving Deputy Carson the clothes and we'll see what happens from there."

"Okay. I'll get the shirt." Finn started toward the foyer.

Liam said, "Wait. Deputy Carson will want to handle the shirt while wearing gloves and put it in the evidence bag herself. Blood is —"

"Dirty. Yeah." Finn came back toward us. "I know about blood. Blood is supposed to be thicker than water. I've learned that's not true, thanks to my mother."

"Did you leave home because of a recent argument?" Liam said.

"You wouldn't get it even if I explained,"

Finn said.

"Try me," Liam said.

"I don't want to talk about it right now," Finn said.

Tom said, "He's being cooperative, but he's been through a lot. Give him time on this one, will you, Liam?"

"Sure," Liam replied.

Tom looked at Finn. "It's all good, man. We'll work this out."

Candace returned with the brown paper sack and Finn, with Yoshi by his side, led the way to the guest room to show Candace where his clothes were. They returned less than a minute later. First she marked the bag containing Finn's shirt and hoodie as evidence. Then she swabbed his mouth for DNA. Everyone stared at this procedure in silence.

The air seemed to have been sucked from my home. My chest tightened and I felt the need to wrap Finn in my arms when she was done. Though both Tom and I couldn't hide our concern, Finn's attitude and posture spoke volumes about his character. He believed he had nothing to hide.

"Finished and ready to go," Candace said, after what seemed an eternity. "Let's get over to your place, Tom, and open your safe."

"I'll go with you," Finn said eagerly.

"Not sure it's a good idea for you to come along," Candace said. "I got a concussion last summer and the doctors told me to take it easy for a couple days afterward."

Something you did not do, as I recall, I thought. "He won't be gone long," I said to Finn, and then turned to Candace. "Tom can come back after he gives you the — the . . . gun, right?" I didn't want to call it evidence.

Candace looked at Liam. From the glance passing between them I thought I understood why Liam was here. This wasn't about Morris's day off. She was probably worried about legalities. When you have to deal with a crime connected to close friends, the boundaries might get blurred. Candace would never want to do anything to compromise an investigation. Gosh, I wouldn't want to be in her shoes.

She said, "Tom still needs to tell us more about —" But she stopped when she saw Tom glance at Finn. "Sorry, I forgot. We can discuss all this later," she finished.

Finn said, "Tell you more about what?" He turned to Tom. "What did Nolan do to you, Tom?"

I said, "I can explain a few things while they're gone — if it's okay, Tom?"

He smiled sadly and my heart ached for all the trouble both Tom and Finn had been through in the last few days. He said, "I'd appreciate it."

Liam, Tom and Candace left.

"Okay, tell me about Tom. Tell me why he never called last night," Finn said, once the back door closed. He sat back down on the couch and picked up a piece of cold toast, but just stared at it.

Yoshi pressed close to his side.

I explained how Tom had to stay at the police station last night, mostly because processing a crime scene doesn't take an hour like you see on TV. Tom's car had been involved, not to mention a man he disliked intensely was dead, so naturally they needed his statement. I decided going into the details of what Nolan Roth did to Tom could wait — for now. Between the concussion and being considered a suspect in a murder, Finn had enough to deal with.

When I was finished explaining, Finn said, "But Tom didn't do anything wrong. Why keep him at a police station practically all night? That's not right."

Oh, to be eighteen again and think the world should be fair. I said, "This is a small town with very few officers. It just took a long time to find out exactly what happened to Mr. Roth. Deputy Carson wasn't being intentionally mean to Tom."

"I guess that makes sense." He finally looked at me. "Are you for real?"

"For real?" I gathered coffee mugs and set them on the breakfast bar.

"I mean, you act like you believe me when I say I can't remember how I got hurt, but are you just being nice?"

"I've learned to trust my instincts now that I'm an old lady," I said with a laugh. "Those instincts tell me you, my friend, wouldn't shoot anyone."

"You're not an old lady," he said. "Okay, not *that* old."

I smiled. "I'm old enough to ask for help. Help me with the clean up?"

Finn gathered mugs and dishes while Yoshi passed out on the throw rug near the utility room. Poor dog had been on high alert for a good long while.

I noticed Chablis slink into the living room. The kitchen and living room area was the sunniest place in late morning and she wasn't about to miss a sunbath. She joined Merlot and Syrah on the window seat. So funny to see them banded together. They never hung out so close to one another for nap time. It must be the dog's presence.

Finn poured the last of the milk into his

glass. Then he sat on the window seat next to the cats and petted each one while he drank. Merlot turned his big body over for a belly rub, a move that practically shoved poor Chablis right off the cushions.

Meanwhile, I sat at the mosaic-tiled table in the kitchen nook and started a shopping list that included clothes for Finn as well as groceries. I hadn't planned on restocking the fridge since I was committed to one more craft show this coming Friday. It would only be an overnight trip, but I'd wanted to delay the dreaded grocery shopping until I returned. Not now. I might be able to live on yogurt and toast and frozen meals, but not this kid.

I'd just finished writing "dog food" when I heard a quick knock at the back door. Before I could even get halfway across the kitchen, my stepdaughter, Kara, walked in and stopped in her tracks when she saw the dog.

Yoshi came to attention and barked repeatedly. *Already playing watch dog,* I thought. His barks sent my three cats running for cover.

"Who's this?" Kara knelt to greet the dog. Her dark, shoulder-length hair hung loose and she wore jeans, an oatmeal-colored sweater and brown knee-high boots. Yoshi sniffed her boots and then put a paw on her knee in greeting.

"This is my house guest, Yoshi." I made a sweeping gesture toward Finn. "He belongs to Finn."

Finn offered a "Hey," but didn't make eye contact.

Once I'd introduced Kara to Finn, he said, "Mind if I lie down?"

"Is the headache back?" Maybe Finn needed a follow-up visit to a doctor sooner rather than later.

"Nah. I'm just tired," he said.

"You've been through a lot. Good idea to get some rest," I said. He had to be overwhelmed by one new person after another coming through my door.

Finn tapped his chest with his palm and said, "Yoshi, come."

The dog raced to him and Finn opened his arms. Yoshi jumped up into them and they left for the guest room.

"He's Tom's stepson, huh? He looks like he could use some serious *z*'s." Kara walked to the fridge and opened it, then looked puzzled. "What? No tea?"

"Haven't had a chance to make any more. But who told you about Finn?" I said.

"I do own the newspaper, Jillian," she said with a smile. "Anyway, I was a little on edge after your call yesterday and I tried to reach Tom myself. He never answered his cell, but some guy at his house picked up on the landline."

I closed my eyes. "You talked to Bob."

"Yup. If there's no tea, how about coffee?" She peered toward the pot and seeing there were still a few inches of coffee, got herself a mug. As she poured, she said, "Tom never mentioned any brother. I wasn't sure I believed the guy I talked to. But he told me there'd been an accident and Tom left to go help or something. He mentioned Finn being with you two. I started to ask him more questions, but I had to hang up because Shondra was on the other line. She told me she'd heard about a wreck on her police scanner, just like Bob said."

"He's a half brother, by the way," I said. "He was a secret; Finn was a secret. Tom apparently can compartmentalize his past. Kind of a guy thing, I've decided. But who's Shondra?"

"Thought I told you about her. I've gotten so tired of listening to the police scanner spew information about fender benders or cows in the road or Jet Ski thefts, I hired her as an assistant at the paper. One of her jobs? Listen to the scanner. She's young and just started out at the community college in communications. You'll like her."

"Maybe we can all have lunch one day." *What a dumb thing to say,* I thought. "Will you listen to me? All sorts of bad things are happening and I'm talking about having lunch."

"You want to share these bad things?" she said.

"I do. But only as your stepmother and friend, not as a source for a story," I said.

Kara frowned. "You know I've changed since moving here from Houston. I would never expect you to be a source."

"I didn't think so, but I'm pretty rattled by all that's happened in the last twenty-four hours. Tom's had all sorts of trouble, Finn got hurt, a man was murdered."

"Murder, huh? I was pretty sure Candace was leaving out something about the wreck. She'll only be able to keep a murder under wraps for another few hours. This town is never far behind the truth." She walked around the bar, into the living room and sat in her late dad's recliner. How we both loved that chair.

I followed, settling on the sofa. Chablis was in my lap in an instant. The scary dog was gone for now and she would take full advantage. I stroked her and she began to purr.

"Finn is the reason Tom went off the radar. Talk to me about him, Jillian," Kara said.

I explained that Finn ran away and how Tom ended up being abducted and beaten up by Nolan, who thought Tom was hiding the boy. Then I told her how, after Tom had gotten away from Nolan, he and I had found Finn walking in the direction of Tom's house. I also mentioned Lydia's visit last night. "She told me the driver they found in Tom's car was Nolan Roth — the very same man who grabbed Tom and beat him up. He didn't die in the accident. He was shot to death."

She said, "Tell me again why this guy was in Tom's car."

"Tom escaped from Nolan and left everything behind — his car, his phone, his wallet — everything but the clothes on his back."

"Wow. Bet Tom is mad at himself for letting this guy get the jump on him," Kara said.

"You should see his poor face," I said.

"I caught a glimpse of him at the scene yesterday when my photographer and I were there for the story. But Morris was keeping us so far away from the accident, I didn't notice any injuries. Will he be okay?"

"He'll be fine — or so he says. I'm more worried about Finn and any post-concussion problems. Worried about why he had blood on his shirt, too."

"Could this kid have had something to do with the murder, then?" Kara asked.

"You know Candace," I said. "She has to run down every lead and every bit of evidence. You ask me, Finn doesn't have a criminal fiber in his being."

She set her coffee on the end table beside the chair. "What you believe in your heart and what the evidence will show might be very different. No matter what, I'll help you and Tom and Finn any way I can."

I felt the tight muscles in my neck relax and smiled. "Thanks. Both Tom and Finn have been through the mill."

"Are you including the arrival of his brother, Bob the Perv, as part of going *through the mill?*" she said.

My eyes widened. "Wait a minute. If you're giving him *that* name, you've met him in person," I said.

"Oh yes. I stopped by Tom's house this morning to talk to the house guest. Turns out, Bob's a chatty guy. As a reporter, I do appreciate the talkative ones, but as a female, I do not appreciate *him.* He wouldn't stop flirting, or making comments that he thought I might find charming. Boy, was he wrong to think I was the least bit charmed."

"The man got on my bad side right away, too. He allowed Tom's cat to get out and poor Dashiell nearly died." I felt in my pocket for my phone. "Speaking of Dashiell, I need to find out how he's doing this morning."

"And I need to make tea. Coffee just isn't enough." She rose and went to the kitchen.

After I learned Dashiell was doing well and could go home anytime, I disconnected. *Go home? Not yet. Not with Tom there delivering a gun to the police.* I'd have to talk to him about his cat — and soon.

"Maybe you can enlighten me," I said while Kara boiled water and filled pitchers with tea bags and cane sugar syrup. "I don't know much about the wreck. Where did it happen?"

Kara cocked her head. "You haven't read the paper? I am shocked and dismayed." She smiled. "Out in the boondocks on Brown Road. Pretty nasty accident. Car hit a telephone pole. Hard to tell if the driver even braked. Of course, if the driver was already dead . . ."

"And you couldn't get close enough to see much?"

"Nope. We were so far from the scene my

photographer stood on someone's shoulders to get the photo of Tom's car we ran in the paper."

"You didn't see the dead man?" I said.

"Nope. Glad I didn't, too. Chief Baca spoke to me and said, and I quote, 'The driver died at the scene.' They wouldn't release his name, which is routine until family is notified. When I get the official word on his identity, we'll print it."

"I'll make sure and get a paper, or . . . since you offered to help, you could get me a copy and do something else for me — for us," I said.

"I'm game," she said.

I handed her my shopping list.

She glanced at what I'd written. "This is easy enough, but can it wait until after I stop by my new house? I have to make sure they're earning the pretty penny this home is costing me. I'd love to be in by Christmas."

Kara's house was being built on acreage at the edge of town. She'd used the money she'd inherited from John to buy the newspaper and build her first house.

"I'll take Finn out for lunch, so there's no rush on the groceries," I said.

"I could pick up Dashiell if you and Tom are tied up," she said.

"Thanks. I'll call you for help if Dashiell needs to leave the clinic by a certain time and I can't make it," I said.

She finished making the tea, took a travel mug from the cupboard and filled it with ice. She poured herself the tea she'd been craving and was ready to go. I hugged her tightly at the back door and again thanked her for everything.

I'd no sooner closed the door than my cell phone rang. I felt like I was living in Grand Central Station instead of my own little house in rural South Carolina.

It was Candace. Seemed Hilary just arrived at the police station and wanted to see her son.

"Bring Finn here, would you? Because I'm not telling this woman where her son is until I've asked her a few more questions." She sounded like one unhappy deputy.

"Getting Finn to the station to see her might take some serious convincing," I said.

"Tom came with me after we got the gun at his house. He was talking with the chief when I learned she'd arrived. You want to talk to him and see if he has any ideas on how to get Finn to talk to his mother?"

"No. I'll tell Finn the truth and say Tom will be around as a buffer."

"Thanks, Jillian. I'm so tired I can hardly

think straight," she said. "Come as soon as you can, okay?"

After she disconnected, I stood in my kitchen wondering how Finn would react when I told him his mother was in town.

No, I had a pretty good idea how he would react.

My fear was what he might do.

Eleven

No surprise Finn balked at the idea of seeing his mother, so after nothing I said convinced him this would be a good idea, I called the police station and let Tom talk to him. After their chat, a reluctant Finn agreed to go with me, but we rode in stony silence to Mercy PD.

As we walked through the pristine corridors of the old courthouse to the police offices located at the back of the building, Finn remained quiet. However, when we passed a few of Mercy's less-than-finest citizens hanging around on the benches and chairs outside the door labeled "Mercy Police Department," his eyes grew wide.

He mumbled "Wow" under his breath.

The smell of unwashed bodies and the droopy-eyed looks of the alcoholics and drug addicts made me tug on Finn's elbow and we went quickly through that door. A sleepy-looking B.J. was sitting at the desk to our left. He wore a headset and was talking on the phone.

"Yes, ma'am," he was saying. "We do have a leash law. Let me give you county animal control's number."

Sitting on one of the two chairs in the small waiting area was Thelma Reese, a retiree with a big heart. She held a plate of scrumptious-looking coconut cupcakes. I smiled at her and said, "Hey, Thelma. Looks like someone was up early baking."

"Hey there, Jillian," she said. "I brought these for Morris, seeing as how he helped me out yesterday. Locked my keys in the Ford 150."

"Uh-oh. I heard someone say Morris is off duty today," I said.

Her face crumbled with disappointment. Rumor was Thelma locked her keys in the car on purpose at least once a month so Morris could come to her rescue.

B.J., now off the phone, said, "Take them on over to his place, Thelma. You know how he loves sweets."

She perked up and rose. "You're sure it would be all right?"

"Perfectly fine," B.J. said.

She was out the door so fast I hardly got a whiff of those cupcakes.

Finn said, "Cupcakes? Really? Between

that lady and the people outside the door, I feel like I've landed on another planet."

"Not like on TV, huh?" I said.

B.J. said, "Let me buzz Deputy Carson — oops, don't have to. Here she comes."

Candace came out of the chief's office and walked down the short hall in front of us, passing the closed doors I knew were the interrogation rooms.

"Thanks for coming, you two." She looked at me. "I'll take it from here."

Finn stepped back and held up his hands. "Wait a minute. She's staying with me, right? And where's Tom? Tom told me —"

"Your mama's been worried about you," Candace said.

Finn shook his head. "She doesn't worry about anyone but herself. Tom said she just wanted to see me, not talk to me."

Candace narrowed her eyes and stared at Finn for a few seconds and then she nodded. "I understand. Come with me."

Finn didn't move. "Mrs. Hart, too?"

"Sure," Candace said. I couldn't read her expression because she was in total cop mode, but she sounded unbothered by Finn's request.

"What did my mother tell you?" Finn said as we followed Candace through the ancient wooden gate separating the waiting area from the hall.

"Hang on," she said, as she opened the door to the first interrogation room.

Before we went inside, I heard a woman call, "Finn. Oh my God, you *are* okay."

She came running toward us. She must have been in Chief Baca's office. She nearly toppled because of her super-high black heels, and was dressed all in black — black wool coat, black tights. Even her hair was such a dark brunette color it was nearly black.

Eyes averted, Finn started to back up, his face ghostly pale.

"Hang on, Finn," Candace said. "I'll handle this." She stood squarely between Finn and the woman I assumed was his mother.

"He's not ready to talk to you, Mrs. Roth," Candace said.

Tom appeared in the door of the interrogation room we'd been about to enter. "Stay away from him, Hilary."

Tom's ex-wife stared at him in confusion at first and then said, "What happened to you, Tom? Were you in the car with Nolan when —"

"You know damn well what happened to me, Hilary. So —"

I held up a hand, my heart pounding in

reaction to this confrontation. In a firm voice, I said, "Tom, why don't you take Finn with you?"

"Jillian took the words right out of my mouth," Candace said, nodding her head in the direction of the room Tom had emerged from.

Tom's anger seemed to dissipate in an instant. He nodded and gestured Finn inside. The door shut after them and I felt as if I could breathe again.

Hilary Roth closed her eyes and shook her head sadly. "I'm sorry if I caused a problem. I'm so glad to see that Finn is all right and so confused by everything that's happened. I've already lost someone I love and —" Her eyes filled. Exquisite, big brown eyes. She raised a gloved hand to her crimson lips. "I'm sorry. I still can't believe Nolan's gone."

Candace stepped toward her. "We here in Mercy are sorry for your loss. We'll do everything we can to find out who did this to your husband. As you requested, you've seen your son, so you're free to leave now."

Hilary didn't seem to be paying attention and instead focused on me. "So you're Jillian? The woman Chief Baca told me about? The one who cared for Finn?"

"Um, yes." I was almost at a loss for

words. When I heard both Tom and Finn disparage this woman, I'd developed a mental picture of someone who looked like a Halloween witch, maybe even cackled, too. Not so. She was stunning. Since I couldn't see a line or a wrinkle on her expertly made-up face, it was difficult to even guess her age.

Candace said, "Chief Baca is finished talking with you, so as I said before —"

"The chief was so very kind," she said, her Carolina drawl thick as sorghum. "Is there a place in town I could stay while I wait for Nolan's —" She pulled her lips in as if trying to gather herself. "For the postmortem to be done?"

"All the motels are maybe ten miles north once you get on the interstate," Candace said. "We do have a bed-and-breakfast in town, though."

"Do you think I could stay there on such short notice?" she asked.

Candace turned. "B.J., would you please help Mrs. Roth call the Pink House?"

"Sure enough," B.J. answered.

Candace and I stepped aside to allow her by. As she passed me, she said, "Thank you for helping my boy. He's been so troubled lately."

Up close, I did see a few fine lines around

her eyes. Her scent was familiar — Chanel No. 5, like Kara wore. I was still surprised by her. She seemed kind and genuine. No, not a Halloween witch at all.

Candace put a hand on my back and told me to join Tom and Finn. "I've got to talk to the chief for a second."

I'd visited the other interrogation room, the one where a suspect could be handcuffed to the table. Pretty awful. This one was different and looked more like a barren kitchen. The maple table had to be fifty years old and the four high-back wooden chairs might have come straight from my grandparents' estate sale.

Finn was sitting next to Tom, and I took a seat across from them. I poured water into a paper cup from the stainless pitcher in the center of the table and took a long sip. My mouth was a little dry after meeting Hilary.

"Water?" I asked Finn.

"No, thanks," he said.

Tom slapped a pack of Trident gum in front of Finn. "How about this?"

Finn smiled. "You remembered." He punched out a piece of gum from the packet and popped it in his mouth.

Tom then offered the gum to me, but I refused.

I didn't want to even mention Hilary, so I

said the first thing that came to mind. "You mentioned you lost your phone. Are there friends in North Carolina you might want to talk to? Like from your high school?"

"I only had one guy I hung with and he left for Duke a couple months ago," Finn said.

"If you want to call him, you can use my phone anytime. Friends are important." I was thinking about how smart Finn seemed, how polite and well spoken. He should be a freshman in college like his friend, not sitting in a police interrogation room. I was puzzled as to why he wasn't in school, but then immediately realized this kid may not have had anyone to help him get into a university. My late husband had told me how he helped Kara every step of the way when she applied to college. But what did kids like Finn do when they distrusted almost everyone in the entire world? They retreated, hid in their rooms. And then, when they got the chance, they ran. Yes, I understood why Finn was now sitting in a police station and not at Clemson or Duke or UNC.

Candace came through the door, strands of hair flying free around her temples. She set a clipboard on the table. When she poured herself a cup of water, I noticed her hand shake.

She sat and smiled at Finn. "Okay. We needed to talk a little more and I'm glad you came."

"Talk more about the gun?" Finn said. "I said I don't know anything about it."

She said, "We've already spoken about the weapon. I'd like more information about your relationship with your mother and stepfather."

"Please quit using any word with *father* in it. He was Nolan. Just *Nolan.*" Finn reached for the pack of gum and took out another piece. He didn't put it in his mouth, just turned the little white rectangle over and over between his fingers.

"I get you didn't like him," Candace said evenly.

"Haven't I talked enough? I don't *know* anything else." Finn remained focused on the piece of gum he was fiddling with.

"Maybe we can go back to before you left home. You remember that much, don't you?" Candace said.

Finn kept rolling the gum between his fingers.

"If Mr. Roth hadn't been murdered," she went on, "it wouldn't be any of my business. But I have to do my job. We're working together — you, Tom, Jillian, all of us —

to find the killer. But I need more facts." She tilted her head down, probably hoping he'd make eye contact.

He didn't. "What did my mother tell you?"

"She said there were problems between you and Nolan," Candace said.

Tom fidgeted in his chair as the topic turned to Hilary. "I'm not about to bad-mouth Finn's mother, but take whatever my ex-wife says with a grain of salt."

"What Tom's trying to say is, she lies. All the time," Finn said.

Candace pulled the clipboard toward her and poised a pen over the blank paper. "About what?"

"She lied about Tom after they broke up," Finn said. "She told me he never wanted to see me again. Only took one text message to him for me to find out that wasn't true. See, she thinks I'm stupid. Thinks I can't figure things out for myself."

"Did she and Nolan get along?" Candace said.

"I guess. But I pretty much stayed in my room since he got out of jail," Finn said.

"How long ago was he released?" she asked.

"A year." Finn finally put the second piece of gum in his mouth.

"You're saying you hardly talked to him?"

Candace said. "Things must have been tense around your house."

Finn looked Candace straight in the eye for the first time. "Oh yeah. By the way, he was a bigger liar than she is. They deserved each other." Finn blinked a few times and then said, "Sorry. He's dead and no matter how big of a jerk he was, I didn't want him to die."

Tom rested a hand on Finn's forearm. "Tell her why you left, Finn."

Finn hung his head. "With my friends gone off to college, I got tired of being alone except for Yoshi. They wouldn't even let him out into the rest of the house. He had to stay in my room. So I stayed with him."

Tears stung my eyes at the thought of Finn and Yoshi alone in a bedroom, day after day.

"What else did you argue about besides your dog?" Candace asked.

"It's hard to argue when you don't talk to people," Finn said.

"You did graduate from high school?" Candace asked.

"Yes," he answered, sounding calmer now.

"If things at home hadn't been such a mess he could have been first in his class," Tom said.

"I know you're a smart kid," Candace said. "And you probably have information you don't even realize — and nothing to hide, right?"

"Nothing to hide." Finn's face clouded with uncertainty. "At least nothing I can remember."

Candace said, "Let's see if I can help you put yesterday back together. What's the very last thing you remember?"

Finn's features seemed to relax since she'd switched her focus off his family. "I got a ride with a trucker in Greenville about midday. He was headed for Atlanta. Dropped me at a gas station in — I don't remember the name of the place. I have maps and GPS on my phone, but I lost it somewhere. Anyway, I hitched another ride with some man in a U-Haul who said he was moving to Woodcrest. I knew Woodcrest was near where Tom lived. The guy let me off on the road into Mercy. Yoshi and I started walking. That's the last thing I remember."

"Somewhere between here and Woodcrest." She scribbled notes on her clipboard. "Should be able to check the timing if we find the guy in the U-Haul. Must be you hit your head bad enough to get a concussion along the highway. You're sure you don't have a clue how it happened?"

Tom sighed heavily. "Candace, he's told you what he knows. Give the kid a break."

"I have one more request," she said. "Fingerprints. Then y'all can leave."

Tom nodded. "Knew that was coming. Let's get it over with, then."

"Be right back." Candace left the room.

"That wasn't too bad, was it?" I said.

"She didn't keep on about my mother and Nolan, so I guess not," he answered.

Tom said, "I hate to tell you this, but you're gonna have to be more specific about why you left home sooner or later. Your mother was in with Chief Baca when Candace and I came back here with the gun. Hilary probably said plenty, not much of it true."

"Do you know how long she'd been here?" I said.

"When Candace and I arrived with the gun, B.J. told me she'd been waiting around for almost an hour before she went in to talk to Chief Baca." He turned to Finn. "Mike only has her version of why you ran, even though he was here last night and knows exactly what I think of my ex and her dead husband. My advice is to set Candace straight in as much detail as possible. But not yet. First I want to find out what cards Hilary's already played. Mike will tell Candace and she can fill us in."

Finn nodded solemnly.

Candace reentered the room holding what looked like a smartphone. Turned out it was a portable fingerprint scanner — a new evidence tool. No wonder she seemed happy. Candace loved anything to do with evidence. She was just finishing up with Finn's prints when we heard a female voice, one I recognized immediately.

"Oh no." Tom rubbed between his eyes with his thumb and index finger.

But Finn's expression brightened. "Is that Nana Karen?"

Twelve

Finn rushed from the interrogation room and the rest of us followed. He flew through the gate dividing the hall from the front office and into the arms of Karen Stewart — Tom's mother.

From their tight embrace, I could tell Karen clearly adored this kid and he seemed to love her, too.

Tom, who was standing next to me, said, "I should have fought for custody even though I wasn't his real dad. He deserved more moments like this."

"Is there any other family — like his biological father?" I asked

"Good question," Candace said as she scrolled through the fingerprints she'd just scanned in. "Has he ever been in the picture?"

Karen placed her hands on either side of Finn's face and started asking him questions. They were in their own world. I'd never seen her smile so big.

Tom said, "The father's name is Rory Gannon. Hilary once told me he's mentally ill. When he was institutionalized, she divorced him, took Finn and got as far from him as her money would take her."

"You ever meet him?" I said.

"Nope. He never paid child support. Never showed his face. A phantom. As far as I knew, she was a single mom, with a fantastic kid, who deserved better than an uninvolved ex-husband."

Candace said, "I have to send these prints to the crime lab, but I have more questions for you, Tom."

He sighed heavily. "About what? I want to help, but I'm tired and I know you are, too."

"I need to know more about what went on between you and Nolan Roth." She started to walk down the hall away from us. Over her shoulder she said, "See, I just talked to the chief. He said Mrs. Roth claimed to know nothing about Nolan making you drive to North Carolina and the dustup between you and Roth."

"You don't believe her, right?" Tom said.

Candace stopped and turned back. "I'd say those bruises on your face are enough evidence for me. But to satisfy the chief, who seems quite charmed by your ex-wife, by the way, I need more details with a time line, Tom. Right now, I've got evidence to examine. So go on, all of you. Get some rest. I know where to find you."

She walked to the end of the hall and disappeared into the office across from Chief Baca's.

Tom's face had gone red with anger. "Hilary knows exactly what happened in North Carolina. I'm sure she planned the whole thing."

I rested a hand on his arm. "Listen, you're exhausted. Come to my house and just . . . *relax* for an hour or two." Even as I said the words I knew he couldn't. The man I thought I'd known so well — a man always in control, strong, kind, generous — was showing a side I'd never seen. The past had come back to throttle him and he was angry, worried and confused.

"Thanks, Jillian, but right now —"

"I understand. Please know I'm with you all the way. Anything you need, well . . . *anything*. I'll do what I can."

He squeezed my hand. "Right now, I need to talk to my mother. Any help you can give me with her would be much appreciated. She likes you."

We walked hand in hand through the squeaky wooden gate and joined Finn and the woman he called Nana.

Karen Stewart, in her late sixties, wore a gray coat and her familiar black cloche hat. She was no longer coloring her dark hair. Silver and black strands escaped the hat and curled on her forehead and temples.

She addressed me, not Tom. "Look where I find my boys. In the police station, of all places. What should I do with these troublemakers, Jillian?"

"Tough question," I said. "I'd say a meal might be in order. Can we discuss this over lunch at the diner?"

Finn's eyes lit up.

I added, "An eighteen-year-old needs more than toast and milk — which is about all Finn's eaten today."

"Let's fix that," Tom said.

The Main Street Diner turned out to be exactly what Finn needed. He looked happy for the first time since I'd met him. The three of us watched him put away fries, three of the diner's famous Texas chili dogs and a root beer float. Karen seemed as cheerful as he was as she nibbled on a salad and drank hot tea.

I still didn't understand why neither she nor Tom had ever mentioned a kid they both obviously loved, but each family has their own way of dealing with problems. After I'd finished my hamburger, I decided to quit wondering and bring up the subject.

"I was so surprised to meet Finn," I said. "You all care a lot about each other."

"We do, but Finnian's home situation has not always allowed us to visit with each other," Karen said. "Especially after Mr. Roth was released from prison last year. I suspect Thomas said nothing to you previously, Jillian. He certainly wouldn't engage me in conversation about what to do concerning Finn's home situation."

"This *has* been a little surprising," I said.

Tom cleared his throat. "I — I felt frozen by the system, what with Finn still being a minor and all. I'd chat with him online and then put away my thoughts. See, I know what Hilary's capable of. Maybe I was being paranoid, but I believed even mentioning him to anyone I knew might somehow get back to her and she'd find a way to completely shut me out of his life. But now that Finn is eighteen, things will be different."

Finn said, "Nolan was just as bad as Mom. He wouldn't let me talk to Nana Karen or Tom. I did anyway, though. He just didn't know."

Didn't know until you disappeared and Nolan

checked your computer, I thought. "Was Mr. Roth so upset with Tom for sending him to jail he decided to punish all of you this way?"

Finn swiped his last three French fries through a puddle of ketchup. "That's about right."

Tom said, "We decided it was best not to let anyone know we were still in touch. Keep the peace, in other words."

"You see, Mr. Roth was extremely controlling," Karen said. "He wouldn't allow Hilary to talk to me either, though she called me without his knowledge on more than one occasion. I have no issue with Hilary, even though Thomas is less, shall we say, *open-minded* when it comes to her." She stared over at Tom, seated next to me in the wooden booth. "Thomas, can you explain why I had to find out via a phone call from Hilary that Finnian was in town? Oh, and I also heard you spent much of last night being interviewed by the police. Did you get all those cuts and bruises from fighting with one of the police officers for some reason?"

"No, Mom." Tom squeezed my knee and I rested my hand over his. "I planned on calling you to explain the minute things settled down."

"The newspaper said the man who died

was driving your car. Did he steal it?" she asked.

"You could say that," Tom said.

"How intentionally vague," she replied. "You always think I'll fall off the wagon if you involve me in less-than-happy aspects of your life. I won't, Thomas. I'm stronger than you think."

"Maybe you are, Mom. But I don't like upsetting you. Anything involving Finn might make you, well . . . overreact."

She looked at Finn, her eyes showing her affection for him. "Perhaps you're right, Thomas. Did you have anything to do with the accident? Is that why the police kept you so long?"

"There was plenty to discuss," Tom said.

I could tell he wasn't about to elaborate because he might not want Karen hearing about Finn's head injury right now. Maybe she'd be upset because Tom called on me to help Finn rather than her.

Finn's gaze went back and forth between Tom and Karen. "He kept the police busy to help me, Nana. When Tom saw it was Nolan who crashed the car, Tom figured he came to town looking for me. See, I left Mom and Nolan to come here."

Tom said, "Can we talk about something else?"

"You ran away?" Karen said. "Oh my goodness, I don't know what to think."

"I couldn't stay there anymore, Nana. I was hoping Tom would let me live here."

"So much for putting this conversation on the shelf for now." Tom sounded exasperated.

Karen didn't seem to hear Tom. She focused on Finn's bruised forehead. "Did they hit you? Because if they did —"

"No. Nothing like that," Finn said. "I don't know how I got hurt. Wish I did. Anyway, it's all part of why Tom ended up talking to the police for so many hours. With Nolan dead and the gun we found in my backpack —"

"Gun?" Karen, sounding aghast, glanced between Finn and Tom. "Was it one of *your* guns, Thomas?"

"Nope. That's all I'm saying about it, too." Tom looked at Finn. "Please let's not talk about any of this until we know more. Words fly faster than hummingbirds around this town. We don't want to start rumors."

"I'm cool with that. But you better tell Bob, since he's the one who found the gun to begin with," Finn said.

Karen blanched. "Bob? *Our* Bob?"

"See, this is why I wanted to wait until I

had all the facts before talking to you," Tom said.

Karen said, "Did you call him? If so, why in God's good name would you do such a thing?"

Tom held up a hand. "I haven't figured out why Bob showed up here. But he's at my house."

Karen rested her hand over her heart. "Oh my."

"You never liked him, did you, Nana?" Finn said. "How come?"

She put an arm around Finn. "You know, I believe Thomas is correct. We can talk about all this later. As for Hilary, I'm certain she's quite distressed over losing her husband. Where will she stay? I could offer to —"

"Please don't, Mom," Tom said, his tone firm.

I said, "I understand she'll be staying at the Pink House."

"I take it you won't be staying there with her, Finn?" Karen said.

"Um, no." Finn focused on his empty plate.

"Then *you* can come to my house," Karen said. "The place is small, but there's always room for you."

"Mom, he has a dog," Tom said.

Karen blinked several times. "Oh. A dog. That would be a problem," she said, obviously disappointed.

Tom looked at Finn. "Mom's friend Ed — you remember I told you about him? — anyway, he's afraid of dogs."

"It's okay, Nana," Finn said. "I'll find somewhere to stay."

"You are more than welcome to continue on at my place," I said.

"Thanks, Jillian," Tom said, "but as soon as I get rid of Bob — which is next on my agenda — Finn can come to my house."

"Poor Yoshi will have to get used to yet another cat," I said, thinking of Dashiell. I pulled my phone from my pocket. "Check this out, Finn." I showed him my cat cam and, sure enough, Yoshi and Merlot were sleeping in the living room. "They're not snuggling up yet, but for only one day, this is progress."

Finn took the phone and smiled. "This cat cam is one fine app."

"Tom set it up for me so I can see what my cats are doing when I'm not at home," I said.

Karen peered over at the display. "Toshi is cute," she said.

"Yoshi," Finn said, playing with the phone to see different angles of the room. Didn't

need any instruction, I noted.

Unfortunately I was being optimistic about Dashiell accepting a dog into his home. Tom seemed to have forgotten that Shawn Cuddahee, Allison's husband and partner in running the Mercy Animal Sanctuary, rescued Dashiell right after he was attacked by two dogs.

"Before I go talk to Bob, I need to pick Dashiell up from the vet — that is, if he's ready to come home," Tom said.

"He is," I said. "I called this morning and Dashiell is doing fine."

"Good," Tom said. "I'll get him after we're done here. Boy am I looking forward to seeing my big old cat, but I think telling my brother to take a hike will be the icing on the cake."

"While you're busy, perhaps Finn could come to my house for a while?" Karen said.

"Sure," Finn said, still fiddling with my phone. "But not for too long. Yoshi will miss me."

"Got any message for Bob?" Tom said to his mother.

Her blue eyes grew frosty. "No message."

The silence hung like a thick cloud over all of us for several seconds. Tom broke the tension by saying, "Let's go. Dashiell probably wants out of the vet clinic."

After we left the restaurant and went our separate ways, I wondered what had happened between Tom and Bob, and between Bob and his mother. No one was offering any information, but then, I wasn't sure I even wanted to know.

I drove home, the wonderful distraction of our conversation at the diner replaced by fatigue and worry. A man had been shot to death and Finn not only had a gun in his possession when we found him walking on the side of the road, he also had blood on his clothes. Candace would surely unearth something from the evidence to eliminate Finn as a suspect in Nolan Roth's death. She had to. No way could she believe Finn was guilty of murder. As I approached my house, those thoughts slid to the back of my mind when I realized there was a car parked on the side of the road, one I didn't recognize — an old banged-up blue sedan with South Carolina plates.

I pulled into the driveway and stopped about halfway up. A man immediately got out of the sedan and started toward my van. He wore no sweater or jacket in this chilly weather and his striped button-down shirt was wrinkled, his jeans baggy and his long sandy hair blew around his head in the autumn wind.

My mouth went dry. I didn't like the looks of him.

The man came all the way up to my car, rested both hands on the driver's-side window and stared in at me.

Thirteen

On another day, I might have rolled down the window and talked to this stranger. After all, folks made wrong turns down my street all the time and needed directions. Today, however, my gut was telling me this person didn't need directions.

I reached for my phone on the seat next to me. Thank goodness I automatically put it close when I'm driving alone. An old habit, one I appreciated right now.

"Can I help you?" I called loud enough for him to hear. I slid the arrow on the phone's screen and pressed the phone button, ready to make a call. I was sure he'd seen me do this, but he didn't make any move to leave.

"They said you have my boy," the man said.

My stomach clenched. Fear can be a gift, I'd read, one that leads you to make the right decisions. Something about this man put me on high alert. I was just about to tap the speed dial number for Mercy PD when I heard the short blast of a car horn. In the side mirror, I saw Kara getting out of her car.

I wanted to yell, "No," but it was too late. The man had moved away from my van when he heard the horn, so I opened the door and got out, still clutching my phone. I couldn't cringe in my car while Kara was confronting this stranger.

A Belle's Beans cup in her left hand, Kara walked up to the man and held out her right hand. "I'm Kara Hart. Who are you?"

This is exactly the sort of thing her father would do in a touchy situation, I thought.

The man tilted his head and stared through narrowed eyes, ignoring her hand. "They told me the name was Jillian Hart, not Kara."

She dropped her hand. "*Who* told you?" she said evenly.

Always the questioner, Kara's even tone not only quieted my nerves, but seemed to do the same for this man.

His expression grew less wary. "The people in the diner. They said I just missed you, that Finn was with you."

Kara briefly looked my way and said, "I didn't catch your name."

"Rory Gannon. Now, where's my boy?" he said.

Finn's biological father. How did the so-called phantom end up in Mercy? This can't be a coincidence.

"Kara," I said, trying to match her cool amicability. "This is Finn's father."

I saw a hint of confusion cloud her face for an instant, but then she was back on her game. She smiled. "Okay. Finn's *father.* When did you get into town, Mr. Gannon?"

He ignored her question and looked at me. "Are you Jillian or is she the one I need to talk to?"

"I'm Jillian."

"Is he with you?" he said.

"I'm sorry, but no," I said.

This obviously wasn't what he wanted to hear. His agitation was evident in eyes that darted everywhere. His gaze finally settled on my van.

I stepped away from the driver's door and gestured toward it. "Go ahead and look if you don't believe me."

He took me up on the offer while Kara and I exchanged "what the heck is going on?" glances.

Once he'd assured himself Finn was not in my car, he walked over and checked out her new hybrid SUV. Finally satisfied we didn't have Finn stashed away somewhere, he returned to us.

"Finn wasn't with you in the restaurant? 'Cause some waitress said you had a teenage boy sitting with you," he said.

I knew better than to give up any information to this strange man. "Can I ask how you ended up in our little town looking for your son — and found me?"

"You can ask all you want." He stared past me at my front door. "Is he in your house hiding from me?"

"Why would he hide from you?" Kara asked.

This question seemed to fluster Gannon. "He doesn't know me too well, is all."

"Does he even know you a little bit?" I made sure the question sounded sincere and not like an accusation, since he'd apparently never been a part of Finn's life.

"What's it to you?" Gannon said. "He's my flesh and blood, so you better tell me where I can find him. I deserve to know."

That's debatable, I thought. But I wasn't about to get him any more riled up than he already was, so I said, "I wish I could tell you, but I'm not sure where your son is." Not *exactly* where he was, anyway.

He stepped toward me. "You're lying."

Kara moved between Gannon and me.

"You need to leave, sir."

Why was she acting like she could take him on? This guy was obviously a loose cannon. Feeling afraid for both of us now, I pressed the speed dial number — something I should have done immediately. "Is this the Mercy Police Department?" I said, loud enough to send a message to Rory Gannon.

B.J. said, "Jillian? Something wrong?"

"I'd like to report a trespasser," I said.

Gannon said, "You're siccing the police on me when you're probably a kidnapper?"

"Am I hearing the voice of your trespasser?" B.J. said.

"Yes. You know the address," I answered.

"Does he have a weapon?" B.J. said.

"Not that I know of," I answered.

"I'm sending someone now," B.J. said.

Kara's hands were on her hips and I saw no trace of fear in her body language. She said, "I suggest you leave while you can."

"I get it. You're hiding him and you're determined to keep him from me." He pointed at me. "I'll be back."

Rory Gannon jogged to his car and drove off.

I still held my phone to my ear and was listening to B.J. dispatching a squad car. I said, "He left, B.J., but I got his plate." I rattled off the numbers. "His name is Rory

Gannon and he's Finn's biological father."

"*Him?* Uh-oh," B.J. said. "He — he said he was Finn's father and seemed nice enough, so I told him where y'all went for lunch. Guess I screwed up."

"Does Candace know he's in town?" I asked. She surely would have interviewed Gannon if that were the case.

"She will in a minute. I am so sorry if he bothered you, Mrs. Hart. He seemed nice, real polite," B.J. said.

"I guess he forgot his manners on the drive over here," I said. "Better let both Candace and the chief know about him as soon as you can." Poor B.J. had so much to learn and was such a good kid, I couldn't be upset with his mistake. Candace might not be so forgiving, however.

"I'll talk to them right away. Let me correct my dispatch to a BOLO. If Mr. Gannon comes back, call me and I promise to do better." He sounded so down in the mouth I felt terrible for him.

"You take care, B.J. No harm, no foul." I disconnected.

While I'd been talking to him, Kara had gotten into her SUV and rolled the window down. When I was off the phone, she said, "Not what I expected to find when I came back here. That guy's seat is not in the full, upright position."

"No kidding. But are you going somewhere?" I said.

"I'm not leaving, especially after a guy straight out of a bad movie just visited. Could you pull your car up so I can get closer to the back door? I did some serious damage at the mall and cleaned out the Piggly Wiggly."

I pulled the van close to the garage, and after I took Yoshi out to relieve himself, I helped Kara empty the back of her SUV of the bags of groceries and the clothing purchases for Finn. I explained what little I knew about Rory Gannon. Yoshi and the boy cats, who seemed to have forged a truce while I'd been gone, sniffed at each sack of groceries. Yoshi was the more interested party, and once I located the dog food, I offered him a dish of kibble.

Syrah sniffed the food while Yoshi sat patiently and watched. My cat took his time and finally walked away, seemingly indifferent. Merlot didn't even bother checking out the kibble and Chablis had only shown her whiskers momentarily and then rushed off to whatever safe place she'd found to hide from Yoshi. Only then did the little dog eat.

As we put away groceries, Kara asked if she needed to pick Dashiell up. I told her

Tom said he planned to do it — and would then be kicking his brother out of the house.

"Do you know anything about Bob and Tom's history?" Kara asked as she stacked cans of cat food on the pantry shelf.

"Nothing, except Tom can't stand him," I said. "I'm pretty sure Karen isn't feeling the love, either." I was checking out the sweatshirts, jeans and T-shirts Kara had bought for Finn. They looked like they'd fit, plus they appeared a lot more teen friendly than what I would have bought.

"Ah, it's logical Karen would know about Finn," Kara said. "From what little contact I've had with Karen, she strikes me as, well . . . odd."

"She's different, yes. But she adores Finn." I told Kara about our lunch and then said, "Tom's ex is in town, too."

"I expected her to arrive and hoped to get an interview," Kara said. "How did you find out she was here?"

"She was at the police station and wanted to talk to Finn, but he wanted nothing to do with her," I said.

"Is Tom going to have her arrested for what she and Nolan Roth did to him?" she said. "You did say Tom thought she was involved, right?"

"There could be a problem. See, Candace

told us Hilary claims she knew nothing about Nolan's actions. Since Tom never saw her when Nolan made him drive to North Carolina, I'm not sure what will happen."

"Uh-oh. A he-said, she-said problem. What's she like, by the way?" Kara asked.

"First impression? Normal. Concerned. Oh, and gorgeous," I said. "She'll be at the Pink House, if you want an interview."

Kara's eyes lit up. "Really?"

I started at the sound of a knock at the back door, but then realized it was Candace's special rat-a-tat. She came in looking even more tired than when I'd seen her last at the police station.

"Hey, you two. I heard about Gannon. He didn't come back, did he?" she said.

"No," I said. "But he said he would. The man's intense, to say the least."

"I'm so glad you called us. B.J. screwed up on this one." Candace took a spot at the breakfast bar. "I sure hope you have tea because I need a sugar boost in the worst way."

Kara poured her a glass and then took her keys from the pocket of her jeans. "I have a paper to run. Call me if you need anything, Jillian."

She waved to us both and was gone.

Candace took a long drink of tea. "Tell

me about this Gannon guy."

"You haven't found him?" I asked, filling a glass with water. My lunch had probably supplied an entire week's worth of sodium and I was thirsty now.

"No. We are so undermanned we only had one squad car to follow up on the BOLO. They thought they'd run into him coming away from this neighborhood, but nothing. It's like he disappeared into thin air."

"He said he'd be back — and I believe him." I drank half my water, realizing my heart had sped up again at the thought of his return.

"What did he want?" she asked.

"He wants his son. Thinks I'm hiding him." Syrah was weaving between my legs and rubbing his head on my calves. Marking his territory in case the curious Yoshi got any ideas, no doubt.

"I searched the NCIC database before I came here," Candace said. "I don't want to scare you any more than you already are, but you need to know this. About fifteen years ago, Gannon served time — first in a hospital for the criminally insane and then when he was competent to stand trial, he did a stint in prison."

I drank the rest of my water, the glass nearly slipping from my trembling hand.

"F-for what?"

"He went nuts when he was pulled over on a routine traffic stop," she said. "Wailed on the officer with a baseball bat he conveniently had in his front seat. Put the officer in critical condition. Seems Gannon claimed the officer was an alien. He was convicted of felonious assault, so this guy is a violent offender."

"Both Kara and I knew he was off, but now I'm even more scared of him," I said. "My question is, how did he find out Finn was in Mercy?"

"Exactly. I have no idea. But I intend to find out. Violent offenders reoffend. He could be our killer — but I have to find him and interview him before coming to any conclusion on that." She stood. "Where's Finn, by the way?"

"He's with Karen," I said.

"I'll ask the squad car out in the field to run by her neighborhood," she said. "If Gannon found you, he might be able to find Karen, too. She was at the diner with you, right?"

"Yes, she was there and so was Tom." I tore at a cuticle with my teeth.

"Guess we should alert Tom to the situation. Trouble is, the man doesn't have a cell phone and I don't have the time to —"

"I'll go to his place and tell him. He planned to pick up Dashiell and then see if he could extricate his brother from the house. He'll want to protect Finn and his mother from Gannon."

Candace pointed at me. "You lock this place up tight and set your alarm — whether you're out of the house or not. You hear me? If anything happened to you, well . . ." She shook her head and averted her eyes.

I walked around and hugged Candace. "I'll be careful. I promise."

FOURTEEN

Fifteen minutes later, the late-afternoon sun doing little to kill the chill in the air, I pulled into Tom's driveway. As soon as I got within five feet of the front door, I heard raised voices. My stomach tightened and I stood still. *What is going on now?*

Then I recognized the voices of both Tom and Bob exchanging heated barbs. I went to the door and knocked loudly so they could hear me over their argument.

Bob was saying, "You owe me, brother. Mom owes me. I'm tired of this family crap."

I knocked even louder, and this time Tom opened the door. His face was flushed with anger and his eyes had what looked like minuscule red lightning strikes mapping the whites.

He said, "Oh. Hi."

"Hi." I smiled, wishing I could relieve the distress that seemed to have taken over his whole demeanor. Too many awful things had happened to him in the last week.

"Come on in." He stood aside so I could enter. "Bob was just leaving."

Didn't look like he was leaving to me. He was standing, arms folded, his cheeks just as red as Tom's. No flirty smile today.

"Where am I supposed to go?" Bob said.

"Back under the rock you slithered out from," Tom answered.

"Um, guys, please. This isn't good for either of you." I felt out of place playing referee, but someone had to. The bad blood between these two must have gone back a long way.

Turned out, a cat accomplished what only pets can do. Dashiell came lumbering into the living room and offered up a pitiful meow.

"See?" I said. "Even Dashiell wants you to stop."

Tom looked embarrassed. Even the brash Bob looked down at the floor.

Tom said, "You're right. The stress isn't good for Dashiell. His blood sugar is stable and I want it to stay that way."

I knelt and Dashiell came to me. He rubbed against my knees. I petted him, glad he could do catlike things again after the major scare of finding him unconscious.

"He looks fine, Tom. I know you must be relieved."

"Guess I should say I'm sorry for letting him escape," Bob said. "I had no idea he'd get so sick."

Tom stared at his brother, looking a tad stunned. "Was that an apology?"

"Yeah, it was," Bob said. "You want to apologize for treating me like dirt on your shoe now?"

"Okay, how's this?" Tom said. "I'll give you money to leave. A thousand bucks. One condition, though. You leave Mom alone."

"You're kidding, right? You think I came here for a thousand stinking bucks?" he said.

"Why did you come, Bob?" I said.

He reverted to his rogue smile and I saw a change in his eyes. Like a curtain dropped. The mask was back on. "Family first, they always say."

"Oh, sure," Tom said. "And I've got a bridge spanning the Atlantic I'd like to sell you."

"Is a compromise possible?" I asked before Tom got worked up again.

"I won't stay long. How's that?" Bob said.

"How long is not long?" Tom said.

"I'll be gone in a week," Bob said. "I've got some prospects and just need a place to hang out until I settle a few things."

"You're broke again?" Tom said.

"Is a week tolerable, Tom?" I asked. Though I wasn't exactly fond of Bob, I was beginning to feel a little sorry for him. I mean, what kind of prospects could he have here in Mercy?

"As long as he stays out of my face, I guess a week is okay. But no longer." Tom turned and walked toward the kitchen. "Come on, Jillian. I need a drink. And I'm not talking about sweet tea."

Tom grabbed the bottle of Jameson's Irish Whiskey from a high kitchen cupboard and poured us both two fingers in water tumblers. I am not really a fan of whiskey, but there are times we all need the comfort of spirits, as my grandma used to say. Tom downed his drink in one gulp. He closed his eyes and said, "I needed that."

Staring down into the glass, I said, "You might need more than one shot after what I have to tell you."

His eyes widened. "What's wrong? It's not Finn, is it?"

"Well, there is a connection. A big connection." I quickly told him about the episode with Rory Gannon.

"Great. How did he end up in Mercy?" Tom said. He wasn't actually expecting me to answer, just voicing his frustration. He went on, saying, "We have to get over to my mom's house right now. If he knew where to find you, he probably knows where to find my mother." Tom started for the back door.

"But how, Tom?" I said, hurrying after him.

"I don't know, but somehow the man's found out about Finn and is here looking for him." He pulled me by the hand as we went outside. "Right now I'm just sorry I got you involved. Since my mother has zero security, even though I've offered to install a system at her house at least a dozen times, Finn won't be safe there."

"There's no room for him here," I said as we practically ran around the back of the house toward the driveway.

"I'll *make* room," Tom said. "If Bob has to go, so be it. Let's take your van. Get over there as fast as possible."

After I slid behind the driver's seat and Tom was beside me, I said, "Let Finn stay with me. You can, too. Bring Dashiell. You know I have plenty of room, and somebody named Tom Stewart installed a state-of-the-art security system at *my* house."

"It won't work," he said. "With Dashiell's blood sugar scare —"

"Being around a dog would be too stressful," I finished. "But you know my house is open to you."

"I have to stay home while Bob's hanging around. If I don't watch out, he might rob me blind or spend his time figuring out ways to get to Mom. Here's what you could do, though. Keep the dog while Finn stays with me. That way I can protect him. I'll roll out a sleeping bag for myself if I have to."

"You don't even know if Gannon intends him any harm," I said.

"What's your gut tell you about him?" he said.

"He's a scary guy," I said, remembering his face and his intensity. "Whatever you decide, I'm with you."

Minutes later, I pulled into the driveway of the house where Karen lived with her partner, Ed Duffy.

Ed, wearing blue jean overalls and a plaid flannel shirt answered the door. I noticed his beard was showing more signs of gray than the last time I'd seen him.

He smiled and said, "Haven't seen Karen this happy in a long time. Come on in and join the party."

Ed couldn't possibly be this jovial if Rory Gannon had shown up. We found Finn and Karen sitting at the dining room table playing chess. The house was chilly and Karen wore a pale blue collared cardigan with every pearl button fastened. I wondered where she bought these vintage clothes, or if she'd bought them years ago and simply taken excellent care of them. I noted a can of Dr Pepper beside Finn's hand. I was glad I had a good supply at my place now and would make sure to hand over a few liter bottles to Tom.

Karen looked up at Tom. She was beaming. "He's beaten me twice already. What a difference a few years make."

"I play chess online all the time," Finn said.

"Hate to break up the party," Tom said, "but Finn needs to come with us."

"But I have supper on, Thomas," Karen said. "The macaroni and cheese is in the oven and Ed was just about ready to fry up the catfish he caught today."

Tom bit the side of his mouth, seeming to consider the importance of a doting grandmother who was fixing what might well be Finn's favorite meal. Finally he said, "Guess we could stay for a spell. Do you have enough food for all of us?"

"We have enough fish for an army," Ed said. "I'll get busy with my part of this deal."

While he ambled to the kitchen, Karen

said, "Guess we'll have to save this game for another time. I almost had you in checkmate, Finnian."

Finn smiled. "Sure you did, Nana."

While Karen and Finn cleared the chess pieces off the table, Tom joined Ed in the kitchen. Karen took place mats and plates from the antique buffet against the wall. Finn and I were helping her set the table when someone knocked on the door.

"Now, who could that be?" Karen asked as she started for the front door.

Tom rushed from the kitchen, saying, "Mom, let me answer." Before she could even react to his words, he looked through the peephole and said, "Jillian, can you tell me if this is the guy?"

"What guy?" Karen asked.

Tom held a finger to his lips while I looked through the peephole.

"That's him." I stepped back.

"Call Candace while I keep him busy," he said.

Finn stepped into the living room. "What's happening?"

"I'll take care of this," Tom replied. "Could you all please wait in the kitchen with Jillian?"

"Did you forget this is my house, Thomas? I'm not going anywhere." Karen fiddled with a sweater button. The words may have been exactly what I expected from her, but I could see a hint of concern in her deep blue eyes.

More knocking, louder this time.

Not ready for another encounter with Rory Gannon, I took Finn's arm and said, "Let's do what Tom wants." We walked to the kitchen together, but Karen didn't follow. We joined Ed, who was preparing the catfish.

I pulled my phone from my pocket and speed-dialed Candace's number. She should be home by now — unless she was working nonstop. She answered immediately.

"What's up?" she said.

"You-know-who is here at Karen's house." I glanced at Finn, who was in the kitchen entry apparently trying to catch a glimpse of what was going on in the other room. "The guy from earlier today."

"Is he threatening y'all?" she asked.

"Tom's talking to him, so I'm not sure." I licked my dry lips.

"I'm on my way. Give me five minutes." She disconnected.

"Trouble?" Ed asked. He hovered over a catfish filet sizzling in a cast-iron skillet on the old gas stove.

"You could say that," I said. "But between

Tom and Candace, they'll get the situation under control. Everything will be fine." I looked back to the entry and Finn was gone. "Maybe I spoke too soon." I went after him.

"Is that you, Finnian?" I heard Rory Gannon say.

I arrived in the living room to see Karen standing on the threshold of the open front door. Tom had stepped outside to speak with Gannon — probably trying to keep him around until Candace showed up.

"Mom, please go inside and shut the door," Tom said.

Finn peered around Tom's tall frame at Gannon. He said, "Do I know you?"

"I'm your dad, son," Gannon said.

There it was, another slug to the jaw from the past.

By his expression, Tom sure seemed to have felt the blow when he turned to Finn. "We don't know if he's telling the truth, Finn."

But Finn was nodding his head. "I've seen your picture. How did you find me?"

"See? He knows me," Gannon said. "Too bad I never saw *your* picture after I left for that hospital, Finnian. Sure wish I had, but your mother took you and disappeared."

Tom tried to block Gannon's view but without much success, since Finn seemed more than interested in this man — and with good reason.

"See? He wants to visit," Gannon said. "You can't keep a boy from his kin."

"Where have you been all this time?" Finn's voice was a monotone.

"Does it matter? I'm here now to meet up with my boy," Gannon said and added a half laugh. "My long-lost boy."

No, I thought. *That's not why you're here.* Though he seemed more in control than earlier today, I thought of the Eagles song about "lying eyes." Gannon had some other motive for coming here, of that much I was certain. I had the feeling Nolan or Hilary Roth might have had a hand in Gannon's arrival. How else could he have known to come to Mercy?

"Your long-lost boy, huh? What a nice sentiment," Candace said. She'd come up behind Gannon so quickly and quietly I hadn't heard her. She must have parked halfway down the block because I surely would have recognized the sound of her RAV4's engine. She still wore her uniform and her hand gripped her weapon. "How's about you come down to the station and you can talk to me about why you've come to Mercy, Mr. Gannon?"

Gannon's eyes locked on me. He raised a

hand and pointed past Tom. "You called the cops on me twice in one day? What did I ever do to you, lady?"

Scared me silly? I thought, wishing I could make myself invisible. As if he'd read my mind, Tom sidestepped to block Gannon's view of me now, though he wasn't completely successful. I could still see Gannon, so he could certainly still see me.

But he abruptly turned to Candace. "As for you, I don't have to go anywhere you say, especially not to a police station. I have every right to visit with my son."

Candace said, "Finn's rights are what concern me, not yours." Candace looked past the two men in the doorway. "Finn, you want to talk to this man?"

Finn's answer was to return to the kitchen without a word. As I went after him, I heard Karen talking, though I couldn't make out what she was saying. Ed was smiling and humming, in his own fish-fry world. He'd placed several pieces of finished catfish filets on paper towels on the counter near the stove.

Finn went to his side, apparently ready to forget what had just happened. "You really caught all these fish yourself?"

"Easy to do. Ever heard of a trotline?" Ed asked.

Seemed like Finn felt the same way I did — that here in this old-fashioned kitchen filled with the smell of a home-cooked meal, the world seemed sane and safe. You could escape and pretend crazy people weren't stirring up trouble only twenty feet away.

"I used to fish with Tom when I was a kid," Finn said. "Is a trotline the one with all the fish hooks baited and you string it out across the water?"

"That's exactly right. You and me, we can do some fishing if you want. I can show you more than the easy stuff," Ed said.

I listened to their conversation while keeping an ear on what might be happening in the other room. Finally I heard the front door close, and soon Candace joined us in the kitchen. Tom and Karen remained in the other room; I hoped not with Rory Gannon in their company.

"Mr. Gannon's gone," Candace said. "I couldn't really arrest him since he hasn't broken the law. But I sure wish he would have agreed to visit with me down at the station. I might have found out more about him and how he ended up in Mercy — that is, if you want to know, Finn."

Candace's question snatched Finn back into the reality of fractured families and serious problems. He wore his sadness in his body language and on his face. My heart ached for him.

Finn said, "I don't care why he's here. I have to say, he sure looked different than I imagined."

"I'll find some reason to pull him in for an interview. For now I told him to keep his distance from you and your family," Candace said. "But I want you to tell me if he bothers you again."

"Sure," Finn said quietly.

Ed smiled at Candace. "Join us for supper, Miss Candace? We'd sure like to have you."

She said, "Love to, Ed, but I have way too much work to do — and just added Rory Gannon to the list of things I have to follow up on. Maybe there's a parole violation I can use as leverage."

I would have thought Finn would be upset by the revelation that Gannon had been to prison, but his face remained impassive.

I could tell Candace was upset with herself for saying anything about Gannon's past. "Sorry I brought that up. Are you okay, Finn?"

"Yeah. I'm good," he said in a monotone.

"Guess I'll be leaving, then. Y'all take care and call me if he comes back." She turned and started for the living room.

"Don't be driving around corners like you're trying for a spot on a NASCAR team, you hear?" Ed said, returning to his job.

I walked Candace back through the dining area and into the living room just in time to hear Karen say, "He's the boy's flesh and blood, Thomas."

"He's also a convicted felon," Candace said.

"Oh my," Karen said. "I had no idea. Poor Hilary had to live with two men who ended up on the wrong side of the law. This is like a Greek tragedy, isn't it?"

Greek tragedy? Karen did have a flare for the dramatic.

Meanwhile, Tom was saying, "Poor Hilary, my ass."

Karen's cheeks reddened so much I could see her cheeks flush despite her heavy rouge. "Watch your tongue, son. She brought Finn into our lives. You need to reconcile your differences with her for Finn's sake — and for your own. She hurt you, yes, but she's a good person who's simply made poor choices."

Since Karen was a recovering alcoholic with multiple failed marriages in her past, I understood how she could relate to Hilary Roth.

"Mom, can we drop this before Finn comes back into the room?" Tom said.

Candace cleared her throat. "Um, I'm thinking paperwork looks mighty inviting right now." She said her good-byes and left.

Ed appeared and called us to supper. Though the food was delicious, I learned a lesson. Do not eat fried fish after two days like we'd all experienced. My stomach was churning when Tom, Finn and I climbed into my van for the short trip back to Tom's house.

Rory Gannon was on my mind, and thoughts of him were not a good thing.

Fifteen

The next morning, I woke up feeling disoriented because I'd slept so hard. But with Chablis on my chest, kneading away and purring, the feeling didn't last long. Her usual morning behavior reintroduced me to the comforts of my daily routine in a week that had been anything but.

Last night, Finn explained to Tom that he wasn't about to stay away from Yoshi overnight. I couldn't blame him. He and his little dog had a tremendous bond.

Tom reluctantly agreed to allow Finn to come with me after he checked Dashiell's blood sugar and found it was high. He didn't feel like he could trust Bob to monitor Dashiell if he were to leave his cat behind and stay at my house. But he alerted Candace to the situation and followed us to my place to make sure all my outside security cameras were operating perfectly and the lenses were clean. He could monitor my house from his computer at home, a setup I appreciated. Last night it had indeed been reassuring to have a security expert as a trusted friend.

After I got up, I took a long, hot shower, with three cats waiting anxiously for me to hurry up and feed them. The house seemed less chilly than when I'd gone to bed, and I suspected the cold front we'd experienced had passed through. Late fall in South Carolina was always a mixed bag of warm days interspersed with cold.

I was surprised when I walked down the hall and found the guest room door open and the bed neatly made. *Uh-oh.* Had Finn risen early and decided to take off? This town — the one where he'd hoped to find happiness — had not offered mercy, so I couldn't blame him if he'd fled.

My fear was short-lived, however. He was sitting on the window seat in the living room looking out at the sun rising over the lake. Yoshi was curled beside him.

"Morning," I said.

Finn stood. "I like how quiet it is here. Funny how I never thought the world could be quiet."

"Nolan and your mom fought a lot, didn't they?" I said.

He nodded, eyes on the cushion. "She'd

break things; he'd yell. So I'd put on my earphones and plug into a game on my computer or listen to music on my iPod. Sometimes Yoshi and I would walk to the park and he'd chase a Frisbee for hours."

"Our fur friends can sure take us to a better place, huh?" I said.

"Yup. He needs to go out, but I didn't want to mess with your security alarm," Finn said.

After I fed the cats and disabled the alarm under Finn's watchful eye, we went out on the porch. Finn and Yoshi chased each other between the big trees. He was wearing a pair of jeans and a T-shirt Kara had picked out. The clothes fit perfectly, thank goodness. The day looked to be much warmer — it had to be sixty already — and the still lake shimmered in the morning light. I thought about what Finn had said a few minutes ago and wondered how quiet it was inside his head with all that had gone on both in his past and since his arrival here. Maybe playing with his dog would help empty his mind for a few minutes.

I wanted to make coffee but didn't feel comfortable leaving Finn alone out here. Rory Gannon knew where I lived, after all. So when I heard a car pull into my driveway, my mouth went instantly dry. I reached into my pocket for my phone in case we needed help.

"Finn," I called and gestured for him to come back to the house. But Yoshi was so invested in this game of chase, the usually obedient dog wouldn't cooperate and come to Finn. He wanted to keep playing.

"Run toward the house and he'll probably come after you," I yelled.

But yelling was a mistake. Our visitor must have heard me.

Hilary Roth appeared at the steps leading up to my deck. Finn had been doing as I suggested and was halfway to the house, but when he saw his mother, he stopped in his tracks. Yoshi caught up with him and sat, staring up at Finn. He held out his arms for his dog and Yoshi leaped up. Finn remained where he was.

"Sorry to bother you, Mrs. Hart, but I wanted to thank you again for caring for my son," she said.

She hadn't looked toward the lake, and thus apparently didn't see Finn standing in the shadows of the pines and oaks.

"No need to thank me," I said.

"I heard you call Finn's name just now and —" Finally she looked to her left and spotted him. "Oh, there you are." She held out one hand. "Can we talk? Please?"

Finn remained where he was, clutching his dog to his chest.

"Can I offer a suggestion?" I said.

She focused on Finn but spoke to me. "Certainly."

"Give him time to recover," I said. "He's hurting right now, both physically and mentally."

"You think his problems are my fault, don't you?" she said.

I would have expected her to be angry but she only sounded resigned.

"I don't have all the facts," I said, "and besides, I've found blaming others isn't very productive."

"You're being nice. All I know is I've made some poor choices. Except for Tom. I regret how I treated him." She kept looking in Finn's direction.

He turned away and walked toward the lake.

Interesting how she mentioned regret when it came to Tom and yet said nothing about her son. Maybe she truly didn't think she was part of the problem. From Tom and Finn's remarks, the issues between Finn and his mother were long-standing. Maybe I needed to hear her side of the story.

"Tell me a little about yourself. Do you work?" I asked, hoping to ease into conversation and get her to tell me about her life before her husband's murder.

From the corner of my eye I saw Finn pick up a stick and toss it for Yoshi.

"I lost my job. This economy has been brutal," she said.

"What did you used to do?" I asked.

She finally took her eyes off Finn. "Administrative assistant positions, mostly for executives. No college education, I'm afraid, but I'm a quick learner. Lately things have been pretty tough."

Having two former inmates for ex-husbands meant not a lot of alimony or child support came her way. Still, if money was tight for Hilary, she was certainly well dressed, her hair looked salon cut and her creamy complexion seemed to have benefited from plenty of expensive care. She was either in debt up to her ears or had some other source of income.

My doubt about her tough times must have shown on my face because she said, "I have family money we've been living on. Nolan hasn't worked since he left prison. He only knew how to be a cop. He couldn't even find private security work."

"Ah. Did he envy Tom for setting up a successful security business?" I said.

"Oh yes. He hated Tom. Jail gives a man

plenty of time to simmer. Nolan couldn't forget Tom was the one who sent him away." She examined a rose-painted fingernail. "Despite Nolan's faults, I loved him. And he cared about my son, just didn't know how to show it."

"That's a lie," said Tom, who had just appeared around the corner of the house. "Nolan cared about Nolan. And he sent *himself* to jail."

I'd been so involved in the conversation I hadn't heard him arrive. I wondered if he'd seen Hilary on his home computer feed from the security camera fixed to the eaves, the one pointed directly at her. Seeing her would have made him hightail it over here.

"You're wrong, Tom," she said quietly.

He pointed to the fading bruises on his face. "He did this to me while you watched from somewhere. I don't care what line of bull you fed Mike Baca; you were there."

Tom isn't about to beat around the bush when it comes to Hilary, I thought.

"I wasn't even in town during the time the police chief told me Nolan brought you to North Carolina," she said.

"That's your story?" Tom laughed derisively and took a step toward her.

I walked down the deck steps and stood between them. "If both of you care as much about Finn as you say you do, you shouldn't argue in front of him."

Hilary glanced in Finn's direction. He may have been pretending to keep his distance, but I could tell he was paying close attention to this confrontation.

Tom hung his head and mumbled, "You're right."

"I'm sorry," Hilary said. "I came hoping my son would talk to me."

"He won't," Tom whispered harshly. "So leave and quit bugging Jillian. Now and in the future."

I never saw this side of him before, I thought. He was so bitter. I wondered if he still had feelings for Hilary since lingering animosity can signal a relationship is far short of closure.

"You know what?" I said. "You two seem to have plenty of unfinished business. Why don't you talk, settle a few things, if only for Finn's sake. I'll be inside making coffee."

Before either of them could respond, I left them together. But as I made the coffee, I glanced out the window at them pointing fingers and seemingly talking at the same time. I didn't see any progress in the peace department. But at least they were speaking. I also noticed Finn edging ever closer to them. He wanted to know what was going on and I couldn't blame him.

I went back outside, if only to offer Finn support by my presence. But I was thinking, *How can such a beautiful morning seem so stifling?*

Just as I closed the door behind me so my curious feline friends wouldn't join us, more visitors arrived.

Candace and Morris.

By the serious look on Candace's face, I could tell this wasn't a friendly drop-in.

"Hey there," she said, her gloomy tone further indicating something was wrong.

"What do you two want?" Tom said. He was on the defensive.

"We need to talk to Finn," Candace said.

"He won't come near the house as long as *she's* here." Tom nodded at Hilary.

"Guess I'll have to go get him." Morris took a step in Finn's direction.

Tom grabbed his arm. "Wait. Can I go with you?" He'd dropped the attitude and I saw alarm in his expression.

"Sure enough," Morris said. "You know the kid and I don't."

As they walked toward Finn, Hilary spoke. "What's this about, Officer?"

"We need to ask your son a few questions," Candace said.

"You already asked him questions yesterday," Hilary said.

"This will be a more, um . . . *formal* interview." Candace averted her gaze, attending to what was happening between Morris, Tom and Finn.

I heard Tom say, "He's not a murderer," before Finn handed Yoshi over to him.

All three walked toward us, the little dog squirming in Tom's grasp.

The whole scene made me sick to my stomach. I managed to find my voice and say, "What's this about, Candace?"

She looked at me, a sadness in her eyes that scared me more than her earlier tone of voice.

"It's about evidence, Jillian," she said. "About blood and fingerprints."

Sixteen

At least when Candace and Morris took Finn away in their squad car, they didn't put him in handcuffs. But from what I'd learned in the past from Candace, the words *formal interview* were a euphemism for "we're about ready to arrest you."

Could Candace still believe in Finn's innocence in light of whatever evidence she now had? From the look on her face, I doubted it.

Tom knew this, too, and he told Candace and Morris he'd be right behind them. He handed me a whining, trembling Yoshi and disappeared around the house in the direction of the driveway.

Hilary had watched in silence as her son was led away by police officers. Once Tom was gone, she said, "They think Finn killed Nolan? He would never do any such thing. He's been sullen and angry, yes, but —"

"He needs your support right now," I said.

Yoshi wiggled in my arms and I swear if I let go, he'd chase the police car all the way to downtown Mercy.

"Should I follow them?" she said.

"That's up to you." The fact she was asking me told me more about her parenting than anything I'd learned about her up until this moment. "I need to put Yoshi inside."

Hilary looked dazed. "Poor Yoshi." She reached her hand out to him, but he buried his head in my chest.

Without another word, Hilary Roth left.

Yoshi and I went inside, and after I set the dog down, I reset the security alarm, the thought of the volatile Rory Gannon ever present.

How could I help Finn and Tom? Should I stay here or join the crowd at the police station? Since Tom still didn't have a cell phone, I couldn't even call and ask him what he wanted me to do. I had to help, but how?

I decided to call Kara and ask her opinion. I needed a level-headed person like her to guide the newly frazzled me.

She answered on the first ring and said, "What's happening? I heard they're taking Finn down to the station to question him again."

I should have known Kara had her finger

on Mercy's pulse. "They just left here. Candace talked about blood and fingerprint evidence, so I'm assuming they've got something important."

"It's called *hard* evidence, Jillian," she said, "and something I doubt is good news for Finn."

"I feel so helpless." I explained how Finn, Tom and Hilary had been here when Candace and Morris arrived.

"I take it Tom went with Finn to the police station. What about the mother? Where's she?"

"I'm guessing she followed, too. Do you think Finn's fingerprints were on the gun?"

"Probably," she said. "If the blood on his clothes belonged to Nolan Roth, well, I'm not sure why they didn't read Finn his rights and arrest him."

"True. Can you find out what they've got?" I said.

"I can try. No promises. Will you do me a favor, too?" she asked. "The contractor wants my approval on the brickwork on my new house. I'd like your opinion."

"It won't take long, will it? I'm not sure if I should join Tom at the police station or —"

"What can you do there? Nothing, really. Why not wait until you have more information? Besides, you need a distraction, Jillian. Yesterday I could see how this situation is stressing you out. You may believe you keep everything inside, but I've learned to read you pretty well."

She told me she'd make a few calls and then pick me up. In the meantime, I made a call myself. Though I'd committed to a booth at the last craft fair of the season, I knew I couldn't leave town now. I'd agonize my way to Greenville and back. The woman who managed the event was more than kind and I told her I'd overnight the raffle quilt they'd been advertising, the one I'd hand quilted. The proceeds would go to a children's charity.

I'd just finished packing up the quilt — a plaid pinwheel design with a flying-geese border — when Kara knocked on the deadbolted back door. No walking right into the house like she usually did, not with Rory Gannon lurking around town.

We drove to One Stop Ship, a mom-and-pop shipping business in the center of Mercy. The store bore Mercy's requisite green awning and the gray-haired Phoebe Langstrom stood behind the counter wearing a green polo shirt.

She said, "Why, if it isn't two of my favorite ladies in all of Mercy. Sending quilts to some lucky folks today, Jillian?"

"One quilt, anyway. It needs to go overnight." I placed the box on the scale. While I filled out the form and Phoebe calculated the charges, we chatted about her grandchildren, her husband who was home with the gout and the new desserts Belle recently added at Belle's Beans. This was normal Mercy chat and for a few moments, I almost relaxed.

Kara had taken a call while I'd been talking to Phoebe and when she hung up, she said, "No prints on the gun."

"How very interesting," Phoebe said. "The only gun you could possibly be talking about is the one that killed the man in Tom Stewart's car."

Oh, Mercy was talking. Why should I be surprised? There were no secrets for long in this town.

Kara smiled. "What else have you heard, Phoebe?"

She smoothed the mailing sticker on my box and then put the box on the shelf behind her. "We do have a multitude of strangers in town thanks to the murder and people *are* talking. Saw Tom Stewart's ex-wife over at Belle's. Pretty thing. Never knew he had an ex. Did you?" She was addressing me.

"Not until recently," I said.

"Hear tell her current husband was the victim," she said. "Well, I suppose *current* no longer applies. Poor man was shot in the head. I'm wondering if he was killed before or after Tom's car crashed. A bullet in your brain makes driving a bit difficult now, doesn't it?"

"It certainly does, Phoebe," Kara said. "So you heard the man who died was driving the car?"

"He *was* found in the driver's seat," Phoebe said. "Strange thing, that. Angie Martin and I were talking and we decided Tom and his ex-wife's husband must have been on good terms if he let the man borrow his car."

Nolan Roth and Tom on good terms? I thought. *Not exactly.*

"You ever consider working for my paper as an investigative reporter?" Kara said.

Phoebe tittered at this suggestion. "You could hire anyone in this town for such a job, don't ya think?"

"I do believe you're right," Kara said.

We left, and as we climbed into Kara's SUV she said, "Why didn't I think about confirming where Nolan Roth's body was found?"

"Because we knew he had Tom's car," I

said. "I simply assumed the obvious."

"As a reporter, I shouldn't assume anything, even if it turns out to be true. Phoebe raised an important question, though. Was Roth shot before or after he crashed into the telephone pole?"

"Why is it important?" I asked.

She turned the key in the ignition. "Maybe it's not. But I know the police are surely asking the same question as they examine the evidence. I may not be a cop, but sometimes I have to think like one."

We drove to the west side of town to the property Kara had bought with money my late husband had left her. The last time I'd seen the construction, the house had only just been framed. Now Kara was much closer to owning her own home.

The contractor's truck sat in the dirt path leading to the brick and stone house. No real driveway yet, but stones had been laid for the front walkway. We walked around the outside with the contractor and Kara examined the bricklayers' work. I loved the natural warmth of the round stones used for the chimney and how nicely they contrasted with the gray bricks.

Once she signed off on the work, the contractor left. Kara held up a key. "Want to see inside?"

"Of course," I said.

The front door was a builder's substitute, not a permanent one, and none too sturdy. Since no appliances or light fixtures were in place yet, I supposed Kara didn't need too much protection from potential thieves.

We stood in the foyer and my gaze first traveled up the curving staircase to our left. She'd decided on an open floor plan similar to my own. From here, we could see most of the first floor. What grabbed me next was the fireplace. The same round stones outside had been used and the effect was dramatic.

"I love this." I stepped forward and realized the foyer was open to the second floor. Kara led me around, pointing out built-in bookshelves in the living room and built-in large drawers for china in the dining room. We reached the kitchen and she told me about the appliances she'd already ordered.

"Are you getting excited?" I asked. I looked out the window above where the sink would be. Not many trees, so she'd have to do some serious landscaping.

"I am excited beyond words," Kara said. "This has been such fun seeing my vision come together. Let me show you the upstairs."

But we'd only made it back to the living

room when the front door flew open and Rory Gannon burst into the foyer.

I gasped and Kara put an arm around me.

"What are you doing here?" Kara said.

My heart thumped against my chest and I thought, *How did you know where we were?* The answer was simple. He'd followed us. Great.

"What have you done with my son?" he said. He wore a navy blue sweater today, the big leather buttons done up wrong. Underneath, he looked like he wore the same clothes he had on yesterday.

I said, "You followed us, so you know he isn't with us." I sounded confident, unwilling to allow this man to intimidate me again.

Gannon's peculiar smile and the gleam of satisfaction in his eyes told me I was right. He knew Finn wasn't here. During the other encounters, I'd believed his concern. Now, though, it seemed like he was merely enjoying the thrill of showing up and scaring us. This was one unbalanced man.

"You never saw me, did you?" he said. "That's how smart you two are." He looked past us and then up the staircase. "Nice place. Too bad if someone were to come in here and smash through some of your drywall or take apart your pretty banister."

Kara had her phone in her hand. "I'm

calling the police again. This time, they'll put you in jail."

"You go right ahead, pretty lady. But I travel like a ghost. They'll never find me — and you won't know when I'm right behind you. I proved as much today." He whirled and left.

Kara started after him, but I grabbed her arm. "Let him go."

"Why?"

"What would you do if you caught up to him?" I said.

She sighed. "You're right. My martial arts skills are considerably lacking. I wouldn't mind giving him a good kick in the butt, though."

I smiled. "At least we know to watch out for him now. Though for the life of me, I cannot understand why he wants to scare us. Or why he's shown up in Mercy out of the blue."

Kara tapped her temple. "Number one, he's not hooked up right. Number two, he's a lurker. He could have been watching Finn's comings and goings back in North Carolina."

"You think he followed Finn to Mercy?" I said.

"I don't know, but I get the sense he's been keeping track of him. Takes a while for someone to work up to an obsession — and I'd say he's obsessed."

"Maybe — but showing up here?" I said. "It's downright creepy. Like I said, he followed us, so he knew Finn wasn't with us. This appearance was all about intimidation."

"Do you think he'll come back and vandalize the place like he implied?" she said.

"Since he's said those things to our faces, he must know he'd be the prime suspect. I think he was just messing with our heads."

"I don't like it and I sure don't like him. Maybe we should call Candace or Morris and —"

"No. Usually I'd agree, but the last thing we need right now is for the police to pick up this obviously unhinged person and take him to the same police station where Finn is being questioned."

"Are you saying we shouldn't tell them he showed up here and was following us — for who knows how long?" she said.

"I'll tell Candace later," I said. "After I know Finn is no longer being interviewed. What concerns me right now is why Gannon came to Mercy. Because, though obsession may be the explanation, he might have had help knowing where to find his son."

Kara smiled slowly. "Ah. Yes."

I nodded at her knowing smile and said, "Tom's ex."

Seventeen

Kara kept an eye on the rearview mirror the entire way back to my house. She had work to do for both Tom and the newspaper so when she dropped me at my house, she made me promise to tell Candace, Morris, Mike Baca and anyone else on the police force about Rory Gannon showing up all over town and in a menacing way.

After I let Yoshi out to relieve himself, he came back inside and I gave him one of the dog treats Kara had bought. I decided to head to the police station and talk to Candace. Gannon accomplished what I believed he'd set out to do — get under my skin.

I expected to see Tom in the waiting area when I arrived, but B.J. said he'd gone home.

That's strange, I thought. "Did he take Finn with him?" I asked.

B.J. shook his head and then whispered, "He knows a lawyer but needed to get the contact information from home."

"This attorney is for Finn?" I said. The news Finn needed a lawyer combined with the stuffy, hot air made me feel queasy. They must have turned the heat up in this place yesterday and forgot to turn it back down.

B.J. put a finger to his lips and continued speaking in a low voice. "The mother left to see if she could get *her* lawyer here first. Tom and Mrs. Roth were spittin' nails at each other when they left."

"Finn's still here?" I said quietly.

"Yeah, but they haven't arrested him. Don't know why, though." B.J. stood and leaned closer to me, speaking even softer. "Between you and me, I can tell Deputy Carson isn't sure about this one, even though evidence is piling up."

"She isn't sure because anyone who spent more than five minutes with Finn would know he'd never intentionally harm anyone," I said. "Candace hopes to find evidence to free Finn, not send him to jail. She can be tough, but she also listens to her gut. She's smart and fair."

B.J.'s eyes were wide when I finished speaking and I realized I'd put plenty of passion into my little speech.

Then I heard the sound of a door opening down the hall and B.J. quickly sat down.

Candace appeared, and when she saw me she walked to the waiting area. Perspiration dotted her hairline and her cheeks were flushed.

"You look like you've been pulled through a knothole backward," I said.

"Morris insisted on turning up the thermostat. Says it helps sweat out a confession." She rolled her eyes. "It won't work 'cause I'm more convinced than ever that this kid didn't do it. All Morris has accomplished is to make *me* about ready to confess to this murder. As for Finn, he still can't remember anything more than he did the last time I talked to him."

The thought of Morris pressuring Finn didn't sit well with me, even though I understood he was only doing his job. "You can't convince Morris to let up on Finn?" I asked.

"You're kidding, right?" she said. "I can only hope Morris will come to his senses and see how things just aren't adding up."

She glanced at B.J., who was doodling on the notebook in front of him but probably taking in every word. "Come with me and I'll explain about what the evidence is telling *me*."

"Only if you turn down the darn thermostat," I said.

Minutes later, I sat at the table in the center of the officer's break room with a chilled bottle of water in front of me. Candace had turned the heat off, but it still had to be eighty degrees in here.

She screwed the cap off her own water and gulped down half the bottle before she took a spot across from me.

"Where's Finn now?" I asked.

"Still in the interrogation room with Morris. He's never asked for a lawyer, but both Tom and Hilary Roth are scrambling to get him one. Finn said he's tired of saying the same thing over and over. And you know what? I'm tired of hearing it."

"Can't you let him go?" I said. "I could take him back to my house, let him play with his dog, ask him a few questions. But I need to know about this evidence first. Otherwise, I'll hear the same things, too."

She held the cold bottle against her forehead. "If you hadn't been so helpful to us in the past — especially to Chief Baca — I wouldn't be allowed to tell you anything. I swear the chief would hire you as a consultant if he could get away with it."

"That's never happening. But I care about this kid, so anything I can do to help, I will. What's this evidence?"

She took a deep breath and let it out

slowly. "We found Finn's prints in Tom's car."

"Uh-oh," I said.

"We can't say when they got there. See, that's the problem with prints. They could have been left on the door handle three days or three weeks ago. But we have other evidence. First off, the lab found traces of baking soda and potassium chloride on the hoodie."

"What does that mean?" I said.

"Those residues indicate he was in a car when air bags deployed," she said.

"So he *did* hurt his head in the car wreck?" This is what I'd feared all along.

"Not so fast. I'll get to his head injury. More important, we also got the DNA back from the blood on the hoodie. It belonged to the victim."

I gripped the water bottle tightly and stared down at the scarred Formica-topped table. "You're saying you're positive he was in the car when Nolan Roth was shot?"

"Or was there immediately afterward," she said. "His sweatshirt came in contact with the victim's blood. Problem is, we found no blood on the sleeve. If he held a gun and shot Roth at close range, we would have found spatter on the sleeve."

"So this is good news?" I said.

"It's a bit confusing," she replied.

"No kidding. Can you make it a little clearer?" I asked.

"The gun was wiped clean, for one thing," she said. "Question. You were there when Tom took the gun out of the backpack. How did he pick it up?"

"He put his index finger through the trigger guard — like I've seen on cop shows," I said. "He carried it to the other room like that."

"He still could have wiped it down before he put it in his gun safe, though he denies doing this. I have no reason to doubt his word. We did find a smudge on the trigger consistent with him carrying the gun with his finger."

"Tom may not tell you everything he knows, but he wouldn't outright lie," I said.

"Like I said, I agree. There's more information in Finn's favor. We know Roth was shot *after* the air bags deployed because we found his blood all over them. If Finn injured his head and the doctor who examined him believes he was knocked unconscious, could he really have woken up in a stupor, shot Roth, wiped the gun down, yet failed to wipe off the other surfaces he touched?"

I nodded, considering this. "You're right.

It doesn't make sense. And why not ditch the bloody sweatshirt if he was with-it enough to wipe prints off the gun?"

"See? We're on the same page. There's something else very interesting — and it's the reason I'm completely against arresting Finn." Candace sipped her water. "I believe I've come up with a scenario that fits the evidence better than Finn being the shooter."

I leaned forward, excited. "Really? What is it?"

"We found skin cells, a small amount of blood and one sandy hair clinging to the deflated air bag in the spot matching up to a round trace of potassium chloride and baking soda on the dashboard beneath the deflated air bag — which means it was deposited there with force after deployment. The blood and hair didn't belong to the victim. We also found saliva on the air bag and it wasn't Roth's either."

I was the one who was confused now. "The air bag would have prevented Finn from hitting the dashboard. Are you telling me he hit his head *after* the crash? How?"

"The air bag might have malfunctioned and he could have been injured in the crash, but we found no evidence to support this. Side and front air bags all inflated and deflated properly. Let me demonstrate what I believe might have happened — something I hope the evidence will back up." She stood and came over to my side of the table. "Sit back in the chair like you're a passenger in Tom's car."

I did as she asked, folding my hands in my lap, feet flat on the floor.

"You've just wrecked, air bags are popping out like inflating parachutes. You're dazed." She stared at me. "Come on. Look up at me like you're dazed."

I met her eyes. "Just pretend I'm dazed."

"Anyway, someone comes up to the passenger-side window and you think this person's a Good Samaritan. Maybe this person even motions for you to roll down the window — we did find the window rolled down, by the way, and Finn's print on the button. You comply. You're even grateful. Then this happens." Candace put her left hand behind the back of my head and pushed my head forward. "Bam!" She shouted so loudly I jumped in my seat. "You are now lights-out thanks to this person you thought came to rescue you."

"You mean someone smashed his head —"

"Please. Let me finish my demonstration," she said, sounding excited. "This is helping me picture the scene. Now, lean forward like you're passed out on the deflated air bag."

I did, and from the corner of my eye I saw Candace pull her gun from her holster with her right hand. As fast as lightning, she pointed the weapon at what I assumed was our imaginary driver. "Another bam, a different kind. A horrible kind. This time Roth is shot in the right temple."

She holstered her gun and I sat up, stunned and a little alarmed by her reenactment.

"You really think that's what happened?" I said.

Candace wore a satisfied smile. "You wanna bet once Finn's DNA results come back we'll find his hair and saliva right where I said it was. And when we receive the autopsy report, the trajectory of the bullet will confirm my theory. The evidence is there. I know it."

"You believe you have concrete evidence to prove Finn is innocent?" I said.

She nodded. "I do. This is good news, Jillian. I've had a gut feeling about Finn's innocence and now I believe I've found what I needed to back up my instincts."

"Thank you for working so hard. This is a huge relief. Can he come home with me, then?" I said.

"I can't in good conscience hold him with what we've got. But I have to convince Morris to let him go because, of course, he thinks the kid's guilty."

"Why? You said there was no blood on Finn's sleeve. And can you even tie the gun to him?" I said.

"Nope," she said. "I checked and the gun is not in the firearm database."

"What does that mean?" I said.

Candace said, "One way to track a gun is to see if the ballistic properties have been entered into the national database after a weapon has been used in a crime. Since this gun hasn't been involved in any crime we know about and since the serial number was filed away and thus we don't know who purchased it, we have absolutely no way of tracing it."

"But you know it's the gun that killed Nolan Roth?" I asked.

"Yes. But that's all. Now, I'm dealing with Morris being Morris. I explained my theory to him, but he tries not to let hard evidence get in his way." She smiled. "He bothers the heck out of me most of the time, but deep down I still like him. He knows when to give in, and he'll give on this one eventually."

"You can really get him to see things your way?" I asked.

"I am becoming a master at getting Morris to see things my way." She smiled, grabbed her water bottle and started for the door.

"Wait. I came here to tell you something," I said.

"Oh. I thought you were just worried about Finn," she said.

"I am worried, but Rory Gannon showed up again," I said. "This time he followed Kara and me out to her property."

She stared up at the ceiling, looking exasperated. "What is wrong with that man? Oh. I forgot. He's crackerjacks. I assume you're both okay?"

"Except for our rattled nerves," I said. "This is like a game to him. Do you have any idea how he ended up in town?"

"I have an idea," she said. "In checking Tom's phone — the one we found in his car — I noticed a call was placed to a halfway house in Greenville. Who do you think might have been living in a halfway house?"

"I can only think of one odd person," I said.

"I'll have to recheck the date when the call was made, but I'm willing to bet Nolan Roth was in possession of Tom's phone at the time."

"Why would Nolan Roth call Gannon?" I said.

"I'm gonna have to think on that one. 'Course, it gives me a good reason to find the guy ASAP and ask him directly." She smiled and nodded. "I do believe Morris would love to bring him in."

"Are you kidding? I thought he —"

"Hates the mental cases? He does. But Deputy Rodriguez is good with them. I've been asking for more help ever since the murder. Maybe the chief will listen when he comes back from his lunch with the mayor and approve some overtime." Candace wiped an arm across her brow. "We're sweating in here like pigs and he's at the Finest Catch having lake trout seared in lemon butter."

"Perks of the job," I said.

"We need to hunt down Gannon and explain how harassment and stalking are serious problems, especially for an ex-con. Then we can bring up any recent phone calls."

"Will police pressure make him stop following us?" I asked.

"Probably not," she said, but then her eyes brightened. "But if we catch him at it, we may learn a few important details. We have his plate number and a description of him and his car. Shouldn't be too hard, if the chief gives his approval."

"Funny how he's acting all concerned about *his boy,* as he calls Finn," I said, "and yet he hasn't shown up here at the police station to see what's going on."

"Because he doesn't give a flip about Finn. You know it and I know it. Gannon came here on a mission — and I wish Nolan Roth could tell us why."

We walked out of the break room together in time to see Morris open the door of the interrogation room and step into the hall. He closed the door after him.

"Where the heck have you been?" he said, ignoring me and staring pointedly at the water bottle in Candace's hand.

"Did he confess yet, partner?" Candace said.

"He's not saying squat," Morris said. "Where's *my* water? Or was visiting with your friend more important than helping your partner?"

"You're the one who decided to sweat the suspect. The suspect who's *innocent.* I told you already I know what happened, but maybe getting you some water will help you turn down your cranky factor." She went back to the break room.

Morris looked at me. "Oh, so she knows what happened. She *always* knows. Sorry. Dealing with juveniles makes me ornery. How are you today, Jillian?"

Before I could answer, Candace returned with two bottles of water. "Let's talk to Finn — all three of us."

This particular interrogation room was less cozy than the one we were in yesterday. For one thing, it smelled like vomit. A bench lined one wall and Finn sat there, his back straight, his hands clenched in his lap. A table bolted to the floor was in front of him and two wooden chairs faced him.

When Finn saw me, his stoic expression softened. "Hey, Jillian. Sorry to cause you so much trouble."

"You haven't caused me any problems," I said. "I want to help you and, believe it or not, these police officers do, too. I never believed you killed Nolan Roth, and now the police have the evidence to show you didn't."

I sat on the bench next to Finn. Candace and Morris took the chairs. Candace set a bottle of water in front of Finn.

"She's right," Candace said. "We do need to find a murderer, though. To do that, we have to process the evidence. You know what that means, right?"

"Just 'cause I'm not in college doesn't mean I'm stupid," Finn said.

"Remember how I swabbed your mouth for DNA?" Candace said.

Finn nodded.

"What if your DNA would help us prove you *didn't* kill Nolan Roth?" Candace said.

Morris, who had finished off his water in two long gulps, said, "Here we go, kid. The evidence queen is hard at work."

The water seemed to have improved Morris's disposition.

"But you told me after Deputy Carson left that you liked the evidence queen," Finn said, amusement showing in his eyes.

Morris almost smiled. "Hey. Don't go telling my secrets."

I said, "As you can see, these are good, honest people." I picked up his hand in both my own and squeezed. "There's a murderer out there, and they'll find out who it is. The good news is, it looks like you left evidence in Tom's car — evidence that explains how you were injured. Candace showed me how it happened."

"Really?" Finn said. "Tell me."

"I might have to show you — just like Candace showed me," I said.

"Go for it," Finn said.

EIGHTEEN

We were all leaving the interrogation room when I saw Tom standing in the waiting room.

"You all look . . . relaxed. Does this mean Finn can leave now, Candace?" Tom said. "And when did you arrive, Jillian?"

"In time to hear about the CSI stuff Candace has been doing," I said.

"Yeah. It's way cool, Tom. She figured out how I hit my head," Finn said.

"Listen, y'all must be as hungry as I am," Morris said. "Take this kid to eat and he can fill you in. He needs some meat on his bones." He turned in the direction of the break room and walked away.

Tom smiled. "Sounds like a plan. I take it Finn won't be needing the lawyer I couldn't reach?"

"Nope, but I have more questions for you, Tom," Candace said.

"About what?" he said. "Because my jaw

is getting tired talking about what happened."

"It's about the calls and texts we found on your phone when we took it from the wreck," she said. "But first, I have to call the crime lab about Finn's DNA results. Can we talk later?"

"What about Finn's DNA?" Tom said.

"I believe his DNA will rule him out as a suspect," Candace said. "Now, I really have to get busy."

"I'll explain what she's talking about," I said. "Finn's interview is over and we can leave."

As we walked through the courthouse toward the front entrance, I offered a shortened version of what Candace figured out and why she needed Finn's DNA results.

"Deputy Carson gets so excited about this forensic stuff," Finn said. "She's way into it."

Before Tom could respond, we saw Karen coming toward us, her straight midcalf skirt making it difficult for her to travel as quickly as she might have.

When she reached us, she pulled Finn to her and hugged him tightly.

"I see Candace has released you," Karen said. "I knew she'd come to her senses. You could never hurt a living soul."

Finn gently pulled away. "They're just doing their job, Nana. I did have Nolan's blood on my sweatshirt."

Karen's eyes widened. "Oh my. But you're free? They didn't arrest you?"

He smiled. "Nope."

"How did you find out he was talking to the police?" Tom said.

"I had a visit from the last person on earth I thought I'd be talking to," she said. "Your brother. He told me you were making calls to find an attorney for Finn and he thought I should know."

Tom's eyes hardened. "I wondered where Bob was going when I left for here. But of course he left his stuff, so I figured he'd be back — unfortunately."

"Interesting how the son I haven't heard from in years is the one who decided to inform me about what's going on." She stared at Tom, a look of disapproval I was certain he was familiar with.

"You're making him sound heroic," Tom said. "Bob wants something — what, I'm not sure yet. It will come out, though. He knows how much you care about Finn and he used it as an excuse to visit you."

"You could be right, but he says he wants to apologize to his family," Karen said. "I had to rush over here, but he's waiting back at the house for my return. We can all go over to my home and talk."

"No way," Tom said.

Finn said, "How will you find out what Bob wants if you don't talk to him?"

"He's right," I said.

Since we'd all ganged up on him, Tom reluctantly agreed to go to his mother's house and we arrived five minutes later in our various vehicles.

Karen didn't smile when she greeted Bob, just said, "Here we are. Time for you to own up, Robert."

His crooked smile appeared. "I — I didn't expect so many . . . well, *everybody.* Glad to see Finn isn't in jail, though." He held up his knuckles and he and Finn exchanged a fist bump. "They grill you, bro?" Bob said.

"It wasn't like that. They're trying hard to find out the truth." Finn glanced around the room, avoiding Bob's stare.

"I have more of the soda pop you like so much," Karen said. "Come with me."

She and Finn went to the kitchen.

I did not want to be left with these two men. The awkward silence now filling the space made me want to run out to my van and not come back until they'd settled their long-running differences. Wait. What made me think they could actually settle anything? A command from Karen to do so? Men resolved things so differently than women, after all.

"Well," I said, clasping my hands and smiling. "Here we are."

"Right where we don't want to be," Tom said.

His voice held a hint of futility and frustration. How could I help Tom? Especially now, with the events of the last few days weighing so heavily on him? I didn't know what to do, so I said, "I'm hungry. Anyone else?"

A meal can unify people for a short time. I guess that's part of why we celebrate Thanksgiving. But as we ate tuna salad sandwiches and homemade vegetable soup, I didn't see much unification happening.

We sat without anyone saying a word and I was beginning to wonder if Karen regretted inviting Bob into her home.

When I could no longer stand the quiet, I said, "Is Ed at work?"

"Yes," Karen said.

"Does he still collect stuff?" Finn asked.

"Too much stuff," Karen said with a smile. At least one person in the room remained in Karen's good graces.

"Why are you here, Bob?" Tom said, staring down at his soup.

At last the elephant of a question was finally addressed.

"Can't a man visit his family?" Bob said.

"Oh sure. After five years you come to town and break into my house while I'm not there. Nice way to visit." Tom still hadn't looked at Bob.

"You broke into his house, Robert?" Karen said.

"I waited outside, but when he didn't show for hours and hours, I needed the restroom — and something to eat," Bob said. "Mom, this soup is awesome, by the way. Just like I remember."

Tom set his spoon down and glared at Bob. "You could have gone into town, to a restaurant and —"

"I'm having a little cash flow problem," Bob said.

Finn watched this exchange like he was at a tennis match, eyes wide with interest.

"You've had money problems your whole life. Why are you here now?" Tom said. "What's the plan, Bob? Because you always have one."

"I was expecting an apology," Karen said.

"I'm sure you were. Answer me this, Mom," Bob said, every drop of charisma evaporated. "If I were being intimidated by the cops, would you have left in a frantic rush to save me?"

Finn said, "I — I wasn't really being intimidated."

But Karen and Bob didn't seem to hear him. Color blossomed on Karen's cheeks. "You're a grown man and yet you're still stuck in the past, believing I favor —"

"You *do* favor. You favor Tom and you favor Finn. Me and Charlie? We're just dirt on your shoe." Bob looked at me. "I have a twin brother. Did anyone tell you about him?"

I didn't get a chance to reply because Bob stood and threw his napkin on the table. "I only took what was rightfully mine." He pointed at his mother. "I will again, too."

"Rightfully yours?" Karen said, her anger building. "How can you say —"

Someone knocked.

Karen rose, but Bob made it to the door in a flash. My guess, he was relieved by the distraction. I feared Rory Gannon was about to make another appearance, but the voice I heard say, "Why, hello there," was female.

Hilary Roth had arrived.

Karen hurried through the dining room and out to the small foyer to greet the new arrival.

Tom leaned back in his chair, his face to the ceiling. "More trouble," he said. "Just what we need."

"It's my mother, isn't it?" Finn said as the murmur of greetings spilled into the room. He stood. "I don't want to talk to her."

"I don't either. That's why you and I are heading out the back door and going to my house." Tom looked at me. "Would you mind running interference?"

"Sure. Go on," I said.

They disappeared through the kitchen and I went to the living room.

Bob was smiling broadly at Hilary, all the resentment from a few minutes ago gone.

"Finnian," Karen called. "Your mother would like to talk to you."

I motioned Karen aside as Bob and Hilary chatted. I whispered, "Finn isn't quite ready to talk to his mother. He and Tom left."

"Oh. I see." She patted my arm. "It's not your fault, so don't look so guilty. Hilary is not the monster those two make her out to be. Please give her a chance by staying for a while and getting to know her. Maybe Finn and Tom will listen to you once you understand her better."

"Sure. I can stay," I said, forcing a smile. But I wanted to be home with my fur friends, not here playing a game of "Get to Know the Ex-wife." I'd give Karen fifteen minutes and then I was out of here.

Karen said, "Can I fix you lunch, Hilary?"

Hilary wore a ruby-red sweater and black slacks, the colors complementing her dark beauty. "No thanks. I ate while I was trying to reach my attorney. Unfortunately, he cannot help Finn here in South Carolina."

"Finn's not in jail," Bob said. "The way he talked, sounds like he might not need a lawyer after all."

Hilary said, "The deputies told me he was gone when I went to the police station. That doesn't mean he won't need a lawyer in the future, though."

"He's not guilty of anything," Karen said. "Not one thing."

Hilary said, "Your belief in Finn warms my heart." She turned to me. "They told me he left with Tom and with you, Jillian."

"Yes, we did leave together," I said.

When I didn't add any more information about Tom or Finn, Hilary addressed Karen. "No one was home at Tom's house, so I figured he brought Finn here. Can I see him now?" Hilary walked toward the dining room. "We need to talk. I need to tell him how sorry I am for —"

"He's not here," Karen said. "At least not

right now."

Hilary halted. "Oh." She looked crestfallen.

Bob said, "You know how stubborn Tom can be. You staying in town?"

Guess he'd gotten over his hurt feelings where his family was concerned. Especially since someone as lovely as Hilary was around to divert his attention.

She said, "I found this wonderful little B&B. Reasonably priced with fantastic food." She pulled a tissue from her pocket and dabbed under her nose. "It's been nice to have such a comfortable place to stay under such stressful circumstances."

"Yes, well, Nolan was a troubled man," Karen said, "though as you told me not long ago, you had no idea how troubled until he was released from prison." Karen looked at me. "Mr. Roth used to be a police officer and Tom's partner. Poor Tom was forced to turn him in to the authorities."

"Forced?" Bob said. "Tom ruined Finn's family because he was jealous."

I wanted to sock Bob Cochran in the mouth about then. I'd had about all I could stand of this self-serving man-child. Instead, I said, "I'm not sure you completely understand, Bob."

"Really? And you do after knowing my

brother for how long? A year, tops?" Bob said.

Hilary rested a hand on Bob's arm. "Please. Don't blame Tom, and be kind to Jillian. She has been so kind to my son. Nolan fooled me. He fooled a lot of people. Now that they've cleared Finn, I believe they should start looking at who Nolan was doing business with."

"Drugs again?" Karen said.

Hilary nodded solemnly. "I tried to tell the police chief as much. But they seemed fixated on Finn and even Tom. He does seem to have been in a fight. Do you know how he got so banged up?"

"He won't tell me," Karen said. "But I'm sure it has nothing to do with Mr. Roth's demise."

"Oh, of course not. Because Tom can do no wrong," Bob said.

Karen leveled one of her famous steely stares at Bob. "It could have been that terrible man who came here last night." Karen turned to Hilary. "Knowing you, it's impossible to picture you with Mr. Gannon. He's a frightful person."

Hilary paled. "Rory? Here? Oh my goodness. Nolan must have called him before — Oh, this is not good. Did Finn talk to him?"

She sounded frightened — and who could

blame her? But I didn't want to listen to a rehash of Rory Gannon's visit, so I decided it was time to leave. I said, "I have quilts to finish for Christmas orders. I did enjoy lunch, Karen. Thanks for having me." I sidled past Hilary and Bob, muttering my good-byes to them.

Once I reached my van and started the ignition, I took a deep breath and let it out slowly. *Why do Southern-raised women like me have to be so darn polite? And why did I want to slug all three of those people?*

NINETEEN

On my way home to get a much-needed dose of kitty and puppy love, I called Tom's landline. When he answered, sounding gruff and as agitated as I felt, I said, "I'm headed home. You can drop Finn off anytime."

Tom said, "Sorry if I sounded rude, but I didn't even look at the caller ID. I thought my mother or Bob was calling, hoping to get me back over to Mom's house for the reunion. Someone needs to tell my mother there's no such thing as time machines."

"What are you talking about?" I said.

"She wants things to be like they were before Hilary decided to sleep with my partner," he said. "Everything went downhill after Hilary hooked up with Nolan."

"Five years ago? What did your marriage problems have to do with Karen and Bob's issues?" I pulled into my driveway, relieved not to see a beat-up blue sedan hanging around the neighborhood.

"Long story," Tom said.

"I wish you'd trust me enough to tell me. What's this something Bob believes rightfully belongs to him?"

Tom lowered his voice. "Finn's in the kitchen, about ten feet away. He doesn't need to hear this. Can we talk later?"

"Promise?" I said, wondering if later would ever happen.

"I swear," he said.

"Good. Now, I know a dog who needs a visit to the nearest tree. When you drop Finn off, maybe we can have some alone time."

We said good-bye and soon Yoshi was racing for his favorite white oak, dried leaves scattering in his wake. When he came running back up the lawn, he checked out the van, sniffing the air for any hint of Finn. We went inside the house and I squatted to pet him. He was such a darling dog, but even though he enjoyed my company, he obviously missed Finn.

Merlot appeared, and he and Yoshi went nose to nose since they're almost the same size. Yoshi dropped his front legs to the play position, but Merlot appraised him as if to say, "I'm not playing chase right now, dog." Seemed like these two were at least getting along, in pleasant contrast to everyone at lunch at Karen's house.

I switched my attention to Merlot, scratching him behind his ears.

Soon Syrah joined us and I saw the cat dishes were empty. With the dog around, I wondered exactly who had licked those bowls so clean. Syrah did figure eights between my legs as I hunted for just the right flavor of cat food. I swore they knew what was available and if I chose the wrong flavor, they'd turn and walk away after the first whiff.

Yoshi still had kibble in his bowl and when Merlot and Syrah started eating — I'd chosen Savory Salmon — he decided to finish his food. Chablis didn't show up, even though with her ability to hear a quilting pin drop, I was sure she'd heard the *pop* when I opened the cat food. I took a small bowl of tuna cat food — her favorite — and went to my bedroom.

At least she wasn't hiding under the bed, but rather crouched in the center of the mattress. When I set the dish on the floor, she sniffed the air and finally stood, stretched and decided she liked her meals delivered.

I sat next to her and stroked her while she ate, wishing she'd stay out of hiding. Every cat is different, however. Chablis was not dog friendly, that's for sure. The memory of cats is about two hundred times greater than dogs, and like people, they have both long-term and short-term memory. I believed Chablis had a memory about a dog — and not a pleasant one. Poor Dashiell did, too. If Finn ended up living with Tom, the adjustment period could be long and difficult.

Yoshi came bounding into the bedroom a moment later and Chablis scurried under the bed. The adjustment period here wasn't going so well, either.

I spent the rest of the afternoon in my sewing room finishing up my Christmas orders — an appliqué on one quilt for a cat in New York named Ralph and some hand quilting on two others. Yoshi, Merlot and Syrah joined me. Late afternoon was nap time for them.

In the last few months, I'd discovered I needed reading glasses for handwork as well as a good, strong light. My eyes were telling me I was no longer young, and though I didn't appreciate the message my body was sending, I accepted it. Anything to keep quilting for as long as my eyes and hands allowed. There is something akin to meditation about the rocking movement of the needle, the in and out, the back and forth.

It took me to such a peaceful place. Worries faded while I quilted.

When someone knocked on the back door, Yoshi jumped to attention and barked. I set my work aside — my last order — and realized it was already dark. As I went through the house flipping on lights, I saw the DVR display read seven p.m.

I let Tom and Finn in, and Yoshi went wild with joy. He jumped into Finn's arms and licked his face.

Tom glanced at the reading glasses dangling from a chain around my neck. "You, too, huh?"

I held them up. "You mean these?"

He smiled and for the first time in days, he seemed stress free. This was the Tom I knew and had come to care about so much. He said, "I've got a drugstore pair for reading at night. I keep telling myself it's those new fluorescent bulbs and not my vision."

"Right. And my quilt stitches are just getting smaller every day."

Tom laughed.

Finn said, "I'm taking Yoshi out back to run, okay?"

"Sure," I said. "The outside lights are to your right before you go out the door."

As soon as Finn and Yoshi were gone, Tom took me in his arms and kissed me. Then, with me wrapped in his arms, he swayed us and said, "Thank you for everything. Thank you for just being who you are — the most normal, caring person I've ever met."

I pulled back so I could look at him. "Why didn't you tell me about Finn before? About your marriage, your brothers, all of it?"

"Because I failed," he said quietly. "I failed Finn, I failed at being married and I couldn't solve my mother's alcoholism or my brother's problems. Another man rescued my mother from her addiction, a man who loved her for who she was. As for Bob? He's a thief. I was a cop. Those two don't mix well."

"I can see how you might feel like calling yourself a failure, but I'm not so sure it's justified," I said. "How does it feel getting all of the old business off your chest?"

"I'm not sure," he said. "It's kind of like hunting through an attic you haven't visited in years. There's dust and cobwebs and surprises — and I'm not talking about birthday surprises, either."

"I want to hear more. How about something to drink?"

"Finn tells me you stocked up on Dr Pepper." He grinned and opened the fridge. Indeed, the door held can after can of Dr Pepper.

I stuck to sweet tea, but Tom popped the top on the soft drink and made a face after he took a swig. "Never did like this stuff. But if the kid likes it, I can pretend."

We sat next to each other on the couch and immediately Chablis was in my lap. Did she have doggie radar or something? How did she know Yoshi was outside?

"You think Finn should be outside while his father could still be roaming around Mercy?" I said.

"I'll give him a few more minutes," Tom said. "He has the energy of an eighteen-year-old and can't stay cooped up all the time. Besides, Yoshi will let us all know if there's a problem."

"He certainly will," I said. "While we have a little privacy, why don't you talk? Clean your attic."

"My family is complicated," he said.

"Millions of people know the feeling," I answered.

He seemed to be staring into the past. "Where do I start?"

"How about chronologically? You're older than Bob, right?"

He nodded. "My mother married my father in South Carolina back in the 'sixties. He died when I was four. She remarried right away — and Bob and Charlie came along a year later."

"How soon did she remarry?" I asked.

"Within months," he said. "Looking back, it was probably too soon. From how she talks about my father, she loved him, but jumped into another relationship right off the bat. Trying to escape the grief, maybe? She's about as good at sharing her feelings as I am, so I can't be sure."

I thought about the grief I felt after losing John. It had paralyzed me, but it sounded as if Karen had taken the opposite approach. "How long did her second marriage last?"

"Couple years. Long enough for her to start drinking. See, my stepfather, Bob and Charlie's father, Henry Cochran, was a successful businessman. He also drank like a sailor. So my mother joined him for all those cocktails at five. She, unfortunately, couldn't hold her liquor. Her liquor held her."

"Things got bad?" I said.

"Brandy in her morning coffee? I'll say. She's not a happy drunk, and she and Henry began to argue. Finally she left him when I was in the first grade. People think kids that young don't understand, but I knew she had big problems." His jaw muscles clenched, but he went on. "I remember her giving us this speech about new beginnings, but she had three boys to raise. The only thing she knew how to do was party, drink and marry men she didn't love. I don't even remember the next two guys we lived with. They paid the bills, though. I graduated high school in, like, the seventh school district I'd been in. Hard to make friends when you're on the move all the time."

"You survived, though," I said. "No, you did more than survive. You found your way."

"I always knew what I wanted to do. Help people. Fix problems. I was long gone when she met her final husband, Gordon. Went to the police academy in Virginia and stayed out of her life. Stayed away from Bob and Charlie, too."

"Y'all didn't get along?"

"That's putting it mildly," he said, adding a derisive laugh. "We beat each other up regularly. I stayed pretty angry with Bob. He was a shoplifter, plus he charmed every rich girl he could find. Charlie didn't piss me off quite as much, but he was a do-nothing. Wouldn't communicate with any-one, was flunking out of school and finally ran away to New York as soon as he could drive. If Mom had only been sober enough to see how much we were all hurting, maybe things would have been different."

"But Gordon came along. Someone who finally helped your mother get sober, right?" I said.

"Yup. Don't know how, but he did. Bob and Charlie and I had all left Mom on her own by then. She cared for Gordon, though I'm not sure she ever loved anyone as much as she loved my father. I'm not sure she even loves her own sons."

"I don't buy it, Tom," I said. "I see how loving she can be — to you and to Finn. I guess that's the reason I don't understand her problems with Bob and Charlie."

"Finn brought Mom and me back together. Like I said, Mom favored him. Loved him from the minute she met him. She finally had the grandchild she always wanted. Bob suddenly reappeared — like he realized he might be shut out, so he had to insert himself back into my mother's life. Of course, what did he do? He stole the diamond earrings Gordon had given her."

"Diamond earrings, huh? Are those what he referred to as *rightfully his?*" I said.

"He's so full of it. For some reason he believed Gordon didn't buy them. He thought Mom bought the earrings herself, with money she got from his father. See, Bob even lies to himself. True enough, his father had money." Tom shook his head sadly. "Great guy who eventually died of cirrhosis because he had a worse drinking problem than my mother. She did find out he was sick, tried to help him like Gordon helped her, but it was too late. He left Mom money in his will. More money than he left Bob and Charlie, from what I understand. She never said how much, and I never asked."

"Bet the reading of the will didn't go over too well. No wonder Bob's resentful," I said.

"The earring theft happened around the time Hilary and I split up. Mom came racing to town — I was in North Carolina by then — and got involved. She thought she'd lose Finn. Bob was living with her at the time — guy's never had a job for longer than a month. She'd just bought her little house in Mercy. Anyway, he took the earrings while she was gone."

"He admitted it?" I said.

"I was a cop at the time. I know how to make a suspect talk — and I did. Can't say I'm proud of how I've handled the problems with Hilary or with Bob. I was proud of my mother, however, for throwing Bob out when she discovered her earrings were gone. They were a sobriety anniversary gift. We couldn't get them back, either. The pawnbroker sold them for cash. No way to find the buyer."

I said, "You didn't have your brother arrested, I take it? Because Morris, who's been around probably since Mercy was founded, never mentioned he even knew about Bob or any legal problems."

"Bob spent very little time here, never got to know anyone. My mother didn't want me to turn him in. I reluctantly went along with her." Tom took a long hit off his soda and made a face like he'd just drank lemon juice. "This stuff is not for me. Anyway, notice she has my father's name now? She changed it back about the same time she and Bob became estranged. It's her time machine mentality I was talking about before. When my dad was alive, everything seemed perfect in her mind. She still talks about him like he was a saint. Maybe he was, but I don't remember him. Obviously his death wounded her enough she went down a dark path for years afterward."

I stroked the purring Chablis and noticed Syrah had taken his spot above my left shoulder on top of the couch. "When I lost John, I felt the same kind of grief. Wounded is the right word. But you talked earlier about how you failed. I don't see what you could have done to make anyone in your family act differently."

Tom stared down at the can he held with two hands. "I just wish I could have made things right."

"Who wants to play with a time machine now?" I asked.

He looked at me and smiled slowly, as if something was shifting in his mind. "You're right. Regrets are a wish for time travel, aren't they?"

"Yes. You are a good man," I said, matching his smile. "Time to let go of the *should haves,* don't you think?"

He didn't answer because the back door opened and Yoshi came racing in. Chablis took off like her tail was on fire, leaving a bleeding claw mark on my arm. The dog greeted me and then Tom by putting a paw on each of our legs, his stubby tail wagging ferociously.

I called, "There's Dr Pepper in the fridge, Finn."

He joined us, holding a can. When he saw what Tom was drinking, he said, "Isn't this the best?"

Tom said, "Mmm. So good."

I almost laughed. He was a terrible liar, but Finn didn't seem to notice.

Finn said, "Did you know they make this in Texas? Every now and then, you can get it in little bottles made with the original recipe. With cane sugar. But this is dope even with the high-fructose whatever." He held up the can and admired it.

"*Dope?* You're using slang like that with an ex-cop in the room?" Tom said with a laugh.

"Okay," Finn said. "It's sick. How's that?"

We all laughed.

My phone rang and I pulled it from my pocket.

The male voice said, "Tom's got you on speed dial. You know what that means." It was Bob — being Bob.

"You want to talk to Tom?" I said.

"Nope. Just tell him to come home pronto. His dumb cat got out again."

TWENTY

Fearing Tom might deck Bob given half a chance, I decided to ride along and help find Dashiell. Maybe I could keep Tom focused on what was important. Too bad his poor kitty got outside again, not only because a cat shouldn't be wandering around in the dark but because Tom had just been mellowing out, getting a lot of old business off his chest.

We left Finn with the security system armed and instructions not to open the door for anyone. I expected to see Bob outside with a flashlight looking for Dashiell, but he was sitting in Tom's living room watching TV. I'd tried to understand Bob, had realized after Tom's story he was probably a bitter man, but any morsel of compassion disappeared when I realized he felt no compunction to find Dashiell. Guess we should be grateful he'd made a phone call.

Tom, to his credit, only offered his brother a dirty look, not fighting words. I followed him into the kitchen and he found a couple flashlights. We went out the back door, which, I noted, was still ajar. Did Bob think Dashiell would come back if he left the door open?

"Be careful out here, Jillian. The drop-off to the creek is pretty steep." He swept his flashlight left and right, revealing the sparkling, dewy lawn.

I pointed straight ahead. "Last time, I found him by a tree over there near the slope."

We both hurried toward the creek. Tom's neighbor to the left had a fence, and I went that way while Tom jogged in the opposite direction calling Dashiell's name. Slowly we shined our lights over the grass and up into the trees.

I passed the spot where I'd found him last time. Not there. If he'd slipped into the creek, we'd need more than flashlights to find him. I pushed such a horrible thought to the back of mind. He wouldn't go far, I wanted to believe. But if his blood sugar crashed, he could be lying unconscious anywhere.

When I reached the fence and ran my beam along the bottom, I took a deep breath and thought about cat behavior. Sick cats hide. This was their instinctive reaction, seeing as how a vulnerable cat could become prey to a larger animal. While Tom eased his way down toward the creek, I called out to him. "I'll search the shrubs around your house."

I continued to focus my flashlight on the ground, looking right and left as I walked back toward the house. Tom had thick holly bushes lining his house in the back and as I turned the flashlight on them, bright red berries glowed like tiny Christmas ornaments. *A great hiding place,* I thought.

"Dashiell," I called. "Come here, baby."

A tiny meow in response. Plaintive. Afraid.

My heart sped, but not wanting to scare Dashiell, I kept a quiet, even tone as I knelt and extended my hand in the direction of the sound and said his name again.

I moved the light along the ground, but at first I didn't see Dashiell — though I heard him again.

I did find something, though. Something my brain couldn't make sense of at first.

A hiking boot.

But as the flashlight captured the shape completely, I realized to my horror the boot was filled by a foot and the foot was attached to a bent leg. The rest of the person was hidden beneath the prickly holly.

"T-Tom," I said. But I spoke too softly for anyone but Dashiell to hear. I backed up and then ran in Tom's direction. When I reached him, I said, "Come with me. Now. Something's very wrong."

"Did you find him? Is he hurt?" Tom said, following me as I ran back toward the house.

I shined the light on the blue-jeaned leg.

Tom knelt and tried to push aside the thick shrubs, but the holly wouldn't budge much. Tom's presence did have a positive effect because Dashiell made his way out. Tom swooped him up.

He said, "Do you have your phone?"

I called 911 and it took only five minutes for a squad car to come squealing around the corner of Tom's street, siren blasting. It was followed close behind by not only the paramedics, but the fire department. In Mercy, it's an all-out effort when there's an emergency.

Deputy Rodriguez rushed to our side. He shook the foot, saying, "Hey. You stuck under there?"

No response.

Tom handed Dashiell to me and ran into his garage. He returned with his hedge cutters.

"Can you pull whoever it is out?" I said.

"Don't move them," Marcy, our paramedic friend, said as she came up and dropped to her knees by the prone figure. "I can check for a pulse on the foot. Might need help taking the boot off, though."

"Let's do it," Rodriguez said, untying the dirty boot.

Once the foot was bare, looking waxy in the artificial lights, she pressed two fingers on the ankle. She moved her fingers around the top of the foot, searching for what was apparently an elusive pulse. Finally she looked up, her lips pressed tightly together, and shook her head. "His foot is cold and there's no pulse. Unless this is a woman with very large feet, you've found a dead man."

Firefighter Billy Cranor came running up, holding a gigantic battery-powered light. "Will this help?"

"Light him up, Billy," Rodriguez said, still kneeling by the body.

Billy only illuminated what we all could see — the leg and bare foot. Nothing more. He said, "How the heck did he get under there? Unless someone was trying to hide him under one of the meanest bushes I've ever tangled with."

"You're gonna have to cut away the holly to get to him," a voice behind me said. "Let me get my camera before you start. We'll probably need crime scene tape, too."

It was Candace. She wore sweats and no makeup. Even in the dim castoff from flashlights, I saw dark circles under her eyes.

"Tom, Jillian, can you go inside, please?" she said.

"Sure," I replied.

Dashiell was purring, but I knew he was purring more from stress than from anything else.

Tom said, "I'll step aside, but I'm not leaving until I know who died in my backyard."

Candace uttered an exasperated sigh. "All right. Just stand back."

I was glad to leave, but when I remembered who was inside the house, not quite as relieved.

"All this firepower for a cat?" Bob said with a laugh when I came in through the front door — the door Candace had suggested I use. "Tom is *the* man in town, I guess."

The police cars, fire engine and paramedics had gotten Bob's attention.

"Are you kidding me?" I said, feeling all my Southern upbringing abandoning me. But I regrouped and said, "There's a dead man out there. Right under the dining room window."

The TV still blasted, sounding about ten times louder than it probably was. I went over and stabbed the off button. When I turned around, Bob was headed for the dining room.

Holding Dashiell close, I followed.

"Wow," he said, peering out the window. "Who is it?"

I pulled the drapes shut because I didn't want to be like the people who stop and gape at an accident scene. I said, "We'll find out soon enough." I went to the kitchen to test Dashiell's blood sugar before we had a feline emergency to deal with, too.

After I finished, with Bob hovering behind me, I read the monitor and found though Dashiell's sugar level was a little high, he wasn't in trouble. I picked up his water dish, walked past Bob and took Dashiell to Tom's room, where his little cat bed sat in one corner. I wanted to find him a safe place to stay because I expected the house would soon be flooded with emergency responders all wanting to hear what Tom, Bob and I had to say. *Now what?* I thought. I was stuck in this small house with a narcissistic, overgrown adolescent. Heck, Finn was more mature than Bob. *Finn.* I needed to call him, let him know the situation.

I'd no sooner disconnected after telling

Finn we'd encountered a problem and didn't know how long I'd be, when Billy Cranor came busting through the front door with Karen in tow.

"Billy Cranor," she was saying, "you take your hands off me or I'll have a serious talk with your mother when we meet at church on Sunday."

Billy gave me a pleading look. "Mrs. Hart, could you keep Tom's mother company while we're busy outside?" He looked past me and saw Bob. "Who's he?"

"One of my other sons," Karen said, shaking free of Billy's grasp.

Billy's mouth agape, he seemed to be processing this information. All he said in response, however, was, "Okay. Whatever." He left.

"What in heaven's name is going on?" Karen said. "I heard sirens and saw the lights. Where's my Tom?" She looked back and forth between Bob and me and I saw panic in her eyes.

"He's fine," I said. "He's outside helping the police."

Her shoulders slumped and she closed her eyes. "For a minute there, I thought something terrible had happened."

"Don't worry. Tom's okay. But something terrible *has* happened," I said. "There's a body in Tom's backyard."

"Oh my sweet good Lord. Who is it?" she said.

"We don't know yet," I answered.

Her fear resurfaced. "Where's Finn? Where's my grandson?"

"He's at my house," I said. "I just finished talking to him. He's safe."

Karen rushed to me and gave me a giant hug. "Bless you, Jillian."

I glanced at Bob, who'd gone unacknowledged by his mother. I could see the hurt in his expression. Old hurt. The kind of disappointment he'd probably experienced most of his life.

"This is all very heartwarming," Bob said. "But since it looks like we're stuck here for the duration, anyone want a drink?" He eyed his mother. "Wine, Mom? Oh, I forgot. You prefer vodka."

Any sympathy I might have felt for Bob a second ago disappeared.

Karen paled and pulled her fleece robe around her. I looked down and could see she was wearing emerald green silk pajamas with cream piping around the hems.

She said, "I will forget you said those words, Robert. This is a difficult situation. I could use a glass of water about now. My mouth is so very dry."

Not wanting to leave her alone with Bob, I took her hand and we went to the kitchen together. I hadn't noticed what a mess the kitchen was while attending to Dashiell. Knowing Tom as well as I did, I decided the overflowing garbage, the dishes in the sink and the beer cans lined up on the counter were all Bob's doing. Tom may have been stubborn enough not to pick up after him, but I wasn't.

But before I could tackle the kitchen mess, I heard Candace's voice in my head: *Evidence can be anywhere. I always preserve the crime scene as thoroughly as I can.*

If the man outside had been the victim of foul play, Tom's home would become part of her crime scene. As difficult as it was to do nothing about garbage, cans and dirty dishes, I poured both Karen and myself glasses of water. With my hand on her back to guide her, we went out to the living room. Karen sat in a padded dining room chair in the corner by the TV. Tom's dining room was too small to accommodate all the chairs around his table, so he used two of them for living room seating.

Karen still seemed stunned but finally looked around and realized Bob was present. "Oh. You're staying here. I forgot. What do you know about this horrible turn of events?"

"About as much as you do. Dumb cat gets out again and then all hell breaks loose in the neighborhood." Bob chewed on his thumb, glancing anxiously back to the dining room.

"Dashiell's smarter than a tree full of owls. Some cats are even smarter than certain humans," I said. I didn't add aloud that Dashiell was probably smarter than Bob, but from his expression, he got the message.

I heard the muted jumble of voices outside and those sounds, combined with the whirling police lights flashing blue and red through the front curtains, made me feel as uneasy as Bob appeared to be. I wondered then if he knew who was lying dead under a holly bush outside. I even went so far as to consider the possibility he had something to do with the man's death. I blinked away these thoughts. The thought of Karen and me sharing space with her son, possibly her murderer of a son, was too unsettling.

We didn't have to wait long for Deputy Rodriguez to join us. He looked at me, probably because I was the only friendly face in the room. "We need you and Mr. Cochran down at the station so we can take your statements."

Karen rose abruptly, spilling her water all over the floor in front of her — and she didn't even seem to notice. "What about me?"

"Were you here within the last several hours?" Rodriguez said.

"No, sir," she said. "But I live right around the corner."

"We'll just need Mr. Stewart, his brother and Mrs. Hart for now," he said.

"What am I supposed to do?" she said.

"Go on home. I can drop you off, if you'd like." He glanced at her slippered feet. "Not safe walking home in the dark without shoes, Mrs. Stewart."

"Perhaps you're right," she said, seeming confused as she stared down at her feet.

I swallowed, finally ready to ask the big question. "Do you know who the dead man is?"

"The stranger who's been causing problems in town. Guess he crossed the wrong person," Rodriguez said.

"Rory Gannon?" I said.

"Yup," Rodriguez answered.

For some reason, I wasn't surprised.

Twenty-One

Tom, Bob and I were escorted to separate rooms at the police station — Tom to one interrogation room, Bob to the other while Rodriguez put me in Chief Baca's office.

I sat in the chair across from Mike's desk and noticed how completely silent it was in here, as if he'd had his office soundproofed. I took a few deep breaths, wondering how long I would have to wait. My thoughts turned to Finn alone at my house. I took out my cell phone and checked my cat cam.

He must have taken Yoshi to bed because, though there were several Dr Pepper cans on the coffee table, he wasn't in the living room. I did see all three cats asleep in different spots.

Then I thought about poor Dashiell, who had been dropped off at Karen's house. Tom had told me once she had no clue what to do for a diabetic cat should there be an emergency, even though he'd tried his best to show her how to test the kitty's sugar. But until we were free to go, Dashiell had to stay with someone. When Tom phoned her with the request, she agreed to take him. Tom made sure to give her Doc Jensen's number in case of an emergency.

I glanced around Mike's office, which was devoid of personal photos. But the walls were filled with police academy certificates, sharp-shooting awards, a commendation from the mayor and town council. For some reason, I'd never noticed these items before. Maybe because I'd never been in his office all by myself. Mike was a good guy, but of late, with all the budget cuts, he'd become much more of a political animal. After all, chief of police was a position appointed by the town council.

As the moments ticked away, I finally allowed myself to wonder about Rory Gannon. Somehow he'd found his way to Tom's house. I guess I shouldn't have been surprised since he'd been showing up anywhere Finn might be in Mercy. There, he'd met his death. Why? And how had he ended up beneath the holly? Like Billy Cranor said, those bushes weren't exactly people friendly. Maybe he'd started to crawl under them so he could peer into the dining room and had suffered a heart attack. But I had the sick feeling something far more sinister had happened.

I realized I was squeezing my left hand with my right, afraid of learning the truth and yet wanting to know at the same time. I hated this anxious feeling and was almost ready to get up and see if Candace had arrived so I could get answers. Before I moved, the door opened.

Lydia Monk flew into the office like she was riding a witch's broom. Her blond hair looked like a lion's mane surrounding her face.

"You again," she said with contempt. "When I heard you were the one who found the body, well, let's say I volunteered to come in here and be the one to interview you. See, I'm getting darn tired of you interfering in Tom's life."

She walked around to the other side of Mike's desk and sat in his black leather chair opposite me. She wore a low-cut purple sweater and a leather vest, along with plenty of makeup. Giant silver hoop earrings dangled near both cheeks. She put a small tape recorder down on the desk.

"Hello, Lydia," I said, mustering every ounce of composure I could.

"Okay," she said, glancing around Mike's tidy desk. "I'm not sure what in the heck you thought you were doing at Tom's house. You don't belong there." She started opening drawers and finally said, "Ah," and pulled out a legal pad. Lydia took a pen from a container on the desk and turned on the tape recorder. "This is Assistant County Coroner Lydia Monk interviewing Jillian Hart at the request of the Mercy Police Department." She gave the date and time, then said, "What do you know about this dead man?"

"Not much, really," I said.

She sighed in exasperation, turned off the tape recorder and echoed, "Not much, really," in a mocking tone. "Listen to me, Miss Prissy. This is the second man in a week dead by another's hand and somehow connected to you. You better tell me everything, starting now."

Dead by another's hand. Murder, in other words. "Why did you turn off the tape recorder?"

"Bothers me. Can't do a decent interview. They can rely on my notes," she said.

"W-where's Candace?" I said.

"You think your friend will come in and rescue you from the hard questions?" she said. "She's busy with the real suspects. Yeah, you're no suspect in her eyes, but I might prove her wrong."

"You believe I killed a man I hardly knew?" I said.

Her eyes shifted, as if she was trying to pull some theory out of the air to confirm her crazy suspicions. "Let me give you a heads-up. Tom has a brother. He has a stepson. He has an ex-wife. How much did you know about these strangers?"

"As much as anyone. They're people from Tom's past." I avoided eye contact with her. Anything not to get her more agitated than she already was.

"I know they've all caused trouble, so what's your part in his problems?" she said.

I would never understand how Lydia's mind worked. I decided my job right now was to be as cooperative as possible and maybe she'd leave me alone. "What exactly do you want to know, Lydia?" I said.

She stared at me for several seconds, eyes narrowed; then, thank goodness, she looked down at the legal pad. "Why were you at Tom's house tonight?"

Feeling less nervous, I explained how Tom, Finn, Bob and I had all been at Karen's place earlier in the day. I told her how Finn and Tom left for his house when Hilary arrived and that I'd gone home. When I came to the part about Finn and Tom coming to my house later on, I saw her press the pen into the paper a little harder, but she didn't look at me. When I told her how Bob allowed the cat to sneak out again and that I'd accompanied Tom back to his house to help look for Dashiell, her almost-rational behavior disappeared again.

She slammed down her pen and leaned toward me. "Why would he trust you? Why can't Tom see you for the Mata Hari you are?"

I shook my head in confusion. "What are you talking about?"

The door opened behind me and Liam entered the office. He smiled down at me and then addressed Lydia. "Did you get the time line I asked for?"

Lydia stood. "Yes, Mr. Brennan, I did. This woman here had plenty of time to kill the man. She *says* she was alone all afternoon. No alibi. Now, I may not be a doctor but, like I told you over at Tom's house, Mr. Rory Gannon was dead for several hours before his body was found." She glanced at me pointedly. "Found by *her* with a knife wound in his back."

The shock I felt must have been written all over my face. She was accusing me of murder in front of the Assistant DA.

I was relieved to see the corners of Liam's

mouth twitch upward. "Your theory is Mrs. Hart murdered Rory Gannon? What evidence have you collected to support this conclusion?"

"She hasn't implicated herself," Lydia said, sounding less convinced. "But she had the time."

"I see. I'm sure you have paperwork to complete for the coroner. Thanks for stepping in when the police needed extra help." Liam stood away from the open office door to allow her to leave.

"Sure." She tore off the notes she'd taken, but before she could leave with them, Liam glanced at the tape recorder and said, "You have her statement on tape?"

She pulled off a few pills on the arm of her sweater. "No. I couldn't work the thing. I don't use tape recorders."

He held out his hand. "Then I'll need your notes."

She looked at Liam, her mouth tight, and then turned them over before she left.

I let out an audible sigh once she was gone. "I am so glad you're here."

He closed the door. "Two murders in less than a week. You bet I'm here. Kara was worried about you, by the way. Her new assistant told her about the 911 call at Tom's house. She was on the scene sooner than I was. Once I learned they'd taken you here, I told her as much. She was relieved you're safe." He perused the yellow piece of paper as he walked around and took a seat in Mike's chair.

"Lydia said Mr. Gannon was stabbed?" I said.

"Yes," he said absently, still reading what Lydia had written.

"No one has confessed, I assume," I said.

He looked at me. "Wouldn't a confession tie this up nicely?" He held up the paper. "This, despite Lydia Monk's propensity to want to find you guilty of anything, is lucid. Thanks to this, I see there's another person we need to bring in. Do you know where Finn is?"

I swallowed. "H-he's at my house. But he didn't even know his father."

"I'm not saying he's guilty of anything, Jillian," Liam said. "He was at Tom's house, probably around the time Gannon was killed. He could know something."

"You just want to talk to him?" I said. "You're aware Candace has a theory about his innocence based on physical evidence?"

"You know me, Jillian. We're friends. From what Candace has told me, that young man doesn't have a serial killer bone in his body. Doesn't mean we don't need to talk to him," Liam said. "I'll drive, since I assume you don't have transportation."

"I drove here, so you can follow me. But can I speak with Tom first?" I said.

"You believe he'll react rationally when it comes to Finn?" he said with a generous dose of skepticism.

I didn't answer. I didn't need to.

Liam stood and offered me a hand up. "Come on. Let's get this over with."

He helped me out of the chair and we went into the hall just in time to see Tom's mother come into the police station waiting area.

She spotted me and ran past B.J. through the gate. I could tell she'd been crying.

Karen gripped my shoulders. "I need to tell what I know. I have to tell someone what he said."

Twenty-Two

"Who are you talking about?" I asked Karen.

"The man who died. Finn's biological father," she said.

The interrogation room door opened and Tom appeared. Candace was right behind him.

"What are you doing here, Mom?" Tom said, walking toward us.

She looked up at Tom. "That man came to see me right after Hilary and Bob left my house this afternoon. I know I should have said something when I found out he'd died, but I didn't and I should have and —"

Tom took his mother in his arms and she wept into his shoulder.

"Hey," he said. "It's all right. You're here now. You can tell us, but first you have to stop crying."

She blew into a tissue she'd been clutching and composed herself so quickly I wondered how truly tearful she'd just been. "When I found myself in my car on the way to the nearest bar I knew I was in trouble. I came here instead."

"You need to call someone from AA, Mom?" Tom said quietly.

"No. I have to tell Candace everything I know. Please, all of you" — she glanced around at Candace, Liam and me — "you have to hear me out."

Candace raised her eyebrows and I could read a hint of amusement in her expression. "Do I have to read you your rights, Mrs. Stewart?" Karen's jaw sagged in surprise. "Oh, my sweet good Lord, no. This is just information you should have. Something I should have said right off the bat. I was so surprised to find out the man was dead, well —"

Candace put her arm around Karen. "Let's go into this room right here and we can talk. There isn't enough space to fit another person's shadow out here."

"Can Tom and Jillian stay with me? Please?" she pleaded.

"You need moral support?" Candace said.

"I suppose. See, whenever I go to AA, the room is full," Karen said. "One on one is so very difficult for me. It's not like I have a whole lot to say but maybe if I'd listened better to what the man was saying, he might not be dead right now."

"Come on in here, then — all of you. Mr. Brennan, would you mind helping out, too?" Candace said. "Might as well make it like one of her meetings."

"Be my pleasure," he said.

While the rest of us took seats around the old table in the interrogation room, Liam remained standing in the corner, arms crossed.

Candace said, "What time did Mr. Gannon come to visit you?"

Karen started pulling her tissue apart. "Maybe two o'clock this afternoon? Maybe as late as two thirty?"

"Why didn't you call me?" Tom said.

Candace stared over at Tom. "Have you decided to apply for police chief next year and need to try out your rusty interrogation techniques?" I was sitting next to him and placed a hand on his knee. I felt the tension in his body and it didn't let up, even when he said, "I know, I know. I didn't mean to interrupt. I'll shut up."

Candace looked at Karen. "Since you'd already had an unpleasant meeting with Mr. Gannon where I had to pay a visit to your house, why did you even talk to this man?"

"He was different this time, Candace.

Nice, even," Karen said. "I let him in."

I glanced down and saw Tom's hand balled in a fist in his lap. Was he thinking about what might have happened to his mother after she let an unstable man into her house? Or did he think Karen had something to do with Gannon's death?

"In the hall," Liam said in a soft voice, "you mentioned you needed to tell us what he said. Is that what has you so rattled now?"

She nodded. "I could tell the man was troubled. Maybe not quite right in the head, though not in a vicious way like before. He kept saying he was sorry. He had to make things right. I've been in the 'sorry' boat on a rocky sea myself. I asked him what he wanted to apologize for and he told me no one would let him near his son, which didn't really answer my question." Karen looked at the ceiling. "He said — let me get the words exactly right — 'The phone call started everything.' "

I swallowed hard and moved my hand over Tom's cold fist.

Candace, seated on my other side, leaned toward Karen. "A phone call from who?"

"Why Finn, of course. Who else could he be talking about?" Karen said.

Candace seemed to ponder this while

Liam tried to clarify by saying, "The exact words were *the* phone call, not *Finn's* phone call?"

"He was talking about Finn before, so I simply assumed he meant Finn. Then the man just got up and left. When I learned he was dead, I guess I was afraid for my grandson. But Finn would never hurt anyone. He's had such a difficult time. Then Hilary called looking for Finn again — right after Deputy Rodriguez brought me home from Tom's house."

Tom said, "What did you tell Hilary, Mom?"

Candace sighed, but she didn't interrupt with another warning.

"I didn't tell Hilary anything — well, except about the body poor Jillian found," Karen said.

"You never told her where Finn is staying?" Tom said.

"No. I knew you wouldn't want me to. Besides, she hung up so abruptly and —"

Candace said, "You honestly believe Mrs. Roth has no idea Finn is at Jillian's house? She'd already seen him there once."

Tom cleared his throat. "Since I'm done giving my statement, I'm out of here." He almost made it to the door, but Liam stepped in his path.

"I'll drive," he said, looking Tom straight in the eye. "We were about to head to Jillian's to talk to Finn anyway."

"We'll compromise. I'll follow you," Tom replied.

"Wait." Candace stood. "Call Finn. We need to ask him if his mother's been there or called the house."

I smiled at Candace, grateful for her sounding so in control, for not racing out of here as if the world was on fire. I took my phone out of my pocket with a shaky hand and dialed my landline number — and let it ring until the answering machine picked up. "Finn? If you're there, could you pick up?" I waited and he didn't answer. "Listen, if you get this message, I'm on my way home now." I disconnected and looked at Candace. "Let me check the cat cam, too. Maybe he fell asleep watching TV." With Candace looking over my shoulder, I saw that all the rooms on my feed — the foyer, living room, kitchen and my sewing room — were empty. No Finn, no Yoshi and not a cat to be seen. Now I was more nervous than ever.

"We need to head over to your house." Candace then looked at Karen. "But, Mrs. Stewart, would you mind returning home in case Finn calls you there?"

"I'll do whatever you think is best," she said.

Since both Tom and I had driven on our own to the police station — only Bob came in Rodriguez's squad car — Tom's work van and my minivan were right on Candace's bumper as she and Liam sped toward my home. Could Hilary have convinced Finn to talk to her? Open the door? Even go somewhere with her? I doubted it, but in the courthouse parking lot before we'd taken off, Tom seemed to think it was possible. He'd said, "She is his mother. Kids love their mother no matter what."

When we pulled onto my block, a dark-colored sedan was parked in the street in front of my house, a car I didn't recognize.

Candace had pulled up beside it while Tom and I drove into my driveway. We both walked back down the drive to see who Candace and Liam were talking to in the sedan.

My stomach lurched. Hilary Roth was out of the car and conversing with them. As we joined them, I could see tears glistening on her cheeks in the moonlight.

When she saw Tom, she addressed him. "I only wanted to talk to him. I called through the door, I begged him to let me in."

"He wouldn't, would he?" Tom said.

She shook her head. "I went back to the car. I waited. I went back several times hoping he would just say something. Anything. See, I knew he was in there. I just knew."

Candace said, "You kept talking through the door?"

"Yelling actually," she said. "So he could hear. He needed to know about Rory. The man was his father, after all."

"You didn't yell out the juicy piece of information about his father's murder by chance?" Tom said angrily.

"I — I did mention Rory died unexpectedly. He had to know. I thought if I told him, he'd open the door. But he didn't." She hung her head and sniffled.

This woman's son ran away and she'd lost her husband all in the last week. I couldn't help but feel sorry for her. But Tom was not swayed by her tears or by the fact she'd been parked here for maybe several hours hoping to talk to Finn.

He said, "You may think you're fooling us with all this fake concern for Finn, but you're not." Tom looked at Candace. "Can you make her leave?"

"Why don't we talk to Finn and see what he wants to do?" Candace said.

Tom said, "Are you kidding me?"

I took his hand and drew him away. His

back was to them and I said, "You can't protect Finn from her forever. With all of us here, what harm can it do to let her see her son?"

"Hilary being in the same room with him is harm done, as far as I'm concerned," he whispered harshly.

But I could tell by his face he was willing to give a little.

I said, "Finn needs to see his mother's concern."

"Jillian, she is *not* concerned. All you're seeing is what I call her beautiful facade. This woman has something else in mind, probably something to do with money. She may not love her kid, but she does love money. You're right, though. With all of us around for support, Finn can decide whether he wants to talk to her or not."

I turned back to Candace. "I'll go in first. Tell him we're here to talk to him, okay?"

We walked around back where I could disengage the security alarm.

And realized it wasn't set.

Tom stood right behind me and knew this instantly.

"Open the door," he said, the urgency in his voice alerting Candace.

She grabbed Tom's arm. "Stand down, Tom. I've got this." She took my keys and unlocked the door — the dead bolt wasn't locked, just the door — and then Candace went into my house with her weapon drawn.

TWENTY-THREE

I saw lights go on in the kitchen and heard Candace calling Finn's name.

Hilary had been standing a few steps back from the rest of us, but moved closer and said, "Does she think Finn is hurt? I don't understand."

Tom turned and glared at her, his mouth white-ringed with anger. "Keep out of this."

Sounding conciliatory, Liam said, "He may be asleep. This is just a precaution."

He isn't asleep, I thought. *Not with the security system disarmed.* Before Tom and I left, we'd made sure he'd armed the system and knew how to work it if he had to take Yoshi outside. He'd picked up the directions easily and wouldn't have forgotten.

Candace returned a long minute later, her face impossible to read. How she managed not to share so much as a morsel of emotion always surprised me. She said, "Come on in."

Chablis was the first to greet me, so I knew immediately Yoshi wasn't here. And if Yoshi wasn't here, Finn wasn't either. I picked my cat up and held her close.

All the lights were on, thanks to Candace's search. Once we'd all stepped into the kitchen, she said, "He's gone." She glanced back and forth between Hilary and Tom. "Either of you know where he might be?"

"How would I know? I've been talking to you about a dead guy I didn't even know from Adam for the last two hours," Tom said.

Syrah arrived to greet us, but stopped before reaching us. Tom's raised voice made him wary. Neither I nor my cats had ever heard Tom sound so upset.

Syrah hissed, turned and raced out of the room past Merlot. My biggest boy hadn't even bothered to come close. He was sitting on the tile near the breakfast bar, his gaze trained on Hilary, his nose in the air trying to catch her scent. Chablis snuggled into my neck and began to purr. She knew I was troubled and wanted to comfort me. How I wished my cats could tell me what had gone on here in my absence.

"Maybe Finn took Yoshi for a walk," Hilary said, a tinge of panic in her voice. "If he went out this back door, I wouldn't have seen him leave."

I said, "Even though the security system was disarmed, the door was locked. You *can* lock it from the inside and leave. If he went to walk the dog, he may have accidentally locked himself out." Why was I being such a Pollyanna? In my heart, I knew Finn was gone, reverting to what he'd done before. He'd run. *Unless,* I thought, *someone lured him outside and snatched him and his dog.* Something pretty darn hard to do with Hilary parked out front. Besides, who would do such a thing?

Just then Tom spotted a Post-it note stuck on the fridge door. He took it down and read aloud, *"Thanks for everything, Mrs. Hart. Finn."*

Hilary looked over Tom's shoulder at the note. "Oh no. I recognize his handwriting."

Tom bolted for the back door and Candace called, "Where are you going?"

"To find him," he shouted.

"Let him drive around," Liam said. "Maybe he'll cool off, and who knows? He might just spot the kid."

The helplessness I felt at watching Tom run out the door made it impossible to speak. He wanted to do right by Finn and, after all he'd told me about his past, I was sure Tom believed he'd failed.

Liam said, "Did you notice if Finn left anything behind, Deputy Carson?"

"Now that I think about it, I didn't see anything that might have belonged to him in the guest room," she said solemnly.

I blinked hard, feeling the unexpected sting of tears. Worry for Finn and for Tom, plus the night's horrific events finally converged. But I managed to fight back the tears and said to Candace, "You'll put out one of those BOLO things for him?"

"If he were simply an adult runaway, I couldn't. But since he's wanted for questioning anyway, I'll do just that." She took her cell phone from her utility belt. "But not out on the radio for the whole town to pick up on their scanners. Don't want the do-gooders in town to spook Finn if he's just walking around, thinking about what he heard his mother say. What was he wearing last time you saw him?"

I described the jeans and shirt Kara had bought. While Candace called in the "be on the lookout" alert with Finn's description, the rest of us listened in silence. I was stunned by the evening's events and I'm sure Hilary and Liam were, too.

After she hung up, Candace looked at Hilary. "We need to talk to everyone who knew

Mr. Gannon. You can follow me to the police station."

She pointed at herself with a manicured nail. "Me? There's nothing I can tell you about Rory aside from the fact he's battled mental illness most of his adult life. I mean, he did. Before he — he . . . died." With the money troubles she had, she still got her nails done. Not unusual, I decided. Denial was a huge issue in a country where people hurt by the downturn in the economy still wanted all the perks they were used to.

"I just need to write down everything you know about Mr. Gannon for the chief. Paperwork never goes away. Let's go." She started for the door and Liam got behind Hilary as if to herd her out.

I stood at the back door and watched them leave, but before Candace disappeared around the side of the house, she turned and said, "I know you'll call right away if Finn shows up."

I shut the door and locked it, making sure the dead bolt was fastened, too. Setting Chablis down, I turned on the deck lights in case Finn decided to come back. Gosh, I hoped he would.

As I walked back into the kitchen, I remembered Candace's words when we were talking about her job once and got a shiver up my spine. She'd said, "The innocent? They just stick around. Guilty folks run."

I opened the fridge and took out the sweet tea. I couldn't remember the last time I'd eaten, but I wasn't hungry. I poured a glass and went into the living room, grabbed a lap quilt and curled up in John's recliner. All three cats soon surrounded me.

I stared out through the picture windows, the deck lights casting faint glimmers on the black lake. Stars shone like brilliant specks through the trees and I hoped one of those stars would lead Finn back here. Why did he feel the need to run away? He seemed to understand we all wanted to help him. The thought puzzled me, and deep down I feared that maybe he didn't run away after all. Maybe someone *made* him write the note and leave it for me to make it seem like he ran. I shook my head. *No.* I couldn't dwell on dark thoughts. There was an explanation. Finn would come back and he would tell us why he left. I was sure of it.

My phone rang and the sound made me jump. Maybe it was Finn. Instead it was Kara, making sure I was all right after what had happened. I told her I was okay and before I could even mention Finn's disappearance, she said she was in a hurry to get a headline in for tomorrow's *Mercy Messenger.* She disconnected.

My eyelids felt weighted and, with Chablis resting on my chest, I closed them. Next thing I knew, a knock at my back door awakened me. I'd dozed off. I rose from the chair so quickly I frightened poor Chablis and she leaped from my arms and scampered off down the hall. But Merlot and Syrah were already waiting in the kitchen ready for me to answer the door.

It was Candace.

I let her in, hugged her tightly and said, "I am so glad you came."

"I knew you wouldn't be in bed," she said. "I take it you haven't heard from Finn?"

"No. But I nodded off. How can I sleep with Finn missing?" As we went into the kitchen I checked the microwave for the time. One a.m. I'd been out for several hours.

"You needed the sleep. And I need tea." She opened the fridge and took out the pitcher.

"I have wine, if you'd rather —"

"Nothing stronger than tea or coffee until I solve this double homicide," she said. "But I'd love a big bag of chips about now."

"Since I had a teenager in the house, I can fulfill your wish," I said.

"By the way, did you check your security footage? I wonder if something important was caught on video. Maybe Hilary lied and Finn did talk to her," she said, taking the bag of chips I offered.

"Can't hurt to check," I said. "We can also get the exact time the security system was disarmed, though I'm not sure how the information will help."

"Any information might be useful," Candace said. "Let's go look."

In my office I booted up the computer and we watched the various feeds from the past evening. Most of the time, Finn seemed to be watching television in the living room. Then we saw him stab the remote and stand up, as if listening to something. Could this be when his mother showed up? He disappeared and must have gone to his room, but without a camera in that part of the house, we could only assume. Then we watched Finn and Yoshi walk through the living room and kitchen, Finn carrying his backpack slung over one shoulder. The time stamp showed Finn disarmed the system around ten p.m. On his way out, he stopped to write the note he'd left me and I noticed he kept glancing back toward the foyer.

I murmured, "He heard Hilary. He left because she was at the front door."

Candace had been leaning over, looking at the screen. "You're right. She was the trigger. He didn't want to see her."

I powered off the computer and we returned to the living room. Candace sat down with her tea and the extra-large bag of Wavy Lays. I felt sad Finn never even had a chance to open them.

"I take it you haven't heard from Tom?" I asked.

"Not a word. He didn't go home. See, Bob didn't have a ride since Rodriguez drove him to the station. But Morris wasn't about to drop Bob off at Tom's house until we can search the yard in the morning light. There could be evidence we missed. He did drive by the place, though. Rodriguez was on watch, parked out front. He said he hadn't seen Tom."

"Where did Morris take Bob?" I asked. "He said he didn't have any money."

Candace finished her mouthful of chips before answering. "Morris dropped him at his mother's house. We made sure not to tell Bob that Finn is missing. We figured he can't tell Karen anything he doesn't know."

"Karen said it was okay for Bob to come to her house to stay?" I said. "You're aware those two have issues."

"I know. But Bob called her from the station, and she apparently didn't put up too much of a stink. You know something? She's been living in Mercy for ten years — since I was a teenager — and I never saw her as hysterical as she was tonight. For that matter, I've never seen Tom as screwed up as he is right now, either."

"I'm worried about him. You think he's still driving all over the place looking for Finn?" I said.

"Not a doubt in my mind. You don't think Tom changed his mind about Finn, do you? Maybe he thinks Finn found Gannon spying through Tom's window and ended up harming his father. Because if that's the case, I wouldn't put it past Tom to help Finn get as far away from Mercy as possible."

"No way, Candace. He knows Finn could never kill anyone," I said. "If he finds him, he'll convince him to come back. I had a thought earlier that perhaps Finn didn't leave here on his own. Maybe someone compelled him to leave. Now we know it was probably Hilary's arrival that made him run."

She used a paper towel she'd grabbed earlier and wiped salt and grease off her hands. After taking a long drink of tea, she said, "Could be, or maybe he *compelled* himself to leave, Jillian. From talking to him, I get the sense he'd blame himself, think he'd caused everyone too much trouble. Distress like that can make people turn to what they know best to solve a problem. In his case, it's running away."

"He'll come back. He has to. Now that he's seen how much Tom cares about him, he won't be able to stay away." I welcomed Chablis onto my lap. Syrah was already asleep above my head on the recliner's back. Merlot, who likes salty fingers, was parked close to Candace.

"I hope you're right," she said. "I want to tell Finn myself how we found a couple important pieces of evidence on Gannon's body."

"What evidence?" I asked.

"Finn's wallet. We also found a prepaid cell in Gannon's pocket. It belonged to Finn, too."

"His wallet? And a phone?" I said. "How did Gannon get these things? Because Finn never mentioned meeting up with his father. Unless . . . Oh my goodness. Could Gannon have been at the scene of the accident?"

"Exactly what I was thinking," she said.

I nodded slowly, deciding it all made sense. "He took those things from Finn's pocket or backpack while he was unconscious."

"I can't think of any other explanation," Candace said.

"That's huge," I said. "But it makes me wonder — and not for the first time — how Rory Gannon ended up in Mercy. And now, how he ended up at the accident scene — or should I say Roth's murder scene?"

"Don't know for sure yet," she said. "But here's another little gem of a connection. The crime lab sent over the phone logs from Tom's cell and we now know a call was placed from Tom's phone to Gannon's halfway house. Once Finn's phone is thoroughly examined by our techies at the county crime lab, maybe we'll learn more about who was talking to whom."

"You didn't look at Finn's call and text record on his phone already?" I said.

"Not completely," she said, avoiding my gaze. "On TV they fiddle around with cell phones, scrolling through the call log and sent messages of phones at crime scenes, but I don't do that. We have techies who know how to access information, relay it to us and preserve the evidence — not to mention preserve the chain of custody for court."

"I can tell you saw something, though.

What?" I said.

She stared at me for a long moment. "Oh all right — but I'm telling you only because I trust you more than my own mother. I saw a text that came from Tom's phone to Finn the day Nolan Roth was murdered. The message said something like, 'Hey, I'm driving around looking for you, Finn. Where are you?' "

"But Nolan Roth had Tom's phone," I said. "*He* sent the message and lured Finn to him. How in the world did he make him get into the car?"

"Good question," she said. "I'm hoping when we find Finn — and I'm sure we will — some of his memory will return and he can help fill in the blanks."

"Remember that the doctor who treated him for the concussion said he doubted what was lost would ever be recovered," I said.

"Call me an optimist. First we have to find him, though. Meanwhile, I'm seriously considering Gannon for Roth's murder."

"What motive did he have?" I said.

"He wanted his son back?" Candace sounded less than sure.

"Then why smash Finn's head into the dashboard? No, wait. Maybe Roth was the one who did that after the crash."

"We just don't know," she said. "Not yet anyway. But we have Finn's and Tom's phones, so we can see how they match up as far as dates and times with those texts and calls. One other thing's been bugging me and I was hoping Hilary Roth had the answer. She claims she doesn't, though." Candace closed the top of the potato chip package.

"What are you talking about?" I said.

"We figured Roth was trying to find Finn — but Rory Gannon seemed to be in town for the same reason."

"Did you ask Hilary about Gannon? Had she contacted him recently?" I asked.

"She says no," Candace said. "She has no idea why he had any interest in Finn."

I blinked several times, considering this. "So we've got an unstable man who hasn't seen his kid in who knows how long. But when Finn runs away from home, Gannon heads here and practically stalks everyone who's had a conversation with Finn. Weird. I hope these phone logs help answer how Gannon knew Finn was here."

TWENTY-FOUR

The following morning, I walked into Belle's Beans hoping for more than a cup of coffee — though coffee was something I desperately needed after staying awake most of the night worrying about Finn and Tom. Even though Candace asked for the BOLO from her cell phone, it had since been picked up by many police officers all over the county and subsequently did get on the police scanner. I was sure people in town were talking about more than the newest murder and a missing adolescent. Maybe someone had seen Finn last night — or better yet, this morning. I sure hadn't heard a word from him — nor had I heard from Tom or Candace yet today.

I forced a smile when the Belle of the Day greeted me. I ordered a large coffee with an extra shot of espresso and doctored it with half-and-half and plenty of sugar. I felt as if my brain was about as functional as a plate of scrambled eggs. Nothing made sense; nothing seemed logical. I couldn't even remember everything Candace and I had talked about last night, but I did recall we both still couldn't figure out how Rory Gannon found his way to Mercy in the first place.

The crowd in the coffee shop all seemed to be staring at me as I wound between tables and took a spot right in the middle of the room. A few people smiled and nodded. If anyone knew anything about Finn or about Gannon's death, I might be able to overhear their whispers.

Belle Lowry, the kind and savvy owner of Belle's Beans, swooped to my table from out of nowhere and sat down across from me. She said, "Whatever have you gotten yourself into this time, sweetie?"

As usual, her snowy hair was perfectly coiffed and her coral lipstick had been applied in a straight line on both lips. At least she hadn't missed below her lips like I'd seen her do at times. Her familiar and kind presence had a settling effect.

"Nothing good, Belle, that's for sure," I answered.

"Did you really find a stranger dead in Tom Stewart's backyard?" she said.

"I did. I was searching for poor Dashiell

and got more than I bargained for," I said.

"Is the young man involved? Tom's stepson?" she asked.

She was fishing for information, but I was the one who needed to do the fishing. I tried to change it up by saying, "What have you heard? And don't be shy. I'm sure it's plenty."

She laughed. "Me? Shy? No one's ever accused Belle of such a thing." She leaned toward me. "Everyone's talking about Tom and Karen, two of the most private people I've ever known. Not to mention Tom's brother. What're the odds of Bob Cochran showing up the same time as Tom's stepson? I can't hardly figure out what's going on with that family."

There it was. Out of Belle's mouth often came the most obvious observations. I'd never even considered the timing of Bob's arrival, but Belle was right to wonder whether it was coincidence. Hoping to mine more gold, I said, "You know Bob's name. What have you heard?"

"Oh, I know Bob. He lived with Karen for a short spell before Ed came into her life. Never had two pennies of his own to rub together, so Karen let him stay with her. Something happened about five years ago and he up and left. An argument is all the grapevine could glean." She smiled. "*Glean* was one of my crossword puzzle words this morning. They say use a word three times and it's yours. Got two more times to go."

"I see. No one ever mentioned him, so I was surprised when I met him," I said.

"You mean Tom never mentioned him," she said. "He was none too happy about Bob leeching off their mother. When Bob left, Tom was singing a happy tune, I tell you. Fresh off his divorce, he'd been pretty mopey beforehand. She's here, too. Hilary. Been in here drinking coffee several times. She's a lovely-looking woman but there's something about her. You are a much better match for our Tom."

I felt the heat of a blush. Tom and I hadn't exactly made our budding relationship public. Before I could reply, Belle's face lit up.

She said, "Speak of the devil, look what the cat dragged in. A man who needs a serious coffee fix."

It was Tom, looking completely exhausted and defeated.

Belle rose and worked her way between tables to the counter. She patted Tom's arm and then pointed my way. Tom looked at me, but couldn't seem to muster even a small smile.

He bought his coffee and came to my table. "You haven't heard anything or you wouldn't be sitting here alone," he said. "I had no luck either. He's simply vanished, Jillian."

I reached across the table and squeezed his hand. "He'll turn up once he thinks things through. But where have you been?"

"At every convenience store, gas station and truck stop within a fifty-mile radius." He withdrew his hand and sipped his coffee, set the cup down and stared into the black liquid. "I plan to make flyers with his picture when I can get back into my house. Finn didn't feel safe here, and that's my fault. I have to make him understand how much he means to me."

"He knows how much he means to you. He's scared, that's all. Wouldn't you be? He didn't want to talk to Hilary when she showed up and maybe he couldn't even stand to hear her voice," I said.

Tom's eyes met mine. "Why did Hilary have to tell him about his father by shouting about his murder through a locked door? I know she's cold, but come on. No wonder he ran."

"She doesn't seem like the kind of person who thinks things through," I said. "She wanted to talk to Finn and thought she could get him to open the door with some shocking news. It was a little selfish."

"A *little?*" He laughed contemptuously. "As for not thinking things through, I'm afraid you're wrong. She thinks everything through. She knew exactly what she was doing. She wanted him to feel guilty and she succeeded. I know how Finn thinks. He's out there somewhere beating himself up for refusing to talk to his father before the man died."

"I've had such little contact with her I was trying not to be judgmental," I said.

Finally he smiled. "Because you think things through in a far different way. You give folks the benefit of the doubt. Wish the cop left inside me would allow me to do the same."

"You had no luck out on the road?" I said. "No one has seen anyone who might possibly be Finn?"

He shook his head. "The only thing I accomplished was buying a new phone. Give me yours and I'll program in the number. If Finn calls looking for me, you can give him this."

I took out my phone and handed it to him. While he started adding the details to my contact list, I said, "You think Finn will call me and not Karen?"

He looked up briefly. "He loves Karen, but he'll call you."

With Tom intent on his task and me watching, I was surprised when a uniformed Candace arrived at our table. Unsmiling, she pulled out a chair and sat down.

Uh-oh. What's wrong? I thought.

Looking straight at Tom, she said, "When were you going to tell me?"

"What are you talking about?" he said, handing me my phone and clipping his new one to his belt.

She said, "A little birdie at the bank called me up. Told me there's something I should know. Don't make me dial Liam's number and get him to go all legal on you, Tom Stewart. Tell me why you gave Finn money."

Tom looked at her. "I didn't exactly *give* him money."

Keeping her voice low, she leaned in and said, "We have your picture at the ATM, standing with Finn right next to you. Last time I checked, those machines don't spit out chocolate bars."

"You think I bankrolled him?" Tom said. "Gave him enough money to get out of town? If I did that, why did I spend all night looking for him?"

Candace's face relaxed and her brows came together in thought. "Sorry. Guess that's true. Why would you?"

I said, "Maybe Finn needed a little cash, Candace. When's the last time you walked around without any money in your pocket?"

Candace looked at Tom. "So Finn needed a few dollars in his pocket because . . . well, just because?"

Tom took a few seconds and then sighed. "He lost his wallet somewhere between North Carolina and here. Lost his phone, too. He wanted to buy a new one. What kid can live without a cell phone these days?"

This jibed with what Candace told me last night — and Tom was right. Every teenager owned a phone. I remembered Finn playing with my phone when we were at the diner, recalled how content he seemed.

"You say you were giving him a gift?" Candace said, sounding skeptical again.

What isn't *she saying? She must know something more,* I thought.

Tom ran a hand through his hair. He looked so worn out and rundown. "Not a gift. The money was his. I'd set up a joint account with him when I split with his mother. Hilary didn't know anything about it. For every dollar Finn earned cutting lawns or doing odd jobs, I matched it. And yes, his asking for cash yesterday doesn't look good."

"You went to the bank yesterday?" I asked softly.

He nodded. "We stopped at the ATM right before we came to your place."

"Anything else I should know?" Candace said.

"You already know what's important," Tom said. "He's a frightened kid. He ran because he heard Rory was dead and he couldn't face it."

"Jillian and I looked at the security videos last night and we came to the very same conclusion," Candace said. "But after talking to Hilary this morning, I'm beginning to wonder if Finn might have left before Hilary came by."

"Why are you wondering?" I said. "The time he left seems to match up with when she said she was talking to him through the door."

"Because," Candace said, "I asked her at the station if she heard Yoshi barking when she was talking to Finn through the door. She said no."

"Ah, yes. He would have barked," I said. "What does this mean?"

Tom folded his arms and seemed to draw into himself. He said, "What it means is that Hilary is a liar. She wants you to believe Finn was already gone. That way, she can try to make us all believe nothing she might have said made him run. Lets her off the hook."

"Tom, you have big issues with your ex — and probably for good reason. But you should know I checked her alibi for the day Nolan died and for the days before," Candace said. "She was at a job fair in North Carolina at the time Nolan Roth was trying to beat information out of you concerning Finn. Plus, she went to several interviews the day Roth died."

"What about an alibi for the time Gannon was killed? Where was she then?" he asked.

"I have her statement," Candace said. "I will talk to people and verify her second alibi. I don't know the woman, and please don't believe for a minute I'm about to take her word for anything." None of us spoke for several seconds and finally Candace continued. "I'm here at this table talking to you because I'm your friend. If you know where Finn is, if you have any idea at all, you need to tell me right now."

"Like I was telling Jillian, I've searched everywhere I know to look. He's disappeared. That's why I need to be at home, in case he calls or shows up. Is the crime scene cleared?"

She nodded. "We just finished up. Didn't

find a thing."

"Good. You know where to find me." He stood, pushed his chair away and walked toward the exit.

He didn't make eye contact with me before he got up, but even so, I could almost feel his sadness penetrating my skin. I looked at his back and then at Candace.

She said, "Go after him, silly. The man's hurting inside."

I caught up with Tom before he reached his van. "He'll come back. I'm sure of it."

He looked down at me. "I want to believe you're right. But right now, hope seems like a scary thing. Mind if I talk to you later? I need sleep. Maybe I can sort this all out in my head after I recharge my battery."

I reached up with both hands and brought his face to mine, kissed him right there on Main Street for everyone to see.

His lips lingered for a moment and then he was gone.

Back inside Belle's Beans, I rejoined Candace, who was ordering a coffee to go.

As she waited, she said, "How'd it go?"

"He's exhausted," I said, "and I know he's still blaming himself for leaving Finn behind when he divorced Hilary."

"He set up the joint bank account and kept in touch with Finn. What more could he have done?" she said.

"Nothing," I said. "But he doesn't see it that way right now."

"We didn't get any tips on Finn," Candace said. "What bothers me most is I went to the Pink House and talked to Hilary Roth this morning, and though she asked about Finn, she never called the station once during the night to see if we'd found him. I'm not a mother, but I've known moms whose kids ran away. Most of the time they're frantic with worry."

"Maybe she didn't seem frantic because she knows where Finn is," I said.

Candace cocked her head. "Hmm. Interesting theory. Hadn't considered the possibility. Maybe she and I need to have another little chat." Candace nodded toward the table where we'd been seated. "Want the rest of your coffee?"

"I *need* the rest of my coffee," I said.

Candace's cell rang and as she answered, my mind began turning over possibilities. If Hilary knew where Finn was, it wouldn't be because he told her. Was her story about telling him about Rory Gannon's death true — or was it a lie, just like Tom said? I didn't know. But just the mere idea that she knew where Finn might be gave me goose bumps.

Candace disconnected from her call. "Got

word the complete tech reports on both phones are in. Maybe they'll give me a lead on who killed these men," she said. "Check with you later."

After she was gone and I was headed for my minivan, I asked myself why Candace hadn't considered the possibility Hilary might actually know where Finn was. Or was she trying *not* to tell me something police-related, hoping I'd figure it out for myself. If so, what?

I took a long sip of my coffee, which was quickly going cold, hoping the caffeine would kick in soon. Fumbling for my keys in my back pocket, I realized I'd parked right by one of Mercy's forest green coin-operated newspaper boxes. I found change as well as my keys and bought a paper. The giant, block-letter headline read: MORE DEATH.

I read quickly, but found nothing in the story I didn't already know. The byline belonged to Kara, and I decided to call her and see if anything new had come to her attention since she wrote the story. When I reached her, she said she was on her way to take tile samples over to her property and maybe I could meet her and help her decide what she should put in her new kitchen.

Sounded like an excellent distraction.

Twenty-Five

The sunny days seemed to be over as dark clouds clustered in the west. I carried my umbrella up the new stone walkway leading to Kara's soon-to-be front door. She greeted me before I could even knock.

We hugged and she glanced out at the sky. "Another cold front on the way, I expect."

Once inside, she led me to the back of the house, where about ten different ceramic tiles were laid out on the kitchen floorboards.

Her hair was in a ponytail and she was wearing a big flannel shirt and blue jeans. She stood, hands on hips, looking down at the tiles. "What do you think of these?"

I let my eyes travel over the tiles, some big, some small and all earth tones. I pointed a toe at a large mottled beige and brown tile. "This one would complement the brown granite you picked out for your countertop."

She nodded, still looking down. "Making all these choices — tile, brick, stone, appliances, paint colors — is proving harder than I thought." She looked at me then. "But in a good way. Your tough times aren't good at all. You okay after last night?" She rubbed my upper arm sympathetically.

"I'm worried, Kara. Finn ran away again. Tom drove around all night looking for him, but no one has seen or heard from him."

"Shondra, my girl who monitors the scanner, told me she heard something about Finn disappearing. Did he go before or after he heard about his father's murder?" she said.

"Apparently it was after." I explained how Hilary had told Finn about Gannon's death.

Kara cocked her head. "What is wrong with her? Though I suppose someone who marries two men who went to jail and who later ended up murdered might not be too competent at thinking through her choices and examining possible consequences."

"Don't forget she also married Tom, who is a far cry from the likes of Nolan Roth or Rory Gannon," I said.

"She slipped into a period of good judgment, then ruined it by cheating on Tom," Kara said.

"You're right," I said. "But after meeting

her and talking to her, those mistakes don't seem to match up with what I've seen. She seems, well, *nice.* Karen really likes her and believes Tom has been way too hard on her."

"Karen loves Finn. I'm willing to bet she'd do anything to keep him in her life — even kiss up to a woman who did wrong by her son." Kara's attention returned to the tiles.

"You're probably right," I said. "Since Hilary was once close to Tom, I've been giving her the benefit of the doubt. Guess I don't want to seem jealous — not that I am."

Kara laughed. "You don't have a jealous bone in your body. You know who's *nice?* You. Way too nice, if you ask me."

"What do you mean?" I asked.

"You don't know how to say no," she said. "You put everyone ahead of yourself. I'm afraid you'll burn out one day."

"No, working in the textile arts business burned me out and is why I left to come here," I said. "I can only be true to myself — and for the most part, that means thinking the best of people before they show me differently."

"I guess I wouldn't want you to change. You're pretty special." She knelt and picked up a creamy tile, one shinier than the others. "I like this one, but I'm afraid it would show every streak and smudge."

"I think you're right," I said. "Sorry I missed seeing you last night, by the way. Were all the neighbors hanging around in the street when you got to Tom's house — now known as *the crime scene?*"

"Of course. Strange how people seemed to lose interest when they found out Rory Gannon was a stranger, not a Mercy citizen. I overheard one man being interviewed by an officer, though. He said he'd seen a guy fitting Gannon's description hanging around Tom's house."

"When did he see him?" I asked.

Kara pressed her thumb on the tile she held and then tilted it back and forth in the dull light coming through the windows. "Ah," she said. "This one even picks up fingerprints. I can narrow the choice by one, anyway." She set the tile on the floor face-down.

"When, Kara?" I said.

"Sorry. When what?"

I repeated the question.

"Day before yesterday," she said. "I talked to the neighbor after the officer was done with him, hoping to get an angle for the paper. The neighbor said he asked the stranger if he was looking for Tom and the guy mumbled something about how his boy, Finn, needed to hear something important, that he had to find him. Then the neighbor said he took off."

"Gannon was all over town and he obviously knew all the places Finn might be," I said.

"Even here." Kara shuddered. "I, for one, am glad he won't be coming back."

My phone rang and while Kara squatted in front of her tiles, her fist supporting her chin, I took a call from Karen.

"Jillian, I need your help. I can't do it. I know I should be able to, but I simply cannot."

"Slow down, Karen," I said. "What are you talking about?"

"This blood sugar thing," she said. "I've tried several times, even had Ed hold the cat for me and still no luck. Dashiell's poor ears don't seem to have a drop of blood left. Ed had to go to the shop for a delivery from a yard sale in Woodcrest. He said I'd figure it out, but he's wrong. I can't."

Tom was probably home, just a few steps down the street, but he'd been up all night. I decided I could handle this problem while he got some rest. "Why don't I swing by and help you?"

"Would you? Oh, how very sweet."

I told her to expect me in about twenty

minutes, since Kara's place was pretty far out of town.

I drove by Tom's house on the way to see Karen. A large wad of crime scene tape stuffed in the garbage can at the end of his driveway brought back last night's events all too vividly. I could picture Gannon's leg sticking out from under the holly and blinked away the image.

Though I expected to find Karen alone with Dashiell, I was at first surprised when Bob answered the door holding a coffee mug. Then I remembered Morris brought him here last night.

After I said hello as politely as I could, I said, "You've seen Dashiell get tested. You didn't think you could help your mother?"

"Cats and I do not get along," he said.

I couldn't hide my dislike for him anymore. "Ah. Maybe that explains why an indoor cat like Dashiell ended up outside not once, but twice while in your care."

"A little fire from the cat lover. I like it." Bob gestured toward the kitchen. "They're in there."

I followed the smell of freshly made coffee and found poor Dashiell backed in a corner with Karen crouched in front of him, her hand extended. She turned to look at me and I saw misery in her eyes.

"I'm no good at this, Jillian. Thank you for coming."

I said, "Has he had his insulin?"

She stood. "I did manage the shot. Those are easy."

I didn't tell her she probably should have tested his sugar level *before* giving him his insulin, because I didn't want to upset her any more than she already was. Seeing how unhappy she was, I guessed the cat wasn't her biggest problem. She was worried about Finn, first and foremost.

"A friend called me and said Finn ran away again," Karen said. The muscles near her left eye began to twitch. "I'm sure Tom didn't say anything because he thinks I'll have another meltdown. But I am determined to stay strong, even though it's difficult after two murders. You don't think he's been harmed, do you?"

"Like you, I'm worried. But from what we know, he left on his own. Maybe he just needs time to think about everything," I said, hoping this was true.

"I trust you, Jillian. You'd tell me if you heard from him, wouldn't you?" she said.

"Absolutely." I squatted next to Dashiell and extended the back of my hand. "I'm sure he'll be in touch. He got a little frightened, is all. Just like this guy."

Dashiell rubbed my hand with the side of his face and began to purr. I said, "Why don't you pour yourself a cup of coffee, go into the living room and I'll take care of Dashiell?"

Karen thanked me again, got her coffee and left us. The glucose monitor kit was lying open on the counter and I lifted Tom's tabby boy and carried him across the kitchen. He seemed heavier than just a few days ago, which was good. Diabetic cats can drop weight fast. Not wanting to set him on the countertop like I'd done when he was unconscious over at Tom's the other day, I took him and the kit to the small kitchen table. I sat and simply held him for a moment, petting and soothing him. Then, without any trouble, I pricked his ear and tested his sugar level. It was one forty, a little high, but he'd had a rough morning and stress affects diabetic cats exactly the same way it affects humans. It raises their blood sugar. His insulin was probably already working.

He jumped off my lap, sat at my feet and began to groom himself. I pulled the monitor, needles and alcohol wipes all together, ready to return them to their little leather pouch. I'd previously set them all on a crumbled paper that had apparently been rescued from destruction. I picked up the paper and smoothed it out.

I realized it was a financial statement of some sort and I wouldn't have paid it any mind if I hadn't seen Finn's name on the top. Did Karen know about Finn's joint account with Tom? I pulled the sheet closer while putting the blood testing equipment away.

Finnian Gannon's name was indeed on the top, but not paired with Tom's name. The other person on this account was Karen Stewart. I wasn't too surprised. No doubt she loved him, but it was the amount of money I saw near the bottom of the page that made me catch my breath. *More than a million dollars.*

Karen Stewart, who lived with our town junk collector in a cute and modest home, was wealthy. Or rather, she and Finn were wealthy. *Wow.*

"Interesting reading, huh?" came a voice from the kitchen entry. It was Bob.

I jumped at the sound of his voice and rested a hand on my chest. "You scared me. This paper was just sitting here and —"

"Made your eyes pop, didn't it?" He walked into the kitchen and sat next to me.

I focused on putting the sugar testing

things back in the leather case and zipped it up.

"You were taking a peek at the reason I'm so pissed off at my mother," Bob said.

"T-this is none of my business," I said, getting up.

"Oh, but you're involved with my brother," he said. "You really should know all the family secrets. See, until I came here and hacked into my mother's computer, I wasn't sure exactly how much money she owed me. Now I do."

"I told you I don't owe you anything, Robert." Karen had arrived in the kitchen. Pretty hard not to hear everything that went on in this small house.

"We have a neutral party who can play mediator. Let's hear Jillian's opinion on this." Bob picked up the paper and waved it in the air.

I shook my head vehemently. "No. Please don't ask me to get involved."

Karen was standing right in my path if I left through the dining room, and I was just about to say good-bye and make a dash for the back door when Dashiell leaped straight up and onto my shoulder. His claws dug into my back and I winced, but he retracted them almost at once. I held him steady and he began to purr. Poor guy had probably been listening to these two argue all morning.

"Jillian, the nice big numbers you see at the bottom of the paper here? See?" Bob pointed at the total. "This is money my father earned. This money belongs to me and Charlie, not to some onetime step-grandson from a cheating mother and a jailbird stepfather. Oops, I forgot. Nolan's dead and so is Gannon."

Karen took a deep breath. She sounded surprisingly calm when she said, "Your father left both you and Charlie a good amount of money. Money he thought would tide you over until you found employment. Money you squandered, Bob. It's not Finn's fault his share has grown because I saved it for him."

Bob's face flushed. "My dad left the money to you, *Mom.* Not to a kid who isn't even related to us. This account should be part of an estate *I* inherit. See, I can wait until you die to get what's mine. Or maybe I should say, I can *hardly* wait."

Karen's face paled. Mine probably did too after hearing him spew such scorn and disrespect.

He turned to me abruptly. "Doesn't my solution make perfect sense, Jillian?"

"No," I said softly but firmly. "Karen can

do whatever she wants with her money. You came here to intimidate her, not visit Tom. Am I right?"

"Tom's latched on to one smart lady," Bob said with a sneer. "I've always envied him. You're not only loyal to him and his cat, you're loyal to his mother. But then you didn't have to grow up with a woman who drank herself to sleep by midday. You didn't have to be embarrassed when she lost her driver's license — how many times was it, Mom? Like five times? Oh, and the number five matches how many times you got married. What a gal."

I swallowed, wasn't sure I should say anything more, but then felt I had to. "Things didn't go well for you, Bob," I said. "I understand your pain. But rather than being consumed by anger, perhaps you could get some professional help."

He stared at me for a second, held up the paper and crumpled it into a ball. He tossed it at Karen and then stomped out through the back door.

I realized I was clutching Dashiell tightly, but he didn't seem to mind. Nice to have a cat in my arms to help keep my blood pressure down.

Karen said, "I am so sorry you had to bear witness to our problems. I've made many mistakes in my life. I hurt Bob. I hurt all my boys by being irresponsible. But giving Bob money would be like throwing gasoline on a fire. See, I'm not the only one in this family battling addiction. Bob is clean now. After this morning, I only hope he stays that way."

Bob is clean? I understood then. No wonder he couldn't hold a job. "Has he been getting counseling, then?" I asked.

"Narcotics Anonymous," she said. "I offered to pay for private therapy. He refused, says he's cured. No one is ever cured of addiction, Jillian. We manage the disease, but we are never cured. I'm concerned about him."

I gave Dashiell a tiny hug and set him down. Then I went and gave Karen a big hug. I tend to be a hugger and, in the past, Karen was always stiff when I embraced her to say hello or good-bye. But we held each other tightly for several seconds as she said thank you over and over into my shoulder.

Twenty-Six

Deciding Dashiell should go home with me was an easy call. I could set the basement guest room up for him like I'd done for cat visitors in the past. Karen's stress would become Dashiell's stress and his blood sugar would end up all over the chart.

When we were leaving, Karen asked me to call her the minute Finn came back. She also asked if she could drop by my house later because she was sure Bob would start in on her again and she just couldn't take it. I told her I would be happy if she came for a visit. Perhaps Finn would show up by the time she came by. Maybe they'd even have a talk about all this money — money he could sure use for his education. But was this just wishful thinking on my part? Both Karen and Tom seemed to have great difficulty talking about their feelings or about the big issues. A million dollars was a very big issue. But then I realized Karen might have kept this secret because she wanted to make sure Finn, and not Hilary and Nolan Roth, ended up with this fortune.

Since Tom had brought Dashiell to my house before, he wasn't a complete stranger to Syrah, Chablis and Merlot. But there was still plenty of hissing when I brought him into the kitchen. Most folks don't realize cats never meow to each other as a form of communication — even cats who live together. But they do hiss and even spit when dogs and other cats invade their territory. Even though they knew Dashiell, it didn't mean they'd throw out the welcome mat.

I carried him down to the basement and spent a good while fixing up his digs, getting him a pillow, a litter box and food. He seemed content when I finally closed the door after me — shutting out my three inquiring fur friends. They didn't follow as I hurried upstairs. I was sure they wanted to play the "paw under the door" game with Dashiell. I was certainly in a hurry, though, as I'd forgotten to refrigerate the insulin.

I put the small bottle of insulin away as soon as I got upstairs. Breakfast seemed an eternity ago and I fixed a sandwich and ate at the small table, watching a drizzling rain through the window without even tasting the ham and cheese. I was thinking how

Tom would awaken soon — hopefully rested and ready to use all his technology tools and contacts in the private security world to find Finn. I sure hoped he'd call me so I could help. I so wanted to help.

Just as I finished eating, Chablis came up the basement stairs, obviously tired of waiting around for Dashiell to learn how to open the door and make an appearance. I was about to cuddle up with her on the couch and maybe take a rest — I'd slept very poorly last night — when my phone rang. It had to be Tom.

"Hey, Jillian. It's Allison," she whispered. My friend at the animal sanctuary didn't sound at all like her cheerful self.

"Is something wrong?" I asked.

"I need your help. Can you come over to the sanctuary?" She sounded rushed and troubled.

"Sure, but what's going on?" I said.

"Just come. Now." She disconnected.

Allison never asks for help unless she really needs it. I decided this weather called for a little rain gear and I put on my flowered Wellies and a slicker. She might need me to rescue a reluctant cat from a tree. I'd helped her before, coaxing stubborn cats from odd places. We were a good team.

The slap of my windshield wipers seemed

to offer a relaxing rhythm on the drive to the sanctuary. I had time to think about the argument between Bob and Karen — and what an awkward and uncomfortable few moments I'd experienced. But Karen opened up, and in his own way, so did Bob. If they wanted a therapist, however, I wasn't the woman for the job. They needed professional help to heal the rifts in their family.

Then I thought about all the money — and realized Bob might not be the only one who knew about a small fortune within Finn's grasp. Maybe Nolan Roth had found out somehow. That would explain why he wanted Finn back at his house. If he'd searched Finn's computer and found his communications with Tom, perhaps he'd found more — found evidence of lots and lots of money to be had. But I still didn't believe Tom or Finn knew anything about the million dollars. Tom may have kept secrets, but in the past few days, he'd told me what I thought was everything there was to know. After all he'd shared, why keep the money a secret? And then there was Hilary. Karen had been in contact with her. Maybe she knew about the money. Tom said that's all she cared about and she would surely want Finn to stay home if he was about to become a millionaire. Yes. It made perfect sense why everyone was after this kid. Candace needed to know and I would call her after I helped Allison.

I'd just about reached the sanctuary when my phone rang. I saw Candace's name on the caller ID and answered, wondering if she was psychic or something. Or perhaps she'd found Finn.

"Get this," Candace said without saying hello.

"Please tell me you found him."

"No," she said. "But things are starting to fall into place. The calls and texts on these two phones are very interesting. I'm still poring over them, but guess who called Rory Gannon a week ago?"

"You mentioned Nolan Roth probably phoned the halfway house using Tom's phone and —"

"No. This is from Finn's phone. He called his biological father," she said.

I pulled into the curving drive leading to the sanctuary. "But Gannon had Finn's phone, so he could have called the place where he was living, maybe to check in at the halfway house or —"

"This was *last week,*" she said. "Before Finn left North Carolina and while he still had his phone. Why would he call his father?"

"I — I don't know. He sure never told any of us he'd talked to him. He seemed afraid of the man." Or was he simply avoiding the subject of Rory Gannon after a conversation that might not have gone too well?

"Not afraid enough, it seems," she said. "Their conversation lasted twenty-seven minutes. Meanwhile, if Tom's time line about when Nolan Roth had *his* phone is correct, Roth also called Gannon, and more than once. Seems like everyone was talking to the guy."

I pulled the minivan into the small area reserved for sanctuary visitors. "You said *if* Tom's time line is correct. What do you mean?"

"Talking to Tom is next on my to-do list," she said. "Now that I have this printout of dates and times, I want to go over it with him. He wasn't completely focused the first time I talked to him about what went on in North Carolina."

"He's home." I checked the time on my phone. "He's had time to catch up on his sleep and you know he'll want to help." Allison appeared in the doorway to the sanctuary and I rolled down the van window and held up one finger asking her to give me a minute. The rain had stopped but the air was chilly.

Allison nodded in understanding.

"Candace, I learned something today you should know." Karen and Bob might not want me sharing about their major money spat today, but a million dollars is a lot of motive for someone to hatch a plan to get their paws on it. I hurriedly explained about the money and the argument between Bob and Karen *about* the money.

"Holy-o-heck, talk about motive," Candace said. "This is huge. Tom's shared account with Finn is small beans compared to this. Did Finn know about this account?"

"Good question. My guess is that he didn't."

"My mind is flying all over the place," she said, sounding excited. "The calls to Gannon, his arriving in town, his hanging around. What if we've been blind, Jillian? What if Nolan Roth hired Gannon to take care of *Karen?* With this joint account, Finn would inherit and become one very rich teenager."

"Oh my gosh," I said. "And Gannon double-crossed Nolan, killed him and kept trying to make contact with his long-lost son — the son he probably didn't care about at all but who would become wealthy and perhaps generous. Maybe Finn's call to him was a return call. Or even a call in response to an e-mail from Gannon."

"This is great information. I need time to piece together scenarios. Meanwhile, we still have a killer out there. Keep your doors locked and your security system armed." She disconnected.

She had no clue I wasn't at home, which was probably a good thing. Seconds later I removed my damp slicker and embraced Allison. I said, "Something is wrong. I heard it in your voice and now see it written all over your face. What can I do to help?"

"I figured you were the right person to call for this problem," she whispered. She fixed strands of her brunette hair over one ear. A smattering of rain dotted her gray sweatshirt.

"Why are we whispering?" I said.

"I'll show you, but be very quiet." She carefully led me through the cramped office where so many wonderful pet adoptions had taken place. Allison cracked the door leading to the sanctuary examining room and told me to have a look.

I peered through the crack. There, lying on a mat with his spotted dog curled next to him, was Finn, fast asleep.

My hand went to my lips and relief washed over me. I quietly shut the door and then whispered, "How . . . how did he end up here?"

She pulled me away from the door and said, "I'll explain. But first, want coffee? Shawn made it about an hour ago — before he left for the feed store to pick up dog and cat food."

Snug, their African gray parrot, was perched above us and said, "Put on the pot, Allison. Put on the pot."

Allison looked up at Snug and put her finger to her lips. "Shhh."

He proceeded to respond with several "shhhs" of his own.

I said, "Yes. Sure, I'll have coffee. I've been living on the stuff, so one more cup might perk me up."

Once we both had our cups full, Allison sat behind her battered old desk and I took the lawn chair she used for visitors. I hung my slicker over the back of the chair.

"How long has Finn been here?" I said.

"He came this morning," she said. "Surprised the heck out of me."

"I don't understand. Why did he come *here?*" I sipped the coffee and was instantly reminded how strong Shawn liked his brew.

"Yoshi was limping. Apparently they'd been walking down back roads and through fields all night, from what little he told me.

He said he turned around and came back this way when he knew the dog was hurt. He still had my card and thought I could help."

"Is Yoshi all right?" I said.

"He had a pebble stuck between the pads on his back paw. That can be pretty painful. I removed it and Finn was ready to head out again. But I pointed out the pebble had done a little damage — nothing serious — but Yoshi needed a day off from walking." She smiled. "I didn't add that Finn looked like he could use some rest himself."

"Did he say anything about this latest journey he was taking?" I said. "We've been worried sick."

"He said he'd caused trouble for everyone," Allison said. "If he were gone, Tom and Karen could go back to the way things used to be."

I blinked back tears of sadness and relief. "He's like Tom. He blames himself for everything. None of what's happened is his fault."

"I figured as much. You'd helped Finn before and you know what's going on with this kid." She paused to drink coffee and then said, "He did ask me not to call the police, which worried me. I took that to mean there's a lot more to this story I don't know."

"There's plenty I don't know, either. I am so grateful you called me." I held the coffee mug between both my hands, considering what to do next.

Suddenly the door to the examining room opened and an exhausted-looking Finn looked at Allison. "Why did you give me up?"

Twenty-Seven

Yoshi dashed through the door and jumped right into my lap. Good thing I'd managed to set the coffee down before his enthusiastic hello. He licked my face and his tail went crazy with happiness at seeing me. I wrapped my arms around the dog and held him close.

He allowed this for a few seconds and then rushed back to Finn. He did his jack-in-the-box routine until Finn held out his arms.

Clutching the dog close, Finn said, "Guess his foot is fine now. I can be on my way."

He wouldn't meet my gaze.

Allison said, "I put some antibiotic ointment with a tad of anesthetic on the abrasion between his toes, Finn. When it wears off, Yoshi will feel the pain in his foot again."

Finn looked at the floor and said a quiet, "Oh."

Allison rose. "Listen, man. I've been

happy to help you out with Yoshi twice. Now it's your turn to do me a favor. Sit here in my office and talk to Jillian. She's the best friend you'll ever have and she'll always be straight with you."

Allison walked over and tugged Finn by the upper arm, leading him to her ripped and worn office chair. "Sit. Yoshi knows how to obey that particular command and so should you."

She left us then, going through the door leading to the examining room and the kennels and cat cubicle room beyond.

Still hanging on to Yoshi, Finn said, "Are you pissed off at me?"

I smiled. "Never. I'm confused, though. Why did you leave?"

"My mother came to your house while y'all were gone. She started shouting things and putting on her hysterical act. The one where she pretends I'm the only person in the world who matters to her."

So she did do exactly what she said while waiting outside my house. "Did you ever consider she might be telling you the truth?"

Finn bit his upper lip and for the first time, even though he'd been through so much, tears filled his eyes. "No one except Tom believes me. Don't you get it? She *doesn't* care about me. Never has. A kid knows."

I sat back and took in the pain now etching his features. This sweet kid knew better than I ever would exactly who his mother was. "I get it. I truly get it. Question is, where do we go from here?"

"If I leave," he said with almost scary resolution, "if I get out of everyone's way, there'll be no more fighting, no more screaming through doors. If you think last night was the first time she ever yelled at me through a locked door . . . well, you'd be wrong."

"When moms aren't so good at being mothers, they sure know how to push our buttons," I said. "Maybe it's time you disconnected the switch."

He stared at me for several seconds and I saw the resolve to run away, the defense he'd used to cope more than once, transform into something different. Was I seeing his burgeoning knowledge there might be another way to deal with harsh realities and how unfair the world can be?

"You sound like you know what you're talking about — maybe from experience?" he said.

"You're perceptive. I'll tell you about my life one day. I was raised by my grandparents and it's complicated. As for now, folks are worried about you," I said.

"I know. Tom and Nana," he said. "I didn't mean to upset them. I just knew my mother would have her way. I'll probably end up back in North Carolina with her, won't I?"

"Why? You're an adult now. You can make your own decisions," I said.

Yoshi's ears pricked and he looked toward the ceiling. He'd noticed the parrot and barked several times in succession.

Snug answered with, "What a good dog. What a good dog."

I'm sure Snug had heard those words plenty of times around here.

Finn stared up in surprise. Guess he hadn't been introduced to Snug. "Whoa. That bird is so dope."

"His name is Snug," I said.

"Snug's a pretty bird," the parrot replied at the mention of his name.

"This would be a cool place to come, maybe volunteer," Finn said.

"I like your thinking. I know Tom and Karen would be so happy if you stayed in Mercy. It might involve some kind of pact about not scaring them to death by running off into the night, though."

Finn looked contrite. "I would promise

not to run — and keep my promise. I guess running away is for ten-year-olds, huh?"

"There is one problem," I said.

"What?" Finn seemed wary again.

"You were probably at Tom's place around the time of your biological father's murder. The police need to talk to you about it."

"I figured as much," he said.

"Did you see Rory Gannon in Tom's backyard?" I asked.

"N-no," he answered.

For the first time, I knew Finn was lying. Knew it as sure as I knew my own name. I placed my forearms on Allison's desk and leaned toward Finn. "You can tell me. Please, trust me. I can't help you if you don't tell me the truth."

Finn released a heavy sigh. "All right, he was standing there when I went outside. Just standing like a scarecrow or something. Freaked me out."

"What did you do?" I asked quietly. He couldn't have harmed Gannon. I was certain he couldn't.

"We stared at each other for what seemed like forever," Finn replied. "Then he said, 'I have to tell you something. It's real important.' "

"What did he tell you?" I said.

"Nothing. I was . . . okay, *afraid.* I told

him Tom needed to hear whatever it was he had to say and I was going to get him. That's when he took off."

"Did you tell Tom about this?" I asked.

"No. He was in such a good mood. We were having a great time and I only went out in his backyard for a minute. He has this creek running along his backyard and I wanted to see if there were fish in there." Finn hung his head. "Did I have something to do with getting the guy killed?"

"Of course not," I said. "Did he happen to show you anything — like your phone, maybe?"

"My phone? The one I lost?" Finn said.

"Yes. See, the police found your phone in his pocket when they searched his body. I thought maybe you'd had contact with Gannon at some point and he took your phone or —"

"Why would you think something like that? He creeped me out." Finn was getting agitated, but I had to plow through all this before I took him to town for a meeting with Candace.

"Here's the problem," I said. "They looked at your call log and apparently you phoned Mr. Gannon at the halfway house where he was living before you hitched rides to Mercy."

Finn pulled Yoshi closer and started shaking his head. "No way. I never called him. Sure, I found out where he was living. Thought about contacting him, but —"

"How did you find him?" I asked.

"Internet search," he said. "Rory Gannon's not a name like John Smith. Pretty easy search to get results for his name. I found newspaper archives about what he'd done to a police officer a long time ago. I'd thought about contacting him. See, once I decided I couldn't live with Mom and Nolan anymore, I thought he might want me. But I swear, after I read what he'd done, I knew he was probably a worse choice than staying at home."

I considered this for a few seconds and then said, "Did you delete the search about Gannon from your computer?"

"If you know anything about computers, you know you can never really delete anything completely. Why?"

I couldn't talk around it anymore. "Nolan searched your computer. He was probably checking it regularly. Pretty much spying on you."

"No way. The guy was a complete luddite. He wouldn't know how to get by my password." But after a moment of thought, I saw Finn's expression transform from scorn to understanding. "Unless he figured it out because he knew where I got Yoshi's name. My password was from a Mario Brothers game, and since Nolan ended up in this town he must have figured it out and discovered I e-mailed Tom saying I was thinking about coming to Mercy. No firm plans — just considering it. Maybe that pissed Nolan off."

I nodded in agreement. "And made him head straight for Mercy when you disappeared. So the password had something to do with the Mario Brothers game? I can see how he might have figured it out."

"Yup. So he came here and ended up dying in Tom's car," Finn said. "Why in *Tom's* car, though?"

"Because he drove Tom's Prius from North Carolina," I said.

"Huh?" Finn squinted at me, completely confused.

"Candace found a text luring you to the Prius. See, Nolan had Tom's phone. We know you were injured in the car and now we know how you got there."

Finn said, "I might have gotten into Tom's car willingly, huh? Pretty stupid thing to do.

"But even though I hated Nolan, I didn't shoot him. Deputy Carson hasn't changed her mind about that, has she? Or does she think I'm guilty of something because I ran?"

"No, she hasn't changed her mind," I said. "She knows you were sitting next to Nolan in the car. What we think happened is that Rory Gannon came upon the accident, or more likely *caused* the accident. He knocked you out and killed Nolan while you were sitting right there and unconscious. Then he took your phone and wallet. He probably didn't even know who you were until he opened up your wallet and saw your ID."

The color drained from Finn's face. "My father could have killed me. Instead, he tried to frame me by putting the gun in my backpack. Did he keep trying to find me afterward to confess because he felt guilty for setting me up?"

I blinked, thinking this was quite possible. "As far as what he wanted to tell you the day he was murdered? I have no idea."

Finn's eyes were closed and he was shaking his head. Yoshi sensed his rising anguish and licked his face. Finally Finn said, "I still don't understand. Why was Nolan in Tom's car? They hated each other. Or was Tom there, too?"

"Tom was with me. See, there's more you don't know, mostly because Tom has been protecting you, afraid for you to hear what Nolan did to him."

"He's not here to protect me now, so tell me," Finn said.

I did, including all the details about Nolan strong-arming Tom, making him drive to North Carolina. Finn's eyes stayed wide the whole time I talked. When I finished, I said, "Let me ask you this. Did you know about a large amount of money your mother and Nolan might have wanted to get their hands on?"

Finn said, "Tom and I have a bank account together. Did Nolan beat up Tom to get the money?"

I took a deep breath and let it out slowly. "How much money did you and Tom have in the account he set up for you?"

"Four thousand, three hundred twenty-nine dollars after what we took out yesterday. See, I needed a new cell, so we stopped at the bank for cash. I never got a chance to buy one, though."

Yoshi began to squirm and Finn released his hold on the dog. He jumped down and began sniffing around the office.

I said, "I'm not sure a few thousand dollars would have brought Nolan to town," I said.

"What money are you talking about,

then?" he said.

"I'm not sure," I said. Not sure it was my place to tell him how much money Karen had saved up for him. "Let me ask you this. During the time before you ran away, could Nolan or your mother have made a call to Rory Gannon using your phone?"

"Why would they?" he asked.

Why indeed.

TWENTY-EIGHT

The rain had picked up again by the time we were on the road back to my house to drop Yoshi off. I called Tom's new cell and it went straight to voice mail. I even tried his landline without any luck. He must still be out cold from exhaustion. So I called Candace to tell her Finn was with me.

"What a relief," she said. "Is he okay?"

"He's tired, but seems fine," I said, glancing at him and Yoshi sitting next to me. I smiled, so glad Allison called me before Finn took off again. I'd feel better, however, if the killer were in custody.

"Where are you?" Candace said.

"Driving to my place to drop off the dog. Then we're coming to see you. Is Tom there by any chance? I couldn't reach him."

"I just talked to him and he planned to take a shower and then come to the station," she said.

"Tell him about Finn as soon as he gets

there. We plan on driving to the station right away because Finn wants to give a statement. He saw Gannon yesterday afternoon, but I'll let him tell you what happened."

"Saw him? Uh-oh," she said.

"It was a brief encounter. Like I said, Finn can tell you what happened."

"Okay, make me wait," she said with a sigh. "Tom will be so happy to see Finn. I'm sure the answers to who killed Gannon are hiding somewhere in these two telephone logs. I've been searching through these calls for hours. It looks like Gannon was even trying to get to Finn through Hilary. A call was made to the Pink House yesterday on Finn's phone."

"How did Gannon know Hilary was staying there?" I asked.

"How did he know where you lived? Where Karen lived? Where Tom lived? Some of the texts on Finn's phone might help explain it. Finn asked Tom for his address in a text that went way back, well before he left to hitchhike here. But this texting jargon Finn used is making me crazy. I need a social networking workshop to understand this stuff."

"Ah, so Gannon read through old texts and found Tom's address on Finn's phone? Maybe hung around and started following whoever came and went from Tom's house?" I said.

"Very possible," she said. "Tom's gonna be pretty upset when he finds out his dear brother messed with his cameras, though. See, we tried to download the videos, hoping to see if they caught the killer on tape. But Bob managed to screw them up and we got nothing. He claims it wasn't intentional; he was just curious. But I'm not so sure."

"Hmm. That seems suspicious," I said. "Listen, we might try Tom one more time. In fact, I think I'll let Finn try to reach him this time."

I disconnected and handed my phone to Finn. Yoshi sniffed at it, but since my phone obviously didn't smell like bacon, he turned his attention to the passenger-side window.

"Call Tom," I said. "He programmed his new number into my phone this morning."

I didn't have to give Finn any instructions. Soon he was talking to Tom and, from the kid's expression, this was the best thing in the world for Finn — and probably for Tom, too.

As we pulled into my driveway, Finn said, "No, Tom. Don't come to Jillian's. We're dropping off the dog and we'll meet you at the weird police station —" Finn looked at me. "How long will it take?"

I said, "We'll get the dog settled, make sure Dashiell is okay — oh, tell Tom I have his cat. His mom couldn't quite manage a diabetic cat right now. We should be at the police station within thirty minutes, tops."

Finn said, "Did you hear what she said?" A pause and then Finn said, "Good deal. We'll see you soon."

I pulled up close to the back door and Finn took Yoshi to pee before we went inside. No cats greeted me when I went inside. They were probably all downstairs waiting patiently for the door to Dashiell's guest suite to open.

I hurried down the stairs.

Sure enough, my fur kids were parked outside the door and I cracked it hoping to see how Dashiell was faring. The second I did, the waiting Dashiell escaped and made a beeline for the stairs.

My three raced after him.

I followed, wishing I had the energy of four cats.

Finn and Yoshi were just coming inside and the dog decided to join this game of chase.

"This isn't how I planned our homecoming," I said. "Can you corral Yoshi?"

The animals were all after each other's tails in my living room. Yoshi was barking, cats were hissing and Finn was shouting commands to his dog. Obedience class works only to a point, I decided. The dog was having way too much fun to obey.

The pursuit went down the hall and ended up in my bedroom. I arrived on Finn's heels in time to see Chablis dart under the bed, but Syrah and Merlot have never shown much in the way of fear. They were on my bed, while Yoshi stood on the floor keeping a safe distance. He was barking like crazy. I had no idea where Dashiell was hiding.

Finally Finn was able to grab Yoshi and hoist him into his arms. "No, Yoshi. You stay with me."

Just then, I heard a voice calling my name. Karen's voice. What the heck was she doing here?

Finn heard it, too, and we both went out into the hall, with him calling, "Nana? Is that you?"

She stood at the end of the hall. She'd changed since I'd seen her this morning and wore a pink fuzzy sweater. Mohair? Really?

She said, "I knew you'd come back and I knew exactly where you'd come. Jillian has been a rock while the rest of us were embroiled in emotion."

Just then Hilary Roth appeared behind Karen. "Hope you don't mind I came along.

I've been so worried about Finn, but I knew he'd show up here sooner or later." She looked like she was wearing one of Karen's skirts — a gray tweed — with the black sweater I'd seen her in the first day we met.

I walked toward them, but Finn hung back. He said, "I forgot to lock the stupid door."

"Finn, don't be upset with me," Karen said. "I know you don't want to see your mother, but we have something so special to tell you. Please. Talk to us? For me, if not for your mother?"

I was standing halfway between Finn and a confrontation he might not be ready for. I turned to him. "You're the only one who can decide what's best for you. If you don't want to sit down with your mother right now, you need to tell her."

Finn's lips tightened and Yoshi whimpered as he looked up at him. He didn't look ready, not at all. But Finn and his mother surely had to talk sometime.

He surprised me by saying, "I'll hear you out. But only because Nana and Jillian think I should."

I led everyone into the living room. Hoping to make this visit brief and to the point, I didn't offer them tea.

Finn set Yoshi down by the couch at his

feet and told him to stay. His tone was harsher than usual with his beloved friend, but I knew this had more to do with Hilary's presence than with Yoshi's earlier failure to obey.

I chose to sit next to Finn for support, and Hilary and Karen sat in my two easy chairs opposite the sofa. I was still holding my phone and held it beneath my thigh. If this conversation got out of hand, I was ready to call Tom.

"What lies has she told you, Nana?" Finn said.

I closed my eyes. Not a great way to begin the conversation. I said, "Why don't we start with how you knew Finn would be here. I'm not sure I really understand."

"Oh, we weren't sure," Karen said. "But if Finn would contact anyone, it would be you or Tom. Since Tom has very hard feelings concerning anything involving Hilary, meeting here is perfect. Since you know about the money I've saved for Finn, we're hoping you can convince Tom I have a wonderful plan." She smiled.

I was observing Hilary, and something about this whole thing didn't seem right. Karen's comment about the money with Hilary present suggested Hilary knew about it. My question was, how long had she known?

"What money? What *plan?*" Finn said warily.

"A plan where you get to go to college," Hilary said. "I know you want to go, and I'm so sorry I haven't been —"

"Save it, Mom," Finn said.

I looked at Karen. "So Hilary knows you've been saving for Finn?"

"Oh yes," Karen said. "When Hilary and Thomas divorced, I assured her I would take care of Finn, though I didn't get specific except to say he would be comfortable for the rest of his life. Today, we've talked about how best to use the money and I've decided college seems a wonderful place to start."

Her naive smile made my chest tighten. Because Karen had no idea.

But I suddenly knew exactly who was behind everything.

I sidled closer to Finn, keeping my hand on my phone and hopefully out of sight. I looked at Finn, who seemed a tad confused at me edging so near. "You want to go to college, don't you?" I said. I tried to speak to him with my eyes, tried to warn him.

He knew the truth, probably the same instant I'd figured it out, because he said,

"You did all these horrible things. Didn't you, Mom?"

I tried to swallow, but my mouth had gone completely dry. I thought, *Only one extremely angry kid would be fearless enough to confront a murderer.*

Twenty-Nine

Karen said, "Whatever are you talking about, Finn? Your mother is contrite. She knows she's done wrong by you. But now she's ready to put her personal problems aside and focus on your future. She suggested once before she could manage any money I chose to share with you and we've agreed your college fund is a good place to start. Once you graduate, then of course, you'll be in charge. And you need a car, of course. She'll get you a car once you return to North Carolina. A little birdie named Tom said you wanted to attend a good college and your mother wants to work with me to make that happen."

Poor Karen, I thought, as I stared at Hilary. *She has no clue.*

Hilary's eyes hardened and her sweet Carolina drawl almost disappeared when she said, "Finn and Jillian don't believe a word of what you're saying. I could fool you, but not these two." She reached into her skirt pocket and pulled out a gun.

Karen gasped and Finn's arm, so close to mine, tensed.

"Do you plan to shoot all of us?" I said, trying to sound bold when I felt anything but. "How will you get your hands on Finn's money then?"

"Shut up and let me think," she said.

I heard a low growl from Yoshi and was troubled about what he might do.

Finn must have been worried too, because he started to get up. He looked like he wanted to attack before harm could come to us or his dog.

If I hadn't grabbed his sleeve and pulled him back down to the sofa, he probably would have gone after Hilary with fists flying. Yoshi, however, wasn't about to back down.

He stood and started barking at Hilary, ears erect. This was a ferocious bark, like none I'd heard from him before.

"Shut the stupid dog up, Finnian." Hilary pointed the gun at Yoshi.

Karen was leaning away from Hilary, her expression one of pure terror.

"Don't hurt him," Finn said. "I'll tie him up."

Hilary was glancing around and locked on

to the pantry door in the kitchen beyond. Then she looked at me. "Is that a broom closet?"

"Walk-in pantry," I said.

"That will do." Hilary stood. "Put him in there. Now."

Finn started to reach into his jeans pocket.

"What are you doing?" Hilary leveled the gun at Finn, her voice bordering on hysteria.

"Getting his leash," Finn said. "Or he might charge you, *Mom.*"

"Go ahead." Her face relaxed a tad, but her eyes were shifting left and right. She was thinking hard.

When Finn bent to attach the leash on Yoshi's collar, I said, "I'll hang on to him while you fasten the leash."

I bent over, in unison with Finn, and carefully slipped my phone into his back pocket. He turned slightly to acknowledge my action.

Hilary said, "Those two working together just warms your heart, doesn't it, Karen? She'd be a much better mother to Finn than I ever was."

"I — I'm frightened, Hilary," Karen said. "I don't understand why —"

"You *caused* all this," Hilary said. "If you hadn't waited until after Tom and I were divorced to tell me you planned to share money with Finn, I would never have left your son." She looked at Finn. "Put the dog away. Now."

Finn smartly held the leash in his left hand, covered his back pocket with the balled-up leash and took Yoshi to the kitchen.

"This is my fault. You're right," Karen said, tears beginning to stream down her face. "What do you want? I can give you money. How much do you want?"

"Bob tells me there's a million dollars in the account you set up for Finn — and here Nolan and I were only imagining maybe a hundred grand." She paused and waved the gun in Finn's direction. "Get back in here where I can see you."

I heard the pantry door close and Yoshi started barking immediately.

Finn returned to the sofa and said, "You will never get away with this. I've watched plenty of crime TV and the mothers who kill their kids don't do too hot in jail."

Hilary surprised us all by laughing. "There is so much you don't know." She looked at me. "I assume you have a computer?"

I nodded, though I didn't want to give her even that much information. But a gun tended to force compliance.

Hilary narrowed her eyes in thought,

seemed to be working through a plan in her head.

What bothered me more than anything, even more than the gun Hilary held, was Finn. Fear is an almost palpable thing and I didn't sense any fear coming from him. I remembered my thought from earlier this week — how fear is a gift we all need to protect us. No. Finn wasn't afraid. He might do something, might risk his life to vent his anger at his mother. Anger that was now so clearly justified. Why hadn't I believed what he and Tom had said over and over about Hilary's character? But there was no time for regrets, for the magic time machine to supply do-overs. I should have seen she was capable of murder.

Yoshi kept yapping and I could tell this was distracting to Hilary. Her face was flushed beneath her ivory makeup and she seemed to be getting angrier by the second.

Then my fear turned up a notch when Merlot came sauntering into the foyer like nothing was wrong. I took a deep breath, my own very real fear now centered on him. The only good thing about his arrival was that Hilary couldn't see him.

Stay there, I tried to telegraph to my big boy. *Please stay there.*

Hilary's back was to him and I was relieved when he sat where the foyer tiles met the wood floor. As he'd done when Hilary was here before, he sniffed the air. Did he smell the fear I felt for all of us? My fear we would all be killed?

"All right," Hilary said, her expression one of intense determination. "Here's what's going to happen." She turned to Karen. "But first, you know I'll use this gun, don't you?"

Karen nodded, abject fright still in her eyes.

Hilary pulled a folded piece of paper from her left pocket. "I was told I'd find this on the floor in your house. Someone who was very upset with you wadded it up."

The savings account statement. The one Bob had thrown at his mother.

Hilary went on, saying, "Bob isn't happy with you, Karen, so he made a deal with me. Or he thinks he did. I'd get my hands on the money — a college fund was something we knew you'd fall for — then I would share with him. Too bad I'll be gone before he can cash in."

Karen's eyes were wide as she kept nodding her agreement. "You can have the money. All of it. Just don't hurt anyone else."

"I plan to take you up on your offer," Hilary said. "Problem is, those two over there will stand in my way. Especially Finn, since he has a stronger dislike for me than anyone I know." The smile she directed at him was truly malevolent.

"You're plain evil." Finn's words carried the full force of his hatred for her. "You couldn't hide it from me or from Tom."

She smiled and said, "Your dog is making a lot of noise. And so are you. Both of you better shut up. Now." She refocused on Karen.

As Hilary kept the gun trained on us while speaking to Karen, Finn reached around to his back pocket.

No, I thought. *Not now. Not yet. She'll see.* I had no doubt Hilary would use the gun if she were threatened in any way.

But from the corner of my eye I saw he'd lifted the phone just enough to silence the ringer.

Whew. Good idea.

"You understand what I want you to do, Karen?" Hilary said.

I was so intent on Finn I hadn't heard. What was about to happen?

Karen stood and picked up the handbag she'd brought with her. She was so wobbly, she nearly fell. She said, "May I use your computer, Jillian?"

So polite. So like Karen, even when she

was obviously terrified.

Merlot stood as well and slinked to the left side of the foyer where a potted silk fern hid him.

"It's in my office down the hall," I said. "I'll have to log on. I assume you plan to have Karen transfer funds?"

"You are *such* a bright woman," she said sarcastically. "I had the foresight to set up an account in the Cayman Islands. Got the number right here." She tapped her temple with her free hand. "Problem is, there are three of you, too many to handle with only two eyes and one gun while we make the transfer. We'll need something to tie up Finn. Something in the house, because I won't be foolish enough to let you near a door to the outside. Stockings? Belts? What have you got?"

"Quilt bindings will work," I said. I figured she wasn't about to let go of the gun, so I would be the one tying up her son. Quilt bindings were flexible enough for what I had in my mind. I just wished I could telegraph my thoughts to Finn.

Hilary got up. "Come on, then. Get up and lead me to this office of yours. We have work to do."

We all started for the hall, Hilary behind us. I still feared Finn might do something crazy, like try to take his mother down. But I never expected what happened next.

Thirty

I heard a slight rustle behind me and turned around in time to see Merlot bounce from behind the fern and streak right in front of Hilary's feet.

She fell forward and I heard her yelp in pain.

Finn started for her, but she hadn't let go of the gun and quickly pointed it up at him. "I don't need you anymore. Take one more step and I'll prove it."

I grabbed Finn's arm. "Don't. She won't get away with this. You know that."

"Aw," Hilary said as she got to her feet. "Aren't you good at playing Mommy already?"

She shook her left hand and I saw her wrist was beginning to swell. But she just said, "Keep going."

I stopped at the door to the sewing room. "The bindings are in there. Can I get them?"

"Bindings. I like the term. Karen, Finn, why don't we stand in the doorway and watch? Make sure Jillian doesn't have any tricks up her sleeve."

She sounded so confident — and so nasty. My concern for our safety was starting to transform to anger. I grabbed a handful of my quilt bindings, the ones my cats love to play with. I always sew them up ahead and have them on hand for when I finish a quilt.

We walked farther down the hall. My office is a small room and we were all close together until Hilary directed Karen behind my desk and told her to sit. She went around and stood over her shoulder.

She pointed the gun at me and said, "Have him sit on the floor and you tie him up. Tight. No fooling around. I'll check your work."

Finn was breathing hard, but I knew he was seething inside. I only hoped he could think clearly through the rage.

Hilary said, "Hands first. Behind his back."

I hoped Hilary Roth had just made her first mistake.

Finn glared at his mother as he put his hands behind his back. I began to tie them together, and when I did, I slipped the phone from his pocket and shoved it under his right butt cheek, making sure his fingers could reach it. I came around and bound his feet under Hilary's watchful eye.

Karen, still sounding petrified, said, "Is this really necessary, Hilary? We've co-operated completely and —"

"Shut up," Hilary snapped. I could see pain in her eyes and glanced at her wrist. The swelling had grown. She was definitely injured.

And perhaps vulnerable.

Hilary walked over to Finn and me. "Stand on the other side of him where I can see you," she said to me.

I wasn't close enough to the bookcase where a heavy hardback might be reachable and useful to bash this horrid woman over the head.

Holding both the gun and her stare on me, she tested Finn's bonds with her left hand. With each tug, I heard a sharp intake of air. She was definitely hurting.

She then walked back around to face the computer. Poor Karen was visibly trembling now and I sure hoped she didn't have a heart condition.

"Come over here," Hilary said to me.

I did so, but as I passed the open door, I saw four cats sitting by the entry, two on either side. By the time I made it to the desk, Syrah and Merlot were already in the room.

"More cats?" Hilary practically shouted. "What are you? A crazy cat lady? Get them out of here."

But before I could make a move, Chablis and Dashiell entered the room, too. I said, "Do you know how hard it is to herd cats?"

Syrah, my bravest boy, made a graceful leap onto the desk from at least five feet away. Karen was so startled, the wheeling chair she sat in moved back about a foot.

"Get it off of the desk," Hilary said through clenched teeth.

I gathered Syrah in my arms, afraid for him now. He'd jump on this woman given half the chance and she wouldn't hesitate to throw him across the room.

Hilary said, "Tell her how to boot up your computer — and hurry. I've wasted too much time here already." Hilary was definitely distracted by Syrah, whose low growl directed her way sounded ominous.

But I noticed with a furtive glance in Finn's direction, the other three cats were behind him, their interest in the quilt bindings obvious. Or perhaps their interest was in Finn's fingers moving on my phone. I sure hoped so.

I set Syrah on the floor and gave Karen

directions on how to boot up my computer and click on the browser. Unfortunately, her hands were shaking and she was so upset, the process took far longer than the impatient Hilary could tolerate. She kept muttering, "Hurry up, old woman."

I said, "I could handle the transfer if I had Karen's account password."

"You keep thinking I'm some clueless Southern belle," Hilary said. "If I let you do this, I doubt I'd end up with a red cent. Karen can do this if she'd just *concentrate.*"

"Hard to concentrate when someone is waving a gun around," Finn said.

From where I was standing, I could detect movement behind him. But was it from the cats inspecting the bindings or from Finn using my phone?

Hilary removed the paper with Karen's account information from her skirt pocket with difficulty. Her wrist might actually be broken.

She set the paper on the desk next to Karen and said, "You told me at your house you have an online account."

"Yes," Karen said, her voice wavering, "but Ed always helps me get to the site. I don't think I can do this without him."

"You can and you will," Hilary said. "If you don't, Finn might not make it out of this house alive."

My growing anger turned to fury with this latest verbal assault on her own child. It made me sick. "You've gotten the browser up," I said to Karen, hoping my anger didn't spill into my tone. "I can read you what you need to type into the bar at the top of page."

The Web site URL was at the bottom of the crumpled paper and I picked it up. I slowly read each letter and punctuation mark and Karen typed with one trembling finger. After what seemed an eternity, she leaned back in the chair and looked up at Karen. "There it is. This is the screen I always see."

"You'll probably need a password," I said, glancing at Finn. He definitely was concentrating on something himself.

"I keep them written down in my little day planner," she said. "It's in my purse."

"You don't remember your password?" Hilary said.

"N-no. Let me get it." Karen opened her bag and I noticed Hilary's breathing had quickened. This drawn-out process was wearing on her patience — or maybe her pain.

I sure didn't like our chances with an impatient, gun-wielding sociopath in the room. It certainly wouldn't make any sense to kill us — how would she get her money then? But could I count on this terrible person to think through what she was doing? No way.

A good thirty seconds later, Karen entered the password. But because of added levels of security, she had to answer several questions before her account finally appeared on the screen — all one million plus dollars.

Syrah had been sitting by Finn, watching the other cats, but suddenly he snapped to catlike attention, listening to something. He ran out of the room and the three other felines rushed after him.

They'd heard something.

But Hilary was paying no attention. She'd told Karen to find the "transfer funds" page, then had to point it out with her left hand.

Karen clicked on it.

I was paying close attention to Hilary's face. She'd reached the money page and was about to make herself rich. That's clearly all she was thinking about.

Though the gun was still pointed in my direction, she was honed in on the computer, not me.

I glanced over at Finn and he gave me a slow nod.

I pounced like a cat.

With my one hand I grasped her right

wrist and pointed the gun to the ceiling. With my other hand I reached around and took hold of her injured left wrist. I twisted as hard as I could.

Hilary screamed in pain, but she was pumped full of adrenaline and began to wrench free.

I feared she'd kill Finn.

Then I felt a surge of my own. But I didn't have to struggle too long.

"Drop the gun," said Candace from the doorway. She held her own weapon in two hands and it was pointed at Hilary's head.

But she remained engaged in our horrific dance, swaying back and forth, trying to free herself.

Then Tom appeared out of nowhere. He hit Hilary's gun hand with his joined fists so hard I thought he'd broken her other wrist. The weapon fell from her grip and toppled onto the desk.

Candace grabbed the gun and stashed it in the back of her utility belt. Then she helped restrain Hilary, while I slipped from beneath struggling bodies and went to Finn's side.

The two of them pulled Hilary away from the desk and into the hall.

"You okay, Karen?" I said, as I untied Finn's hands.

She seemed frozen, her face gray, her eyes wide. "I — I . . . Yes."

Finn grinned as he rubbed his wrists. "It may be an old word, but I can't think of a better one. That was *awesome,* Jillian."

"Thanks. I've never been in a *cat* fight before." I smiled, relief and the remaining adrenaline making me feel nearly euphoric.

Finn laughed.

I cocked my head at him. "What'd you do to get help?"

Finn picked up my phone. He tapped a button and played a video. At first it wasn't exactly clear what I was seeing — but then I recognized tied fingers and many cat paws swiping and pulling at the quilt bindings tied around Finn's hands.

He said, "Since the call to Tom was the last one made, it was easy to send him the video. I was sure he'd be smart enough to figure out something was wrong here. I mean, we had to be here with these cats, right?"

"But you did this without looking?" I said, dumbfounded.

He said, "Come on, Jillian. What self-respecting kid my age doesn't know how to work a smartphone practically blindfolded?"

"Ah yes," I said with a laugh. " 'Geek' isn't a derogatory word anymore."

Thirty-One

Finn and I helped a shaken Karen walk out of my office. Tom met us to warn us Hilary was still in the house.

Karen stopped in her tracks. "I can't see her right now. Can I wait until she's gone?"

"Sure," I said. "I have the perfect spot for you."

We took her to my sewing room, and she sat in the most comfortable chair in the house. As soon as she was settled, she released an audible sigh. Chablis appeared from who knows where and jumped in her lap. At times, my girl kitty could heal by her presence alone. Karen began to stroke her gently.

Tom addressed Finn. "You want to stay here with Nana?"

"I will, if you want me to," he said. "But I'd sure love to see my mother leave here in a cop car."

I was glad to see Finn angry. He needed

that anger to help him deal with what he'd been through. Both his mother and father had left him with a tragic legacy, and I knew he'd need our help in dealing with it in the years ahead.

Karen said, "Go, Finn. I need the time to collect myself, anyway. Seems appropriate to say I'm still as nervous as a cat in a room full of rocking chairs."

I reassured her she would be safe in here and we all went to the living room.

Hilary sat on my couch, her right wrist cuffed to the end table leg. She had her head down, hair surrounding her face.

The look I gave Candace must have betrayed my confusion because Candace said, "Her wrist is so swollen I need a zip tie rather than cuffs. Morris is getting one from the squad car."

"Why, Hilary?" Tom said. "How could you do this to your own son? What kind of monster are you?" All the bitterness I'd heard in his voice over the last four days was gone. He just wanted to know everything — and so did I.

She jerked her head up. "You don't have a clue. Do you, Tom?"

Candace held up a hand like a traffic cop and quickly said, "Hilary Roth, you have the right to remain silent . . ."

When Candace finished reciting the Miranda rights, Hilary said, "No lawyer can help me now. Besides, I hate lawyers. A lawyer and judge put a kid I never wanted in my home. Made my life hell."

Tom gave Hilary a bewildered stare. Finn chose to look at the floor.

Candace took a small tape recorder from her pocket. "I will repeat your rights, Mrs. Roth." She clicked on the recorder and held it in Hilary's direction. She went through the Miranda rights again and said, "Do you understand these rights?"

"Yes," she said. "I said I *don't* want a lawyer. I want out of here. Out of this house and away from these idiots."

"We have a jail cell ready and waiting," Candace said. "Just have to make sure we take you there in a fashion worthy of a person who murdered two people."

Just then, Yoshi started barking — a hoarse, faint sound. He'd yelped away his voice, poor thing. No wonder we hadn't heard him since being herded to my office for Hilary's desperate attempt to get her hands on the money. I wasn't a financial wizard, but I truly believed her ploy never would have worked. Her desperation to get her hands on the money had obliterated all logic.

Finn looked at Candace. "Can I let Yoshi out?"

"Sure. If the cats don't mind, that is," she said. She almost smiled, but I was sure she wanted to remain professional — and what had gone on in Mercy over the last week was no laughing matter.

Dashiell was lingering close to Tom and my two boys were sitting side by side at the far end of the couch, their eyes trained on Hilary. They conveyed the disdain only cats are capable of offering with a simple look.

Tom swooped up Dashiell when Finn opened the pantry door. Yoshi did a few jack-in-the-box jumps. But when Finn opened his arms, he didn't do his usual leap. He raced into the living room — and straight for Hilary.

Before anyone could make a move, Yoshi clamped onto her skirt and began to shake his head and growl. Finn ran to stop the assault, but good old Yoshi managed to come away with a mouthful of gray gabardine before Finn pulled the dog away.

I smiled and so did Tom.

"Keep your dog away from me," Hilary said, visibly shaken.

"I've heard you say those words plenty of times," Finn said. Yoshi's leash was still attached and Finn held tightly to it. "I'll keep my dog away from you while you tell me the truth for once. What did you mean about lawyers and judges?"

"Maybe this can wait for another time," Candace said, giving me a warning glance. "Where the heck is Morris anyway?" She turned on her two-way radio and asked him the question directly.

He replied, sounding as grouchy as usual. "Can't find the zip ties. Where the heck did you put them?"

"*You* put them somewhere, remember?" Candace said. "Check the fingerprint kit or the camera case."

"Ah. The camera case," he said.

"Bring a Miranda waiver while you're at it." Candace switched off her radio. "We'll be out of here right soon."

"No. I want to tell Finn what he needs to know," Hilary said. She sounded haughty again, as if she wasn't sitting in my living room handcuffed to a table.

Candace said, "We'll take your statement at the station, relay all information to Tom and your son —"

"He's *not* my son," Hilary said. Her smug smile made me want to rip a chunk of fabric off her skirt myself.

A heavy silence followed.

"What are you talking about?" Tom finally said.

"I married Rory when Finn was a year old. Then Mr. Mental Case gets himself sent to prison. Since his birth mother was dead, the court said he was mine until Rory was out of jail. I did get welfare money and food stamps because of him on and off through the years. Kept me from starving in between jobs. I considered him my paycheck."

I glanced at Finn, concerned for him. No matter what she'd done, how cruel she'd been, she was the only mother he'd known.

But he was nodding, a small smile playing on his lips. "You don't know how many nights I went to bed wishing you weren't my mother. Guess dreams do come true." He turned, and with Yoshi at his side, started for the hall. He would need time, I knew. Time to heal from her last verbal assault.

"Wait," Tom said.

Finn looked back over his shoulder. "It's all good, man," Finn said. "Right now, Nana Karen could use some company."

Turned out we all ended up down at Mercy PD, answering questions for official statements. Even Karen, who was still so shaken by what had transpired, Candace asked the paramedics who'd splinted Hilary's wrist to check her out, too. Karen finally shooed them away, saying she needed time and she'd be fine, but promised to see her family doctor the following day.

We took her home late in the evening. Her car, the one she drove over to my house with Hilary, was still parked in front of my place. Karen didn't want Ed to learn what had happened from police officers. He would hear it from her in person. We left her in Ed's loving care to explain.

Famished, we drove to the Main Street Diner and settled into a booth near the back. Word was out and folks were already beginning to stare at us and the new kid in town.

Tom and I watched Finn enjoy his food, which was more fun than eating my own chili burger and cheese fries. The kid could put away a mountain of chow. It would be back to salads and yogurt for me tomorrow. But tonight, we celebrated.

Once Finn seemed satiated, he looked at Tom and me, sitting side by side, and said, "You two like each other, huh? I mean *really* like each other."

Tom looked at me and smiled. "Yeah. We do."

"Why don't you show it, then?" He smiled.

"I mean, I see the looks you give each other. Kids at school hang all over each other when the hormones are raging."

My cheeks heated up. *Hormones raging?* It was so much more.

Tom said, "Maybe we don't hang all over each other because we're not in high school."

"Doesn't sound like as much fun. I've never had a girlfriend, but I think about it. A lot," Finn said.

"Seems like you'll be free to find a girlfriend once all this trouble is behind you," I said.

Finn's expression grew serious and he pushed his almost empty plate away. "This bad stuff has been going on a long time. I saw her leave in the police car like I wanted, but it wasn't enough. I still see her face. Still hear her voice threatening me and Jillian and poor Nana. Still see her face the times I asked her to take me somewhere for school or give me lunch money. She really did hate me."

"Time heals," I said quietly. "But I think you should talk to someone — you know, like a shrink."

Tom said, "He'll do fine. Guys are different. We don't need to talk about every little thing."

"Every *little* thing?" I said.

"Finn's tough. He chose to be smart and come here to Mercy," Tom said. "Problem solved after a tough week. A woman who deserves it, goes to jail."

Finn looked at Tom for a moment. "Would I be less of a guy if I *did* want to talk to someone? You know, someone who knows about stuff like I went through with . . . *her.*"

For the briefest moment, I saw Tom's eyes glisten. Then he blinked back the emotion. "You'll never be less of a guy no matter what you decide. In fact, you're the bravest kid I know. You want to talk this out, I get it. We'll make it happen."

"Thanks, Tom," Finn said. He pulled his plate back and began the job of finishing the remains of chili dogs and fries.

THIRTY-TWO

More than a week passed, with Candace continuing to sort through the evidence against Hilary Roth. Though Bob had played a part in Hilary's plan to get the money Karen had earmarked for Finn, he was all talk and did nothing he could be arrested for — or nothing Candace could find to indicate a conspiracy. He'd slipped by without consequences — seemingly a pattern for him.

Kara put out several special editions of the *Mercy Messenger* as the complete story began to come out. The gossip was still going on at Belle's Beans, the Main Street Diner and the Finest Catch, as well as all the other spots people gathered in Mercy.

Dashiell and Yoshi, it turned out, seemed surprisingly compatible. They'd remained at my house since the Bob problem still existed. He was slow to move out of Tom's place after finding such a comfortable spot to crash. Dashiell wasn't safe until he left. Tom, meanwhile, spent most of his free time at my place and even bought an Xbox and hooked it up to my flat screen so he and Finn could play games together where pretend swords were the only weapons involved.

Tonight, however, I'd invited the entire family to dinner, Bob included. It was a risk — especially since Bob thought he was coming alone and the rest of his family had no idea he would be there.

Ed and Karen arrived early, bringing the catfish Ed, Finn and Tom had caught that morning on one of Ed's trotlines. Finn and Tom then took off for the mall. Apparently the clothes Kara bought were passable, but not exactly "dope," as Finn put it.

Karen brought a casserole of hash browns, sour cream and cheddar cheese, which she said needed only an hour in the oven. More important, she'd brought one of her famous lemon icebox pies. I only had to supply salad, sweet tea and plenty of counter space for Ed to do something he did so well — prepare the fish.

Karen took Yoshi for a walk to give Ed a little time to get used to the idea of befriending a dog. Seemed he was truly phobic, and it had taken a lot of persuading to get him to come here rather than do the meal at Karen's house. In the end, he'd said, "How can I refuse Jillian's invite? She protected Karen and the boy with every tool in her box — including her genius cats."

Ed brought his own filet knife and showed me how to prepare a catfish. Four felines were showing a great interest in this process — and I even wondered if they were considering how to manage a filet knife themselves. Syrah, Chablis, Merlot and Dashiell were lined up in a row near Ed, waiting for so much as a morsel of raw fish to drop on the floor.

"You're so handy with your knife, Ed Duffy," I said. "Bet you've had plenty of practice."

"You betcha," he said.

I'd supplied separate flat pans for flour, milk mixed with egg, and bread crumbs to coat the fish. I thought, *No wonder I never cook. This room is about to become a fish-fried kitchen.*

Ed drank a Dr Pepper while he worked carefully, piling one pink filet on top of another. When Tom and Finn arrived with department store bags and a couple shoe boxes, they were talkative and happy. I was certain the atmosphere would change once Bob arrived, so I enjoyed their happiness.

After putting the purchases in the guest room, they sat next to me on the stools at the breakfast bar where we could oversee Ed's preparations. Tom had grabbed a beer and Finn began downing a Dr Pepper like he'd never had one before.

"So," Ed said, skinning one of the few remaining fish adeptly. "Karen won't talk about everything that happened and I'm pretty confused concerning this woman Hilary who pretended to be her friend all these years. Did she really kill two grown men?"

Tom took a slug of his beer, then said, "She's responsible for Roth's death and did the actual deed on Gannon. Stabbed him with a knife from a set she bought in some tourist-trap housewares store on Main Street. I'm thinking her purchase goes to premeditation — and I like it because they'll tack on plenty more jail time."

"You mean the House and Home store near the end of Main Street?"

"That's the one," Tom said. "Never been in there myself."

"How did they find out she bought the knives there?" I asked. "Receipts?"

"Owner came forward with security camera footage after reading about her arrest in the *Messenger,*" Tom replied.

"She confessed, but not to buying the

darn knife?" Ed asked.

"She's vain. She knew she'd screwed up," he said. "Anyway, here's what we now know from Hilary's confession. She and Nolan were watching Finn closely, but even more so once he turned eighteen. They were worried he'd run off again, especially once he learned about all the money my mom had been saving for him. See, she told Hilary she'd take care of Finn and asked when would be the right time to have a chat with Finn in person. Mom was worried about his schooling. With Hilary not working and Nolan the ex-con not contributing, Mom was justifiably concerned. Hilary was formulating a plan to get her hands on the money, but wasn't sure how. She needed time to figure it out. So she convinced Mom to wait, saying Finn wasn't responsible enough to handle money yet. Hilary was planting a seed, hoping Mom would turn the money directly over to her. I'm sure glad she didn't."

"Well, Hilary may have known about all that money, but I sure didn't," Ed said.

"You're not the only one," Tom said. "Mom has since told me that because the money didn't come from my dad and I always said I wanted to take care of myself financially, it wouldn't be an issue if I didn't know. She's right. It's not."

"Typical of Karen not to talk much about such things. Maybe 'cause she knows I'm not concerned with those matters aside from helping her get to her accounts on the computer. A little bit of cash goes a long way in my book." He looked at Finn and smiled. "Come to my place of business and see how you can stretch a few dollars. You'll see I'm serious."

Finn said, "I'm looking forward to visiting your shop. You got any Xbox games?"

"Indeed I do," Ed said. "You wouldn't believe the perfectly fine items people toss in the garbage. Go on, Tom, because maybe if I hear the whole story, I can make sense of it for Karen. She's had more than one nightmare in the last week."

Tom said, "Here's where things started to go wrong. When Hilary looked at Finn's computer — she'd been monitoring his phone and his computer for months — she saw he'd been researching his father. She was concerned because she knew darn well Rory Gannon would like to line his pockets with Finn's money."

"Did she believe Gannon would want anything to do with Finn after all these years?" I said.

"She probably had a fleeting thought,"

Tom said. "But she knew exactly what he'd be most interested in — any payday to be had." Tom glanced at Finn. "I didn't mean to put him down. You understand the man didn't know you, right? Didn't —"

Finn held up his hand to stop Tom from explaining Gannon's motive. "Save it. I didn't know *him,* either, though I think in the end he did want to tell me Hilary wasn't my mother — which could be one reason she killed him. Anyhow, we may have had the same blood, but that's all. I only hope I don't turn out like him."

"You will *never* be like him," I said.

Ed said, "Listen to Jillian. She knows what she's talking about. Heck, we know what you're like and you're one fine young man. But here's where I'm a little confused. Hilary's husband, Mr. Nolan Roth, was in cahoots with her to get Finn back home after he ran off. Maybe milk the account Karen set up. What changed?"

"I believe it was indeed the original plan," I explained. "But according to what Candace told me, Nolan Roth expressed doubt to Hilary they could ever get Finn back after he learned Tom and Finn were communicating. Added to that, Nolan was becoming obsessed with getting revenge on Tom for sending him to jail. Hilary didn't care about getting even and didn't like Nolan focusing on his own agenda. Didn't like it enough to get rid of him. See, she'd already contacted Gannon, using Finn's phone. She figured Gannon might take a call from his son. He did."

"Gives you great insight into Hilary's character," Tom said. "Gannon was her back-up plan. When Nolan wouldn't toe the line, she quietly seethed, but she played nice with him. She talked to Nolan all along the route to his second visit to Mercy to find Finn — sending her calls to *my* phone, which shows she knew Nolan had it."

I said, "Candace might not have told you this, but she busted Hilary's alibi. She signed into the job fair, but was seen leaving on a security camera. She used your phone, Tom, to contact Gannon, not just Finn's. This was during the time you were being held in Roth's garage."

Tom smiled. "She always thought she was so darn smart. Apparently she knows nothing about cell phones except how to make calls."

"When Finn ran away," I said to Ed, "Hilary figured he'd head straight to Tom. There was even a text Candace located where Nolan spotted Finn and lured him to the car saying he was Tom. He and Tom had similar hair and body build from pictures I've seen of Roth, so Finn climbed into the car not suspecting who was really driving."

Finn shook his head. "I still don't remember climbing in Tom's car. I don't even remember walking down the road, not until you and Tom picked me up later. It's weird to lose parts of your memory."

I said, "Maybe it's a good thing you don't remember."

Finn smiled and nodded. "Yeah. I think you're right."

"In her confession," Tom said, "Hilary admits she told Gannon to run the Prius off the road when he found my car and" — Tom glanced at Finn — "and take care of business. Heck, she practically gave him the GPS coordinates since she'd been chatting it up with Nolan. If she'd known you were in the car, Finn, who knows how this would have turned out."

"Why didn't he kill me, too?" Finn said.

"Because knowing Hilary," Tom said, "Gannon would have received explicit instructions not to go off script — at least at first. He was supposed to get rid of Nolan; that's all. When he looked at your phone and realized who you were, I'm sure he called Hilary and was told not to hurt you. You were the paycheck, after all. Only

Hilary didn't have him completely under her thumb. He started showing up everywhere — really did go off script."

"Hilary was sure a cold one," Ed said. "But a coward. Stabbed Gannon in the back. If I ever felt an urgent need to kill someone, I'd look them in the eye."

"Unlike her, you wouldn't ever hurt anyone, Ed," I said.

"Nope. I catch catfish, though. But I don't think it hurts them." He chuckled and went to the sink to wash his hands before breading the filets.

"She *was* cold," Finn said, his mood more melancholy than I'd seen in the last week.

"We don't have to talk about this anymore," I said. *It's too much for him,* I decided. *He needs time to heal.*

"No. Don't stop," he said, sounding determined. "I want to know everything that was happening behind the scenes — because see, I *knew* what she was capable of. I saw how she manipulated Nolan. I also dealt firsthand with Nolan's frustration over her bossing him around. Tell me this. How'd she find my father the night he died?"

"Hilary made a decision to get rid of anyone who might want a share of Mom's money," Tom said. "With Gannon showing up all over town, saying he needed to tell

Finn something, she thought he might have grown a conscience. Might even confess to killing Nolan. He was a risk. Heck, she probably told him my address and instructed him to meet her there."

Risk, I thought. I was reminded Bob might be here any minute.

But it was Yoshi and Karen who arrived through the back door. I saw Ed nearly jump out of his skin when he spied the dog.

"After his long walk, maybe Yoshi could use a nap," I said, eyeing Finn.

He got the message. "Yeah. I'll take him to the guest room."

But before he could take the leash, Yoshi took off and ran down the basement stairs. Four cats were hot on his tail.

"I'll get him," Finn said, pounding down the stairs after the animals.

Karen looked at the door to the basement, toward where Finn had gone, her smile heartwarming. We all had a wonderful job ahead — to make up for all the love Finn had lost.

An hour later, with Bob still not making an appearance, we all sat down at my dining room table for another wonderful fish-fry dinner — one I truly enjoyed. Meanwhile, Yoshi and the cats seemed content to stay in the basement for some reason. About halfway through the meal, I heard my phone ding. But I wasn't about to be rude enough to check my messages while we were eating.

Good thing the animals didn't reappear until we'd cleared the table. Karen and Tom insisted on doing the dishes and I sat down with Ed and Finn in the living room.

I heard the pets race up the basement stairs and was about to tell Ed he might want to hide, but there was no time.

Yoshi came running up to Ed. He had a mouse in his mouth.

I covered my mouth in horror and saw four cats who seemed completely disgusted that a dog had muscled in on their territory.

With Yoshi's tail wagging furiously, he seemed to be offering Ed a gift.

Ed smiled. "What's this?"

"Yoshi's a rat terrier," Finn said. "Good as a cat at catching rodents."

Ed nodded and took the mouse from Yoshi's jaws. "This is a dog I just might like."

Finn laughed and the cats converged, hoping to get a taste of mouse for themselves.

While Ed and Yoshi continued to bond, with Finn's help, I went to the end table where I'd set my phone.

My first thought after I read the words on the screen was something Candace once told me: "You can't con a con man." I tried to fool Bob by omitting that his whole family would be here for dinner. It hadn't worked.

The text message I'd received from Bob was simple and to the point: *Can't meet with you. I'm gone.*

EPILOGUE

Dashiell hadn't liked the idea of getting into a cat carrier — but then what cat did? I was now searching the nooks and crannies in my house for spots he might have hidden, glad he would finally be going home. Of course, he thought he was headed for the vet and had taken off the minute I pulled the carrier up the basement stairs.

With Thanksgiving come and gone, and the Christmas season upon us, I smiled at the thought of what a wonderful holiday this would be for Finn and his family — his real family. Not blood relations, but the people who cared deeply about him.

I'd managed to close the basement door when Dashiell ran off, but the rest of the house was Dashiell's playground for this game of hide-and-go-seek.

As my three cats followed me around — and were no help whatsoever — I thought about how Dashiell was the one who started this latest journey of mine. I felt very lucky I'd met Finn — and gotten to know Tom so much better.

I was on my belly, looking under the guest room bed for about the fourth time, when I heard someone knocking loudly on my back door. Syrah took off immediately, his curiosity piqued.

Merlot decided on a more leisurely stroll out of the guest room, while Chablis decided she'd wait right where she was — in the fairly safe guest room. Yoshi's stay here had spooked her and convinced me a dog wasn't in my immediate future, even though I adored dogs. Yoshi had gone with Finn to live at Tom's house and my home had felt a little lonely without them. Now it was Dashiell's turn to go live with Tom, Yoshi and Finn. I'd agreed to allow Yoshi an adjustment period at his new place by keeping Dashiell with me, even though the two seemed to get along just fine while they'd been here together.

I made it to the back door and said, "Who's there?"

"It's me," called Tom. "Is something wrong with Dashiell?"

I unlocked the dead bolt and the other door lock and when I let Tom in, he said, "Good job keeping this place secure. But we expected you over at the house at least thirty minutes ago."

I stared up at him. "You could have called — and I would have told you the problem. Dashiell is a reluctant traveler. I don't blame him, either. Cat carrier equals Doc Jensen in his cat mind."

"He's hiding?" Tom asked.

"Yup," I said, blowing up at the bangs that had fallen into my eyes.

"No, he's not," Tom said with a smile.

"Yes, he —" I heard a small meow. The elusive Mr. Dashiell must have heard Tom's voice.

"He has a pitiful voice for such a big cat," I said.

"I still love him." Tom pulled me to him and gazed down into my eyes. "But not as much as I love you."

Before I could respond, he kissed me.

I liked the kiss, liked the words and liked how, when we came apart, four cats were staring up at us looking, well . . . happy.

ABOUT THE AUTHOR

Leann Sweeney was born and raised in Niagara Falls and educated at St. Joseph's Hospital and Lemoyne College in Syracuse, New York. She also has a degree in behavioral science from the University of Houston and has worked in psychiatry. A former registered nurse, she has been writing in the mystery genre for many years, and writes the Yellow Rose Mystery series. Leann is married with two grown children and has lived in Texas for most of her adult life. She resides in Friendswood with her husband, Mike, her three cats, and her ADHD Labradoodle, Rosie.

The employees of Thorndike Press hope you have enjoyed this Large Print book. All our Thorndike, Wheeler, and Kennebec Large Print titles are designed for easy reading, and all our books are made to last. Other Thorndike Press Large Print books are available at your library, through selected bookstores, or directly from us.

For information about titles, please call:
(800) 223-1244

or visit our Web site at:
http://gale.cengage.com/thorndike

To share your comments, please write:
Publisher
Thorndike Press
10 Water St., Suite 310
Waterville, ME 04901

CPSIA information can be obtained
at www.ICGtesting.com
Printed in the USA
FFOW021659150113
702FF